THE ACCIDENT

A chilling psychological thriller

NATALIE BARELLI

Also by Natalie Barelli

Until I Met Her (The Emma Fern Series Book 1)

After He Killed Me (The Emma Fern Series Book 2)

Missing Molly

The Loyal Wife

Chapter One

I had a math teacher in high school, Mr. Cunningham, who would begin each class by picking one student at random and asking a tricky question about the previous lesson. A wrong answer would strip a point in your final grade. A correct answer gave you nothing. You could feel the dread in the room as we sat in silence, trying to make ourselves as small as possible, heads down, eyes raised just enough to follow that pointing finger, praying that it would settle on someone else.

Except for me. I would sit there, secretly hoping he'd pick me because I always knew the answer. But then I also knew the value of fitting in, and if that meant looking petrified, so be it.

"You may think that the odds are in your favor," he intoned once. "Since there are thirty of you, you've got it in your head that there's only one chance in thirty that I'll pick you. But you're wrong. The odds are fifty-fifty: either it's you, or it's not. Think about that."

I already knew enough about probabilities to understand these were not the odds. Not by a long shot. But I

1

was also awed by the audacity of the lie, and maybe because it was so weirdly convincing, I never forgot it. Take getting into a car, for example. I know the odds that I'll die behind the wheel are one in twenty thousand, give or take, but still I think of Mr. Cunningham.

That's not how it works, Katherine. Get in the car, maybe you'll die, maybe you won't. Either it's your turn or it's not.

And in this very moment, when the pain in my chest feels like shrapnel and my neck gets whiplashed by the force of the impact and I can't catch my breath and someone is screaming—me, I think—the first thought that comes into my head is, *Shit. It's my turn.*

But then immediately I know it's not that bad. We've hit something, yes, and I don't know what it is yet. I know we've hit it hard enough that my neck hurts real bad, but nothing fatal. The car has come to a standstill, but the engine is still running and the headlights shine their beams through the rain. I squint, trying to make out what's out there.

"What the fuck was that?" Something is wrong with my voice. It's hoarse. I try to swallow but my mouth is dry and my throat feels like sandpaper. The radio is still blaring that happy country western tune we were singing along to just seconds before, and I reach across to turn it off. Now all I can hear above my own ragged breath is the squeak of the windshield wipers. I sit very still, both hands gripping the steering wheel, knuckles white, like I'm bracing myself for something else to happen, and then suddenly I'm laughing.

I'm laughing because this entire evening has been so strange. I'm laughing because I don't know why I'm laughing. Probably because I'm stoned. I'm high. I'm drunk.

And I'm laughing especially because guess what, Mr. Cunningham, it's not my turn.

"Jesus. What the—"

Then I hear Eve next to me. At first I don't realize it's Eve because she's making such a weird sound that I think it's something wrong with the car. I turn to her, and my stomach flips.

"Oh, God. Oh, my God. Eve." She's hunched over, wailing softly, her chest straining against the seatbelt, her forehead pressed against the dashboard. Her breath is loud, raspy.

I'm not laughing now.

"Eve, what's wrong? Are you okay? No, of course you're not okay."

I'm shaking so much, I struggle to find the clip to my seatbelt, and even when my fingers grasp at the latch it takes a few goes before it releases.

"Oh, Christ. Eve, talk to me."

I lean over to her, put a hand on her shoulder, bend down low so I can see her face.

"I think I'm all right," she says, her eyes closed, her voice still raspy. "I need a minute…get my breath back… can you unhook me?"

"Yes, yes, hang on." I manage to unclip her seatbelt and she takes in a bigger breath.

"I'm all right," she says at last, lifting a hand to her forehead. I rub her back.

"I don't know what happened," I say, to myself as much as to her. "Did we hit something? Oh shit, look at you, you're not okay, are you. I'll call an ambulance."

My eyes dart around for my cell but I have no idea where it is. My head hurts. My chest hurts, too. Do I even have phone reception here? We're in the middle of nowhere. No, we're not. We're on the Parkway, that's all. We're surrounded by civilization, just over there. I can see the lights in the windows of the taller buildings, over the trees. We're okay. We'll be okay.

Eve is sitting back into her seat now, but her face is pale. "I don't need an ambulance, I'm fine. Just a bit winded, that's all. I just need a minute." She coughs and I rub her back again.

"I don't know what happened," I say again. "But we must have hit something, maybe it's a tree that's fallen over. I'll go and have a look."

I open my door and step outside. I have to walk slowly because the road feels slippery and I don't have the right shoes on. Then something comes into my view, right in front of the car. Something big and dark. At first, I think it's some kind of wildlife, like a wild boar maybe? I'm really stoned, but I still know there are no wild boars this close to the center of Boston.

Are there?

I crouch down to take a closer look, and that's when I know. I stand up quickly but I am dizzy, nauseous, and I have to turn to the side of the road and vomit while the world tilts around me. I want to speak, but I can't move my mouth properly.

I wipe my lips with my sleeve. "Eve?" My voice sounds pinched, like my chest is too tight and it can't get out.

"Eve?" This time I yell out her name, but she's already here, standing in front of the car, one hand over her mouth, staring down at the shape. I have to put a hand on the hood to steady myself.

4

Chapter Two

Two weeks ago, I thought I was stressed. I thought my life was hard because I'm juggling a high-pressure job that I love and a teenage daughter who I believe has taken up too many extracurricular activities and her school grades are suffering. But she's happy. She loves hockey, she's good at it, she wants to do drama. She's in the chess club. Should I let her make these choices for herself? Or should I impose restrictions until her grades catch up? These were the kinds of brain loops I fell asleep to.

Two weeks ago, I was planning Abigail's birthday dinner at Barolo because she loves it there and they have big, long tables so it's easy to bring together the half dozen school friends she invited and the three adults I did. Okay, maybe *planning* is a big word here. I made some calls. Come on down this Saturday, I said. It'll be fun.

When I called Hilary she paused for a moment, as if considering it, then she said, in her thoughtful voice—I could just picture her eyebrows drawn together even though I couldn't see her—"Really? You're having Abigail's birthday party at a *restaurant*?"

I closed my eyes but I didn't reply. I'd just called to say exactly that, after all, so yes, I'm having Abi's birthday at a restaurant.

She went on. "Well it's up to you I suppose. I can't imagine doing that for Paige's sixteenth birthday. It *is* a milestone, for a girl. Henry and I certainly would want to host Paige's party at our house."

Well of course you would, I wanted to say. Look at your house, for goodness sake. It's magnificent. Just like you, Hilary. You're stunning and your skin is glowing and your hair is always glossy and your clothes are beautiful and you're always so pristinely put together and you don't have to work because your perfect husband makes a trillion dollars a minute and you take care of your adorable children and you will absolutely throw the perfect birthday party for Paige. But Abi and I, we're doing it at Barolo, so there you go. Be there or be square, as Abi used to say.

I don't know why Hilary gets to me like this. It's not that I don't like her, because I do. I can see under that perfect Martha Stewart carapace there's a human struggling to get out. And Hilary can be funny and sweet at times. Usually when she thinks no one's listening. I just wish she'd refrain from taking jabs at me whenever the occasion presents itself. Which, granted, is often.

But I couldn't shake the guilt after that, so I called Sasha. "Do you sometimes think you're the worst mother? No, of course you don't. You're a fantastic mother. Maybe I should ask you to adopt Abi. I'm just the worst. I'm terrible at motherhood."

"I don't know why you beat yourself up," she said. "Kids love eating out. I know my girls do, so it's a safe bet Abi's the same. Face it, Kat, it's much more of a treat than your tired old carrot cake." I laughed when she said that, even though I was so tired I could cry.

I miss Sasha so much. She's funny, she's generous, and I love her to bits. When I talk to her I can't help wishing we hadn't left LA. I lived there for almost half my life until just over two years ago. That's a long time. I don't have friends like Sasha here, not yet anyway. And I don't think Hilary is a contender.

So yes. Two weeks ago, along with Hilary, her daughter Paige and the rest of Abi's guests, I watched my daughter blow out sixteen candles. We sang, we laughed, and I marveled at what a perfect evening this was in the end.

Two weeks ago, I didn't even know Eve existed.

It was Sunday morning, early, and I could tell from the silence of the house that Abigail was still asleep. I swung my feet to the floor and with one foot, dragged my slippers out from under the bed and stepped into them. I unhooked my dressing gown from the back of the door and shivered as I put it on. It was freezing on this winter morning. As always, I forgot to set the timer on the thermostat.

This was the day after Abigail's birthday, and I wanted her to have a nice day. Birthdays last a full week in our house, and I promised to bring Abi breakfast in bed. I turned on the heating, and it immediately clanked noisily to life. I prepared some eggs—scrambled and not too dry, just the way she likes them—and popped a couple slices of bread into the toaster.

Then she appeared in the doorway of the kitchen, still rubbing sleep out of her eyes. She's tall with willowy limbs, like a dancer, and when she sat down at the kitchen table it was like she was folding herself. She's at the stage where she grows out of clothes in about five minutes.

"I was going to bring this to you in bed."

"Thanks, Mom, but I'm awake now. I'd rather have breakfast with you."

It was lovely, just the two of us, eating breakfast together. She said she had a really nice time last night, and she loved her presents. Her aunt Sue had given her a hundred dollars, and she wanted to go to the mall with her friends. She wanted to buy herself a leather jacket. I told her a hundred dollars might not be enough, but if she found something she liked, we could go and buy it together, and I'd cover the shortfall.

"You're the best mom." She put her arms around my neck and briefly rested her head against mine. I inhaled the scent of my child. She smelled of lemon and soap. I love this grown up person my daughter is turning into. She's becoming happier, more at ease with people and with the world. Recently, she had begun to talk about where she wants to go to college. She said her dad will help pay for it. Her dad lives in South America with his own family. I wouldn't trust what he says as far as I could throw him.

"You can study wherever you like, sweetie, but you're only sixteen years old, you've got plenty of time for that."

Which is code for, *Please don't go yet.*

Not much happened after that. It was just a perfectly ordinary, lazy Sunday. Abigail went out with her friends; I pulled out cookbooks that I hadn't looked at in months, but Hilary was still in my head. *I suppose this is all right,* she said through pursed lips when the cake shaped like a castle came out and the kids were all dancing and Paige yelled out, 'Can I have my birthday here too, Mom?' But I hadn't cooked a proper dinner in months. I thought that today might be the day.

Is this too much detail? Because we haven't gotten to the phone call yet, the call that will change everything, although not right away. So yes, I'm taking my time. I don't want to rush through the memory of that day because up until this moment, when Abigail is at the mall and I have pulled my coat off the rack in the hall, when I scribble a grocery list for the week and slip it in my pocket, when I step outside into the grey day, right up to that moment, everything is fine.

It's better than fine. It's perfect, and I don't even know it.

Chapter Three

I was walking down the street with my grocery list and thinking about Abi's new hockey uniform. Where was I supposed to get it from? I'd forgotten. I'd need to ask the coach again. Then I thought about my mother's abandoned house, and what I should do with the contents. I think about that a lot. My mother's house, crammed with decades of hoarding. I told myself that the way to make it happen is to get some help, but I didn't even know who to ask. Maybe Mark would know.

Mark. I thought of calling and asking him right then and there. *Come and tell me what to do with all this stuff,* I'd say, and he'd laugh and say, *You just can't get enough of me, can you.* And I'd say, *You got me there.* And then he'd say, *I'll be there in half an hour.*

We're still at the stage of our relationship where although we see each other every day, on days that we don't I miss him terribly. I am like a schoolgirl with a crush around him, even though I sure didn't get to be that kind of normal teenager back when I was one. Maybe that's why. I'm still playing catch up with my own teenage-hood.

And anyway, it's not the same being at work together. I don't get to hold him and kiss him and rip his clothes off when we're in the office.

I wanted so badly to call him. I'd ask him about the house, then we'd meet there, as we often did, and we could talk about the SunCell project. We have so much riding on that. We're both obsessed with it.

It began to rain, and I pulled the hood of my coat over my head. I was holding my phone, ready to call Mark, when it rang in my hand. I stopped abruptly when I read the name on the screen. It was Atwood House, the nursing home that cares for my mother. And on a Sunday. They never called on a Sunday.

"Katherine, it's Fiona from Atwood House—"

Fiona is Scottish, and she has the most charming accent. The kind of lilt that makes you happy just hearing it, like a song. But there was a certain tension in her voice today.

"Fiona, is everything okay? Has something happened?"

I was standing in the middle of the sidewalk, and a little boy balancing on a skateboard almost ran into my calves.

"Nancy is fine, don't worry," Fiona said quickly. The boy picked up his skateboard, and his dad shot me a dirty look, as if I were the one who ran into his child. If I hadn't been on the phone I might have said something. Like, get real.

Instead I moved out of the way and stood by the house behind me. "What happened?"

"It's nothing serious, but she had an unfortunate episode just now."

"An unfortunate episode?" Was that a euphemism for something? Had she wet herself? They wouldn't call me for that. She does things like that all the time. "Did something happen to her?" I felt my stomach churn as I said this.

She hesitated just for a beat. "She choked, over lunch, but—"

"She choked?" I cried out. "My God! On what? Is she okay?"

I saw a cab coming up the street and stretched one arm high. Fiona assured me again that my mother was fine. There was someone with her, just at the right moment.

"She gave us all a scare, but she's absolutely fine."

"I'll come over now," I said, the phone wedged into the crook of my neck as I negotiated the door of the cab and slid into the backseat.

"There's no need—"

"I know, I was going to come anyway. I just want to see her. I'll be there shortly."

"Of course. See you soon, Katherine." I heard her sigh just before she hung up, but I didn't care if she thought I was overreacting. I've had so little time with my mother over the last sixteen years, her disease may have forced her to let me go, but I wasn't ready to let her go. Not yet.

As my mother's mind slowly became hollowed out by dementia, keeping contact with her became more difficult. At some point she stopped calling. Then her letters slowly trickled to nothing as she gradually forgot about me, one fact at a time.

I missed her so much, I wrote to my father, desperate for news, but he never replied. When I called, he hung up on me. That's the kind of relationship we had. Or didn't have, depending on how you look at it.

But he's gone now, and instead Abi and I are here. We moved from LA so I could care for my mother, to the best of my ability, which feels never enough no matter how hard I try.

I entered her bedroom, and I was relieved to see her sitting comfortably in her large armchair. Her eyes were closed. I crouched next to her. "You're all right, Mom?" I whispered.

There was another person in the room. A woman, sitting on the other side of her, holding my mother's hand. She stood to greet me. "Hello, you must be Katherine. I'm Eve." We shook hands and I mumbled something, then I watched her rearrange the blanket on my mother's lap, talking the whole way through in her nice, soothing voice, and I felt a small pang of jealousy because I saw my mother open her eyes and smile, and I thought she liked her better than me. If I didn't know any better, I would assume this person was a relative. She wasn't wearing a uniform and she didn't have that rushed manner about her, that the staff often have. But she couldn't be because that would just be too weird since I didn't know her. I decided to take my rightful place by my mother's side, elbow out the usurper. I pulled up the other chair until it touched my mother's and took her hand in mine. She turned to me, eyebrows raised.

"Yes, hello." She raised a hand to her hair. Like she wanted to make sure she looked decent for this visitor, this stranger. Me. Her grey, curly hair was getting long and I wondered when she was due for a cut.

I smiled. "Hello, Mom." Her skin felt dry and papery. I was looking around for her moisturizer when I heard a voice behind me.

"Katherine?"

I turned around. Fiona at the door, beckoning me outside with a tilt of her head. I joined her, leaving this stranger in charge of my mother.

"Who's this?" I asked, throwing a thumb over my shoulder. Fiona was walking quickly, and I had to rush to catch up.

"Eve, she's one of our volunteers. She's the one who helped your mother, she saw it happen."

Ah. I felt guilty, instantly, that I hadn't been more friendly. Let alone more grateful. We'd reached the nurses' desk and I lowered my voice. "So what the heck happened?" I hadn't meant for the question to sound so abrupt, and Fiona bristled at the words then recovered quickly. "Come into my office. I'll explain. Do you want tea or coffee?"

"No thank you." I mumbled. My hands were sweaty and I wiped them on my thighs. It happens when I'm stressed, and I was stressed.

Fiona clasped her hands together on top of the desk. "We served lunch at 12:30pm. Chicken Schnitzel, green beans, mashed potatoes, and broccoli. Barbara—she does the service on Sunday—did everything correctly. She straightened Nancy's reclining chair so she would be more comfortable, and rolled the tray closer to her. Nancy was watching TV."

There was a small bowl of mints on the corner of Fiona's desk. She picked it up and offered it to me. I shook my head.

"And then what?"

"Eve, whom you've met just now, was walking past your mother's room when it happened. She saw her, she called out for help, pressed the emergency button, and assisted your mother right away."

"Assisted how?"

"She slapped her back, your mother coughed, and the morsel came out. By then the nurses had arrived in the room and confirmed there was no more blockage in the airway."

Blockage? Airway? Jesus! "She must have been terrified. Did my mother almost die? Choking?"

"I'm terribly sorry, Katherine. It was an accident. We constantly monitor our residents so that—"

"Don't you cut up her food? You know you have to cut up her food, right? She forgets to chew."

She glanced toward the office door, no doubt wishing she'd closed it.

"Of course, we cut up Nancy's food, we always do. Always. It was an accident, Katherine, and it was averted immediately."

"Sorry. I didn't mean…" I felt myself deflate. It was an accident, not the result of neglect. I knew that. The care in this place is second to none. It should be, it costs a small fortune.

I bit a fingernail. "And she's okay now?"

"We gave her a full check-up immediately. She's completely fine. She had a wee bit of a scare. We all did."

"I'll go back and see her," I said, pushing my chair back. "And I should thank Eve."

Fiona stood. Resting the tip of her fingers onto the desk, she said, "I'm really sorry about all this. But I promise, Nancy is fine."

"I know. Thank you."

She held the door for me. "You'll like Eve. Nancy is very fond of her. We all are. She's extremely popular with the residents. We're very lucky to have her, actually."

I smiled and returned to my mother's room. Eve was

still there, reading to my mother from a magazine. She stopped when she saw me and gave me a sweet smile. I felt a bit embarrassed; I should have spoken to her earlier.

I kissed my mother's cool cheek.

"Yes, hello," she said and immediately returned her gaze toward Eve.

"Hi, Mom." I took her hand. "I'm glad you're okay. I'm going home now, you'll be going to bed soon." I turned to Eve. "Can I speak with you for a minute?"

"Sure." She put down the magazine. "I should be going home, anyway," she said. "I'll walk out with you."

She said goodbye to my mother in a lovely, warm manner. As we walked out together, I thanked her as profusely as I knew how. She brushed my words away with a flick of the hand. "I happened to be there. Lots of us happened to be there, it wasn't just me."

"But Fiona says you were the first to spot something was wrong."

"I was, but only by a few seconds." She stopped and looked at me straight on. "She's safe, Katherine, really. I'm glad I was able to help, but it could have been any one of us. Your mother is safe."

I'm a crier. Even at my age, I still can't control it. The tears came, uninvited and unexpected. They hurt the back of my eyes as I tried to hold them at bay. "Thank you, that's exactly what I wanted to hear."

She squeezed my arm and said she had to sign off and get her things from the nurses' area. I watched her lean on the counter and chat with the other nurses. I looked at her properly for the first time. She was very pretty, but not in an intimidating kind of way. More like a cheerleader kind of way, with bright blue eyes, shiny blond hair, rosy skin and a kind, open face. The face of someone who does good deeds for people. A volunteer's face.

She returned. "All done," she said. In one quick gesture she tied up her hair loosely on the nape of her neck before tightening the collar of her coat.

"I'm getting a cab home," I said. "Can I drop you off somewhere?"

She bit her bottom lip, like a child, thought about it, then she smiled. A megawatt, all teeth, big mouthed, movie star smile. I remember thinking that she could sell toothpaste to an anteater with that smile.

"You know, Katherine, a ride sounds great, but I'm starving. Have you had lunch?"

I shook my head.

"There's a great Italian place a block away. You want to join me?"

It was so unexpected that I didn't know what to say. I quickly thought about all the things I was going to do this afternoon. I thought about Mark. I glanced at the clock on the wall. It was only one o'clock. I could still call him later, after lunch. We'd still have plenty of time to see each other.

"I'd understand if you're busy," Eve said.

"No, no. I'd love to have lunch with you. But it's my treat."

Chapter Four

I called Abi while we waited for the elevator, made sure she was having a nice day, which she was. She was with Paige, at the mall, with a hundred dollars in her pocket. What's not to like?

The elevator arrived with a ding and Eve and I took our passes out at the same time. Since residents here all have varying degrees of dementia, the security is paramount. The elevator won't go anywhere unless you flash the pass against the sensor. But as nice as this place is, the residents are always trying to sneak past you and get out. I wish I understood why, because if you ask them where they're going they'll look at you blankly. They don't know. They just want to go somewhere. And yet this place is so nice, the food is excellent, there's a cinema and a theater, in the spring they have concerts on the lawn, the staff is lovely and everything is done for you.

Sometimes I think it would be nice to have dementia.

From the outside the restaurant was pretty uninspiring. It had a brick facade with bright pink neon signs in each window announcing its name: *Mario's* (window 1), *Table* (window 2). But step inside, and you were instantly warmed by the smells, the music, the cheery décor—a bit kitsch, too, with its red and white checkered tablecloths and candles dripping wax over Chianti bottles. I liked it.

Suddenly I was famished. Eve ordered a linguini with clam sauce, and I settled for the veal scaloppini. We ordered a bottle of Sangiovese because, when in Rome and all that, and as Eve pointed out, neither of us were driving.

"I find life is much easier without a car, don't you?" she said.

"Oh, I have a car. I couldn't do without it. It so happened it was quicker to grab a taxi."

Then it all came over me again, how she saved my mother's life, and I took her hand and thanked her again and again, and I told her lunch was on me, of course, and every lunch and dinner after that for the rest of her life, because I could never repay her, and all the while she brushed off my thanks. "It's in the past," she said, and she laughed and wondered where that Sangiovese was because Christ, she needed a drink.

She must have conjured up the waiter because suddenly he was there, with the wine. We waited in silence while he poured, both of us smiling at him although he wasn't looking at me, only at Eve. I didn't mind. I had Mark, I wasn't looking for love and certainly not from a waiter in an Italian restaurant, no offense, but I'm told the hours aren't family friendly. Then he said something in Italian I didn't understand and I doubt Eve did either, but we smiled and thanked him anyway, then he was gone.

"To you," I said, holding my glass aloft.

"And you." We clinked our glasses and the wine tasted nice. I began to relax.

"So tell me about you," I said. "What brought you to

Atwood House? You don't look like a typical volunteer in an old people's home."

She lifted her napkin to her lips while she finished swallowing. It left a faint mark of lipstick, in the shape of a heart.

"My grandmother was a patient there until recently. She died. I just kept coming anyway. Is that weird? Sometimes I think it is, but I'm not ready to stop." She shrugged.

"Oh, I'm so sorry. I feel like an idiot."

She flapped her hand in the air. "Don't. You didn't know."

"It sounds like you two were very close." I was thinking about my own mother. Would I still come to Atwood House after she died? And tend to another elderly woman in her bed? God no! No way.

"We were close. She meant the world to me." She sighed. "What about you? What's your story?"

My story. I liked that. Everyone has a story. Everyone *is* a story. I told her bits about mine, about Abi, about living in LA, about college. I stopped as our friendly waiter arrived with our meals.

"What did you study in college?" she asked, before blowing on her steaming pasta, like a child.

"Math. I have a Master's degree in statistics. Probability theory. I started a PhD, too, but life got in the way."

"Wow! Katherine! Well done, you! I'm impressed!"

"It would be more impressive if I finished it, but I will, one day, hopefully."

"Still, better you than me. I couldn't balance my checkbook if my life depended on it."

I shook my head. I may even have slapped my hand on the table, I'm not sure. "Why does everybody hate math? Math is wonderful. It's magic! One day—" I picked up my cutlery, loosely pointed my knife in her direction, "—I'll make it my personal mission to find out who's responsible for giving math such a bad name. And when I do, I'll spend the rest of my existence discrediting them. Because if I had a dollar for every time I heard the line, 'math? Not me. I couldn't even balance my checkbook,' I'd be richer than Bill Gates."

Then I cut a piece of veal.

"Okay, I can see you're passionate about it," she said, amusement in her eyes.

"I am. I mean, who goes around saying, 'I couldn't string a sentence together if my life depended on it?' Or, 'I couldn't spell a single word to save my life?'" I only stopped talking to chew my food. And even then, barely.

"At least this point of pride is gender agnostic," I resumed. "Men are just as likely to think that not being able to add two numbers together is cute and charming. No offense, Eve, by the way."

"None taken, Katherine. And what do you do for a living?"

"I work for an investment firm. It's a boutique VC firm. Rue Capital, they're called."

"VC firm? What's that?"

"Venture Capital. I help startup businesses find investors. We do tech startups mostly. If we think the company has potential, we sign them up, organize a funding round. Investors get a return, hopefully, and the company does well. Everybody's happy. There's a demand for this service because everybody wants to 'discover' the next Uber or Airbnb and get in on the ground floor."

"Do you enjoy it?"

"I do, I love it."

I told her how lucky I was to get this job considering

they wanted someone with experience. I'd spent so many years trying to raise my daughter, earn a living, and study all at the same time. The café where I worked used to joke I was probably the most qualified waitress in all of California. I guess I could add up the bill and give the right change without a calculator, so there was that. Then I got a job in marketing, which paid better and had better hours, but my father died shortly after and we came back this way. Abi settled into a new school. I was pretty desperate and going for anything. Mark told me later he picked me because I was a 'Stanford dropout'. He thought it would look good on paper.

Not the 'dropout' bit surely, I remember saying.

Especially the 'dropout' bit. Very Silicon Valley, he said. Investors will love it.

"Anyway," I said to Eve, "turns out I have a knack for picking winners. I seem to be able to identify startups that then do really well really quickly. Or maybe I'm just lucky. Either way, I'm an entrepreneur at heart. I see a business opportunity, and I seize it with both hands. In the end everyone's happy. We even got a mention in Forbes last month. *Twenty Up and Coming VC Firms to watch out for.*"

"Wow, that's so cool, Katherine. What number were you?"

"Twenty," I laughed. "Anyway, sorry for rambling on like this. It must be the wine. Please, tell me about you."

"Don't apologize, I'm really very interested," she said. At least I didn't tell her what the article said about me. *Rue Capital's secret weapon* they called me.

"Your turn, Eve. Come on. Tell me everything."

She shrugged, grew silent, picked at the cold melted wax on the base of the bottle.

"Nothing as exciting as what you've just told me," she

said finally. "I'm twenty-six, almost thirty, which makes me feel scared—"

"Don't be," I told her. "Thirty is great. And anyway, you're not thirty yet, you're twenty-six."

"Wow, you really are the math genius."

I laughed. "Do you have a family?"

She shook her head. "My boyfriend and I moved around a bit. We were in New York for the last three years, then we moved back here because he got a job offer he couldn't pass up. A month later he met someone at work he loved more than me, so he dumped me!" She made a face as if to say, *and here I am!*

"Oh, Eve, I'm so sorry! That must have been awful."

"You can say that again. On top of that I haven't been able to find a proper job yet, just bits and pieces here and there. The job market isn't great right now, that's also why I volunteer at Atwood. I think I'd just curl up and die if I didn't keep busy."

She took a sip of her drink and it seemed all that sparkle and light had gone out of her eyes.

"Wait." I put down my cutlery and leaned forward.

"What?"

"There's a job opening where I work, and—"

"Where you work? Oh, Katherine, what the heck would I do there? I don't know anything about ... whatever it's called, capital something?"

"It's actually an executive assistant position, can you type?"

She shrugged. "Sure, I can type."

"And you can answer the phone, right? So there you go! You're qualified." I could feel my heart race with excitement. Maybe it was the wine, or the delicious food, or the fact that Eve had saved my mother from choking only hours earlier, but I knew that the one thing I wanted most in the world was to make her happy. I was going to find her a job. I would invent one for her if I had to.

Her whole face lit up. She reached for my hand and covered it with her own. "You'd do that for me?"

"Are you kidding? Yes! Of course!"

"And you think they'd consider me? Oh, my God! I'm a really hard worker, Katherine, I swear. I'd be happy to do anything if that helped. You know, like make coffee, sweep the floor, clean windows…"

"You're hired!" I laughed. "I'll talk to Mark, he's the boss. I'm sure he'll be thrilled to have you. And he's a really nice guy, you'll see."

Then I said, more seriously, "It's actually a position in my office, you'd be working with me."

"Oh, Katherine, are you kidding? That'd be truly awesome. Honestly, this is the best news I've had all day. What am I saying! All week! All year!"

I did have a moment of regret for saying it out loud. What if Mark didn't want Eve for the position? No, he would. Of course, he would. Why wouldn't he? She was as qualified as anyone.

We exchanged phone numbers, and I promised to call her in a couple days with an update. She looked happy again, and I was filled with pride that I had done that, returned the sparkles to her eyes. And when we left the waiter flashed her his best and brightest smile. I bet he would have liked her phone number, too.

Chapter Five

Our office is very sleek, very modern. It takes up two whole floors of a historic building. It even won an architectural award, too. All the offices have glass walls, so you can see pretty much everyone, from anywhere. In the middle is what we call reception, even though it's the combined reception area, conference table, and even an open kitchen at the far end of the room with all the gadgetry you'd expect in a hip firm like ours, and a long breakfast bar against the brick wall. Then there's another level upstairs which you reach via the open steel staircase. That's where we make our presentations, and where the IT people live. All two of them.

We're pretty small. We have two researchers, a legal expert, there's Mark of course, and his assistant Caroline who I suspect doesn't like me much, which is unfortunate since she does most of the admin around here, and as anyone who works in an office would tell you, you really want the administrative staff to like you. Then we have Amy at reception, and finally a two-person marketing team.

Until I started working here, the company was really limping along. Would I say this out loud? Sure I would. It's not a secret. I do have a talent for picking winners. I can do the research and crunch the numbers and pull out the right contender from a field of a hundred, knowing that the time is ripe, and the market is ready, and I can almost predict how much our investors will make and over how long. Rue Capital went from hobbling to the twentieth VC firm to watch out for in just under two years, and I had a lot to do with that.

A few weeks ago, armed with the *Forbes* article, where I had highlighted the words *Katherine Nichols, Rue Capital's secret weapon* in bright yellow, I approached Mark.

"I want in," I said.

He dropped his glasses on the desk and smiled.

"Okay, let's hear it."

So I told him. I want to buy out Sonya, I said. I remember he winced when I said her name. Sonya is Mark's ex-wife. Or soon to be ex-wife. It sounds much more sordid than it really is, but they're not a couple anymore, not exactly, whereas we, Mark and I, are. And I want to buy her out of the company, even though I don't have enough money to do that. But I am a secret weapon. That's got to count for something.

We do have a very promising client, a new company that produces solar powered batteries. Which doesn't sound particularly innovative, except they've been able to store the power in tiny cells. You can power your house for a week with something the size of a watch. Small volume, large capacity. Products like these are great, because they're easy to test and they don't fall within too many regulatory hoops. There's so much potential that I can't see how they cannot bring in a truckload of money to their investors, and that makes everybody happy. With Mark's share of that transaction, plus what I already made for him, he will have enough to lend me the money to buy out Sonya. I will repay that loan through my share of future successful funding rounds. I'll still draw a salary, as he does.

So that's why SunCell is so important to me. It requires a lot of funding. Like, a lot. A hundred million minimum, maybe more. But it's my future. If I pull it off, Abi and I are set financially. Maybe not for life, but for a good while. But even more than that. I really think this one is going to rock the world.

Mark's office is opposite mine, across the central area. He shares it with Caroline, his executive assistant. I was itching to talk to him about Eve. I caught Mark's eye through the glass walls. He winked at me, did a little flick of the head, which I had to admit I kinda love.

I walked briskly across to his office. "Do you have a minute?" He was standing and putting his laptop into his bag. He smiled. "I'd love to chat but unfortunately, I have to run. Is it urgent?"

"No, we can talk later. Hi, Caroline," I added, belatedly.

"Hello," she replied drily, without looking at me.

After he left, Mark sent me a text.

Sorry babe, had to run, can I see you later? 4pm? Usual place?

I got all tingly just reading that. I replied with a *yes please*. Even though it meant I'd have to take work home to finish later.

I grew up around the corner in Kirkland Place, not very

far from where I live now. It's the house of my childhood and it has stood empty ever since my father's funeral. It's the security for my mother's long-term care at Atwood House. I could sell it and give them money instead, but that would mean emptying it of its contents, and I don't know how to do that. It's not just their furniture, it's a lifetime of souvenirs, knick-knacks, my father's files, my mother's journals, and forty years of history. My parents were more enthusiastic about decorating in the seventies than in any other decade. There's even a set of ceramic ducks in increasing size on the wall of the living room. Mark joked they're probably worth something by now. It's a joke because a lot of things here are worth something, like my father's collection of antique clocks, some choice antique pieces of furniture, a small sketch by Giacometti—which is a study for a larger work but would certainly be valuable—a lovely small bronze sculpture by Gaudi, and on and on. It would be a mammoth undertaking to sift through this stuff. But most of all, these are still my mother's things, and it doesn't feel right to get rid of them.

This house has become our refuge, our place of intimacy. It's where Mark and I meet because I don't want to be sleeping with Mark at my own house yet, because of Abigail. I want to wait until our relationship is official, and cemented, before I even tell her about Mark.

We were lying in my parent's bedroom, our hair tousled and our legs caught in the sheets, me with my head on Mark's chest. He was lying back, his hands crossed behind his head, his eyes closed and a serious expression on his face. I took in the smell of him. He put his hand behind my neck. "I love you," he said. I raised myself on one elbow and pressed my lips on his mouth. I love his mouth. I love the shape of it, I love the taste of it. I pulled back and rubbed my knuckles against his stubbly chin. "You need a shave," I said.

He caressed the spot slowly. "People tell me it makes me look like a young George Clooney."

I laughed. "People say the darndest things, don't they?"

He laughed and punched me playfully on the shoulder.

"You got plans to update this museum yet?" he asked, crossing his hands behind his head again.

"Funny, I was going to ask for your help with that."

"Good. Because frankly, it's a little creepy."

I was surprised at that. "You really think so?"

"It's like Madame Tussaud without the wax figures."

"Oh haha. Good one, Mark."

"Or Jurassic Park without the dinosaurs."

"Stop it." But I knew what he meant. Everything was dusty and jaded. Dated. Like the dresser over in the corner, with a vanity mirror above it, round with cut glass decoration along the edge. Still now, the top drawer is filled with my mother's beauty products, what's left of them. Half empty jars of caked foundation, dusty sachets of potpourri that stopped smelling of anything a long time ago. Dried up tubes of lipstick. Hair clips and old bus tickets. It smells like her, that drawer, even with the touch of rancid. But this neglect isn't recent, and it's all over this house. What happened to her? When did she stop seeing?

I ran my fingers along Mark's arm. "Hey, about that position, the executive assistant we're recruiting," I said.

"What about it?"

"I have someone in mind."

"You do?"

"Yes, I think she'd be terrific. And I sort of owe her." I knew as soon as the words were out that it was the wrong thing to say. I do that sometimes. Speak before I have time to think about it.

"Sort of owe her what?" he asked, predictably. "What kind of basis is that anyway, to hire someone?"

"That came out wrong. I'm not asking you to hire her. I'm asking you to interview her, that's all."

"Who is she?"

"Someone I met recently. I think she'd be very good in the job, but like I said, just an interview. That's all I ask."

He thought about it for a moment. "I can interview her. She's qualified, isn't she?"

I beamed. "She was a legal secretary, in New York."

"Yeah, I don't know, Kat—"

"I didn't have any experience when you hired me."

"Yeah, but you're different. You're crazy smart. Anyone can see that."

He said that to me a lot. *You're crazy smart, Kat. Scary smart.*

Then his cell phone rang, with the familiar ringtone that made my heart sink a little because I knew it was Sonya calling, and that she needed him.

Mark swung his legs out of the bed without looking at me. Our clothes were strewn all over the floor and it took him a moment to find the phone. He pulled it out of the pocket of his jeans and ended the call without taking it. I rubbed a hand behind my neck.

"I should go," he said.

"Why?" I whined, reaching out to him. "She'll be fine. Stay."

"Don't be like that, Kat."

I didn't know what he meant. Like what? I knew Sonya wasn't very well and Mark was a caring soon-to-be-ex-husband, but I'd been very understanding, hadn't I?

He put on his trousers and tightened his belt. Then he leaned over to me, kissed me softly on the lips. "Your friend. Send her in. Actually, tell Caroline to make a time for her interview."

I pouted. "Okay," I said. Then I added, reluctantly, "Thanks."

"No problem. What's her name?"

"Eve."

Chapter Six

Eve got the job, as I knew she would. Mark was a little hesitant, but as he pointed out, she would be working mostly with me, so if I was happy, he was happy. When I called to tell her, she squealed in my ear so loudly I had to pull the phone away.

I was talking to Liam over a cup of coffee on the morning of Eve's first day. Liam is our IT guru. He builds software for us, analysis tools, that sort of thing.

Some people find Liam difficult to be around. He told me once that he always had issues with boundaries as a kid. He can't tell how close or how far he should stand from people. I suspect that's more common than you'd think. If anything, I used to have the opposite problem. I was always reaching out, touching, standing close, until I was made to grow out of it. Liam said that because of that, he's always careful to leave plenty of space around people, and as a consequence they think he's unfriendly. I told him, Liam, I hate to break it to you, but I think it's your looks. Get a haircut for one thing. He's a tall, gangly guy with floppy, jet-black hair that falls over his eyes all the time. People want to see your eyes, you know? And then his skin is kind of grey, probably because he never goes outside if he can help it.

He was showing me something on his phone when I heard Eve's voice beside me. "Oh, wow. Kat, hello! This place is awesome!"

"Eve! Hi! Welcome!" I chirped. She kissed me on the cheek, and I introduced her to Liam, who muttered a greeting and narrowed his eyes at her just before his hair fell back over them.

I led her away to show her around. "Friendly," she said. I smiled indulgently. "Not," she added, once we were out of earshot.

"He's all right," I said.

"I sure hope so. He looks like the type of kid who'd take a shotgun to his high school because his classmates wouldn't let him play Fortnite. Or something."

I was so shocked I stopped walking. I stood there, frozen, mouth open, speechless. She was three feet ahead of me before she noticed I wasn't there. "I was joking! Come on, let's get to work," she said gaily.

"That's one hell of a sense of humor you've got there, Eve," I snapped. "You might consider toning it down a notch. You don't even know him." I was surprised at how strong my own reaction was, and I didn't think it was because I wanted to defend Liam. I think it was because I was scared she wouldn't turn out to be the person I thought she was.

"Katherine, I'm sorry. I'm really nervous," she said. Her face crumbled in sorrow. "I'm an idiot. Forgive me?"

I nodded. I understood the urge of appearing more

confident than you really are and ending up looking like a complete tool. I decided to let it go.

"Let me show you around." I said. I forced myself to lighten up as I took her to our office. "Here we are, that's where we live, you and me. You're here," I pointed at one desk, "and I'm there."

She glanced around the room. "Very nice."

I checked my watch. "Every Monday morning we have a meeting, where everyone discusses any new business we should be looking at, and how our current ventures are tracking. It's about to start, come with me. You'll get to meet the team."

Everyone was already seated when we joined them. I introduced Eve. She said sweetly how delighted she was to be here and thanked everyone for making her so welcome.

"I brought a little thank you present," she said, her index finger pointing up. She turned around and walked over to reception, and we all watched her pick up a large white box from the counter and return with it, her skirt flowing sideways with every step. She opened the box and laid it on the table with a flourish. I recognized the pink ribbon and the Flour Bakery logo on the sticker.

Everyone stood and peered inside. There were brioches and those heavenly little chocolate muffins, cinnamon rolls with cream cheese glaze, and what looked like apple walnut scones that I knew Mark loved.

"You didn't have to do that!" Amy said, diving in. Then there was a blur of hands reaching and elbows pushing as we all picked our favorites. There was more than enough to go around and for a few minutes all you could hear was the licking of fingers and the smacking of lips.

"Well that was awesome, thank you Eve!" Mark said, and everyone agreed and started to clap so Eve stood and gave a little curtsey. It was funny and cute, and there was a lot of smiling and nodding and finally we got down to business. I felt strangely proud of her. I glanced over at Mark to gauge his reaction. He was looking at me, smiling. He winked.

I'd given everyone a copy of the SunCell strategy report and they all flipped their copy with their sticky fingers. Aaron the legal guy asked a million questions, and I was pleased to have an answer for every one of them. We didn't bring up any new business because we'd taken so long with SunCell and Mark does not like meetings to overrun.

We wrapped it up and I took Eve back to our office and got her settled.

"Wow," she said. She said 'wow' a lot I noticed. "That was so interesting, Katherine. I can't say I understood much of it, but you were awesome in there!"

I laughed. "You will, you'll see. It won't take long." Then Mark popped his head in the door and said, "Welcome again, Eve. Good to have you on board. Good job, Katherine." Then he walked off back to his desk without waiting for a reply and it occurred to me that having Eve here, in my office, was going to change things. No one knew about Mark and me—yet—so normally, when Mark came into my office, to anyone watching he would seem perfectly professional, but then he would always whisper something inappropriate. The conversation would go something like, "Good job, Katherine," and in a soft low voice, almost like a ventriloquist, he'd say, "now please take your top off." Which was hilarious and would make me laugh every time, and anyone watching would wonder why I was laughing because they thought all he'd said was, "Good job, Katherine." An inside joke if I ever saw one.

It goes without saying he left that last part out.

Chapter Seven

The following day, I was surprised to find Eve already there. It wasn't even eight thirty, but there she was, and not only that, she was talking to Liam over in the far corner of the reception area. She was nursing a cup of something steamy, and while Liam had his hands deep in his pockets, he looked like he might be enjoying himself, although with Liam it was hard to tell.

Eve saw me, smiled, said something to Liam who nodded, and then she pointed at her cup, her eyebrows raised. *Coffee?*

I gave her a thumbs-up, and five minutes later she joined me in my office with an espresso for me. Neither of us spoke of it, but I was pleased that she made the effort with Liam. It meant a lot to me.

Over the next few days, all my doubts—not that I had many—vanished. She turned out to be pretty fantastic, actually. She was a fast learner, and she worked hard. She asked all the right questions, even the ones not directly relevant to her position. She wanted to understand what we did here, how it happened, how it worked. She made me feel like a mentor to an eager disciple. She quickly took such a load off my shoulders that I found myself leaving work at a decent hour without having to take work home, and even having the odd coffee break.

We were eating lunch at our desks, Eve and I, straight out of take-out containers. We were talking through strategies to complete the funding round for SunCell when Caroline walked past our office and waved at Eve, who waved back.

"Did you know Caroline before you came here?" I asked.

"No, why?"

"No reason. I just wondered." *What's your trick*, is what I really wanted to say. *Why is she so nice to you?* But then you could tell that Eve made friends easily. She had that type of personality.

"Are you with someone?" she asked, picking out an olive from her Greek salad.

My eyes flicked involuntarily across to Mark's office. He was on the phone, he caught me looking at him and winked. I turned my attention back to Eve as she spat the small olive stone into her palm.

"Sorry, am I with someone? Yes, I am," I guessed.

She tilted her head at me. "You are?"

"Yes. Why so surprised?"

"It's just that, you never said, I mean, you never mentioned anyone, you don't seem to take personal calls, as far as I can tell."

I took a moment to chew through a bite of my bagel.

"It's still early," I told her, wiping a crumb from the corner of my lips.

"Ah. How long?"

"Six months."

"That's nice," she said. "I find six months is the tilting point, don't you? If you make it past six months, it's probably going to be fine."

"I sure hope so," I said. I kind of wanted to change the subject, I'm not used to talking about my private life, or the lack of it mostly. But then I remembered asking her similar questions when I first met her.

"So? What's his name?" she asked.

I hesitated, but only for a moment. "Mark." Surely that was safe to say. There are a million Marks out there, she wouldn't jump to any conclusions. But I hadn't said it out loud before, and it felt strange, and nice.

"Are we going to play twenty questions?" she asked, but not unkindly. She was taking a sip of water, looking at me over the rim. Eyebrows raised, waiting.

"Sorry. It's just that, well, considering what you told me before, about how your relationship ended…"

She put the drink down. "What do you mean?"

"He's kind of married." I made a face. Like a grimacing emoji with clenched teeth.

I could tell she was shocked.

"It's not what you think," I said quickly.

"Kat, first off, you don't know what I think. I'm not judging you, but when people say, 'it's not what you think', I find invariably that it is."

She was smiling, but I think she was hurt. Like I'd betrayed her somehow. She was identifying herself with Sonya at that moment, not me. *Note to self. Stop blurting.*

"Do they have children?"

"No!" I said too loudly. I lowered my voice. "They're in the process of separating."

"They are?" She popped a cherry tomato into her mouth. There was a definite irony to her tone.

"Yes, Eve. Actually they are."

"So they're still living together?"

I shook my head, unable to hide my frustration. Now I really wished I hadn't said anything. "It's complicated," I said.

"That's not an answer, Kat."

I snapped my head around but her face softened.

"I'm not trying to give you a hard time, and of course, it's none of my business—"

"Correctamundo," I said, trying to make a joke and sounding like an idiot instead.

"—but take it from someone who's been there. It doesn't take six months to tell your spouse you're leaving for someone else. In my experience, it takes three minutes and twelve seconds. If he's saying to you that he's going to leave his wife for you, and six months later he's still there—"

"He's not leaving *for me*. They were already splitting up when we met."

"Splitting up?"

"It was going to happen, anyway."

"I see." She patted my hand and wiped her mouth with a paper napkin, which she then scrunched into a ball and dropped into the empty salad container. I didn't know what to say. I watched her get up, gather the mess to put into the garbage.

"You're so smart, Kat, you should listen to yourself. That story you've just told me? I know it already. It's as old as time, and it always ends in tears."

Chapter Eight

It wasn't an affair, exactly. But it was illicit. It had started at the beginning of summer. We went to a conference together in Denver. I suspect this sort of thing happens a lot at conferences. Three days of being cooped up with colleagues and strangers, nice hotels, lots to drink, a company credit card. And there's always some kind of function at these things, where you're supposed to mingle and network. And then there are the dinners, the gatherings in bars, all of it away from the prying eyes of husbands and wives.

I suppose that's how it was with us, a shared bottle of wine over a meal, then when they closed the bistro we went up to his room because we didn't want to stop talking. Who made the first move? I don't know, and I don't care. All I know is that our bodies fit so well together, and that I was hungry for him, I suppose I was already in love with him, and it was wonderful.

I'm not proud of it, but I'm not embarrassed, either. I knew he was married, so yes, the morning following that first night, I did feel confused, guilty. I wanted to get up and get the hell out of his room. He didn't stop me, but later, in the hire car that was to take us back to Boston, he told me about his marriage.

He and Sonya had married young and tried to have children for many years. Subsequent tests revealed that Sonya was not able to get pregnant. They talked about IVF, adoption, but without much enthusiasm on either side. They came to terms with the prospect of not bringing up children into the world, and decided they were fine with that.

But—because there's always a but—as Mark's success grew, and Sonya threw herself into her interior decorating business, they drifted apart. They started to talk about separating. It was all very amicable, but last year, Sonya became ill with chronic fatigue syndrome. She's much better now, she's undergoing treatment and it's working, but Mark didn't bring up the separation anymore, and neither did she. He wanted to wait until she was well again. Then I suppose the routine set in—until he met me, and according to him, that's made everything change again and the time has come to finish the separation that they started.

There's nothing wrong with that story, as far as I can tell. It's a story of two people who care about each other deeply. They're still entitled to have their lives. But after talking to Eve that day, for the first time since Mark and I had been seeing each other, I thought it might be time to move this relationship out of its cocooned closet and into the sunshine.

After work, I went to visit my mother. I asked Eve if she wanted to come with me to Atwood House, but she said no.

"I'm exhausted," she said. "I guess I'm not used to working full time anymore. I'm going home, and I'll try to get some rest. If I can, with all the noise in my house."

"What do you mean?"

"Well, you know how I told you my relationship broke up recently?"

"I remember."

She made a face. "I'm couch surfing, staying with my friend Allegra right now. She's a good friend but still, it can't last forever." She shook her head. "I feel like such a loser sometimes."

"Oh, Eve! On the couch? In the living room? Every night? No way!"

"I know, tell me about it. But hey, not for much longer! Let me tell you, Kat, this job is a Godsend. *You* are a Godsend. I'm so grateful to you, you have no idea."

I told her not to worry about that, it was the least I could do, I said, after what she did for my mother, for me. It's me who's grateful, I said.

It was very quiet at Atwood House. My mother was asleep. She looked so peaceful. I sat next to her and just held her hand.

After a few minutes I pulled my cell from my bag. There's a photo of Mark and me from that Denver function. I'm looking toward the stage, eyes squinting in concentration. Mark is looking at me, a small smile on his lips. There is an air of such gentleness about him, and I think, of love. I adore that picture, so much so I keep it on my phone. I look at it sometimes.

I called him. He picked up immediately.

"Hi, Katherine," he said, a little brisk, a little formal, and I wondered if Sonya was there.

"I was hoping we could talk, are you busy?"

"Yeah, a bit busy, what's up?"

And just like that, my sense of Mark shifted. I had wanted to push Eve's words aside, mentally shove them to the bottom of the trash. I wanted to discard them in a *she doesn't understand* garbage bag and tell myself that what Mark was going through with Sonya was really hard.

But instead I felt a wave of resentment rise up. "Can you unbusy yourself? We really need to talk."

"I can meet you in thirty minutes," he said.

We were sitting at the dining room table at my mother's house. He was slumped into the chair, looking pained.

"It's true, right? Everything you've told me? You and Sonya, you're really separating, aren't you? If it turned out I'm just a fling on the side, I don't know what I'd do Mark. I think I might have to kill you." I meant that last bit as a joke to lighten the mood, but my stomach was clenched with nerves and it just came out harsh and wrong.

"I wasn't going to have a relationship with a married man. I would never do that," I said, as if that mattered. As if that wasn't exactly what I'd been doing.

"Of course I know that," he said, and I couldn't remember the question.

"What are we really doing, Mark?"

He tried to take my hands but I pulled them to me.

"Mark?"

"You know what. Sonya and me, it's over. It's been over for years. You know that."

"Please stop saying that. I know nothing of the sort, you've been saying that for months."

"I just need more time."

"Mark, I swear, if you throw one more clichéd platitude at me, I'm going to kick you. Or bite you. Or both."

It was strange and unexpected, but it felt good to argue. I hadn't realized until my conversation with Eve just how overdue this fight was. Maybe I'd been asleep at the wheel, coasting on his tail wind. Maybe I'd just parked this conversation in the 'too hard' basket. It had been easier to pretend that everything was fine, and everything was going to resolve itself, by magic, thanks to some fairy dust I happened to carry in my back pocket.

"You're right. I need to do something about this," he said, running a hand through his thick, black curly hair. He looked so sheepish, I wanted to take him into my arms and tell him everything was going to be okay. But I didn't.

"If you've been lying to me—" He flinched at my words, "—and your marriage was never going to end, then you better just tell me right now. Or should I end it myself and spare the both of us?"

He just cocked his head, and his eyes swam in sadness. I immediately regretted my words.

"Kat, I love you. I'm begging you, wait for me, please."

"How long?"

"Do you trust me? Look at me, Kat, do you trust me?"

"How long!" I repeated, because we were having this conversation now, for real. And I thought, fuck it, I may as well get a deadline, an end game. I'm here now. And it did occur to me that I never had one from him. Not really. Just vague promises.

"One month."

"What's going to happen in a month that hasn't happened yet?"

"Two weeks then. Please."

"Two weeks?"

"Yes. That's all I need. I swear to you."

Two weeks I could do. Two weeks, at this point, was kind of easy. Two weeks was exciting.

"Okay," I said. "Two weeks."

He leaned forward until his lips touched mine, and we kissed, tenderly, for a long time, and I let the words dance in my head.

Two. Weeks.

Chapter Nine

A few days later I found myself navigating the streets of Danvers, a suburb I'm not familiar with, leaning forward to read the streets signs through the rain. This was a really bad night to be out. I wished I was home with Abi, curled up with a good book, instead of out here on this wet and dreary winter evening. But Eve was so insistent, I didn't have the heart to turn her down.

"I want to thank you properly," she said. "For everything you've done for me."

I told her fifty million times that it was me who was indebted to her, but it was no use. She announced with much flourish that she was taking me to a *very* special restaurant for dinner, and I was to pick her up on the way. This is the kind of situation I find myself in often, where someone says they want to do something for me, like a favor, and somehow I end up going out of my way to help them do it. It sure happens with Hilary a lot.

I finally found her street and turned onto it, and there she was, just a few feet ahead, waving at me from beneath an umbrella. I'd hoped right until then that she wouldn't be there. That maybe she'd felt sick and had forgotten to call me. But I put on a bright smile and pulled up in front of her.

"Hi!" she chirped—bright and happy, classic Eve—flashing her radiant smile. All doubts about the evening left me, just like that. I was already having a good time.

"So where are we going?" I asked, pulling away from the curb.

"Chestnut Hill," she said.

"Okay, it's a bit vague, but Chestnut Hill it is."

Everything about that night is a blur. She took me to an upmarket, eye-wateringly expensive French restaurant where we possibly drank more wine than we should, but she kept ordering it and what the heck. Being out with Eve was very different from my usual nights out with girl-friends. Not that I have those often. But when Hilary and I get together, we talk about the kids, about school, about her husband Henry, about responsibilities. Even going out with Sasha back in LA is nothing like being out with Eve. That night she was funny, engaging with everyone around her. She told me hilarious stories that had me crying with laughter in my celery root velouté with crabmeat and candied lemon. She talked about the future, the things she wanted to do, the places she wanted to go. She was interested in me. She wanted to know all about Abigail, and why I liked numbers so much.

"My father was a mathematician," I said, twirling my spoon into a crème brulée. "Mathematics made us close, my father and me. Until we weren't."

"What happened?"

She coiled a lock of hair around her finger and waited.

48

"I got pregnant."

"How old were you?"

Do the math, I almost said.

"Fourteen."

"Wow!"

"I had a crush on a boy at my school called Harry. We lost our virginity to each other ... on his parents' sofa. They were at the movies, and we were supposed to study for a history test."

What are the odds of getting pregnant the first time you have sex? The same as any other time.

Or maybe it's fifty fifty, either you get pregnant or you don't.

"Two months before my fifteenth birthday, I found out I was going to have a baby. I told my mother, she told my father, he ordered me to have an abortion. I said no. He threw me out of the house. I begged him to let me stay. My mother threatened to leave him if he didn't. But he wouldn't budge. It was too late, he said. The trust was broken. I had brought his good name into disrepute. I told him to fuck off, and his good name, too. Then I got sent to live with an aunt and uncle in LA, and I never saw my father again."

"What about Abigail? He must have softened when he met her. Surely."

I shook my head. "He never met her."

"You're kidding! Why?"

"He didn't want to."

"What about your mother?"

"She did, she would come over to us regularly. He couldn't forbid her to see us, or if he tried, she never said. She doted on Abigail."

"Your father sounds like a total asshole," Eve said.

Sometimes I think keeping my baby was my one and

only act of defiance. After that, I became more of a people-pleaser. Finding out at a young age how dependent you are on others will do that to you.

"Yep, that's my dad."

We finished our meal and I started to yawn.

"This was really, really lovely Eve. Thank you."

"You're not going home yet," she said. "I'm taking you out, remember?" She told me about a nightclub that was all the rage apparently, as if that would mean anything to me. "I've never been there, have you?"

"Me? You must be joking. I've never been anywhere," I said. Which is true, I never went out much. When Abi came along, I was still too young to go into places like that. Amazing, when you think about it.

We went. I can't say I was 'wowed' by the place, but Eve was excited. She wanted to dance in the blue, pulsing light of the dance floor, so I let myself be guided. And then I was floating, my arms high, I felt languid and light. Even when my heart was thumping, it wasn't unpleasant.

I have no idea what the time was when we left. The rain had turned to a drizzle, and I was freezing. I pulled the belt of my coat tighter and shoved my hands deep in my pockets. Eve hooked her arm into mine. She was still laughing.

"I'll call an Uber," I slurred, fishing around for my cell phone.

She punched me on the shoulder. It kind of hurt. "Don't be silly, you can drive us home."

I laughed, rubbing at the spot. "I don't think so!"

"Oh, come on, Kat. Don't be such a sissy." She dragged me toward the car and I remember thinking that I didn't know exactly what a sissy was, but I sure didn't want to be one.

"We'll go via the Parkway, over there." She waved, swaying a little, pointing to the distance. "You know the one. There won't be any cops there. My uncle's a cop, did I tell you?"

"No, you did not."

"Yeah, he's in traffic or something. He tells me those things. Like where the cops patrol at night and where they don't bother. He's a nice guy, Uncle Bill. I'll introduce you some day."

Back in the car I turned the heat on and rubbed my hands together.

"You think I'm okay?" I asked. "I think I'm okay."

"You're definitely okay," she said. "Definitely."

"I don't feel drunk, I just feel relaxed."

"Exactly."

"But I don't really know the way home that way."

I started to fiddle with the GPS.

"It's easy. I'll direct you, it's just down there," she said.

"All righty then." I turned off the street and followed her directions.

"This is so eerie," I said. "I've never been down here at this time of night. It's beautiful."

"Go this way," she said. "Just for a minute." I drove into an empty parking lot.

"Here?"

I thought she wanted to pee on the side of the road and I remember thinking, hey, this woman is wild. Instead she pulled what looked like a hand-rolled cigarette from her pocket.

I turned off the ignition and squinted at it. "Is that what I think it is?"

"Uh-huh." She brought up a lighter. The flame threw a yellow glow onto her face as she lit it up and in that light for a moment, she looked kind of scary. It made me jerk away.

She let out a long stream of smoke and passed it to me. "Trust me, this is super fun stuff. It'll make you focus, too."

"Focus would be good," I said.

I took the joint from her and inhaled a nice long drag. I don't know why I did it. Because why not? Because I didn't want to kill the party? Because it was Eve?

Because all of the above.

The hit was instant. It didn't burn my throat, which I figured was a sign that this was 'top-grade' stuff, as she put it. It brought a rush of pleasure and I felt mildly euphoric, like I had back at the club.

I leaned back against the seat and let the feeling engulf me. Eve laughed, and I did, too. Soon we laughed so much that I could barely get a breath.

"Stop, I'm going to pee in my pants!" she said, and eventually we calmed down. I started the car again as Eve tapped on the GPS screen.

"I have a setting in there for 'Home'," I said. "I'll do it."

"That's okay, I got it," she said. "It's just a straight line. Turn here, left," she said, just as the GPS said, "turn left," which sent us both into another fit of laughter.

I knew I shouldn't be driving, but I told myself we were only fifteen minutes away, and Eve has an uncle who is a cop who says it's perfectly all right apparently, as long as you don't get caught.

"Slow down," she admonished. I checked the dash and it was true, I was speeding. She had her hand on my arm, her eyes on the speedometer and I pulled off the accelerator until we were cruising at a leisurely 30 miles per hour.

"Better," she said, pulling her hand away.

We were back among trees, and I wasn't sure where I was. It was strange how quiet it was, how alone we were. I remember thinking it must be very late. I remember the rain starting again. I remember being thirsty.

"Take it all the way to Beacon Street, and we'll be almost home," Eve said. I knew my way from Beacon Street so that was good. I started to relax.

There was a song on the radio, and Eve turned it up and we started to sing along. I was buzzing. I felt mildly scared but fantastic. I felt free, driving on the windy road, slicing through Hammond Pond Reservation. It was beautiful, the forest lit by the yellow hue of the overhead lights through the rain.

Eve said something, but I only caught the beginning, *Hey*, because the music was so loud.

"What?" I yelled back. She was laughing. She was so pretty. She said something else but I still couldn't hear so I reached for the volume button.

And then I screamed.

Chapter Ten

I'm shaking, my hand on my mouth. I can smell the vomit from moments ago. Eve is crouched down next to the shape.

"It's a ... a person," she says.

"I know it's a person for fuck's sake."

It's a man, to be precise. He's wearing a dark hoodie, a grey scarf around his neck, dark jeans. Boots. His clothes are frayed, old, like he's been wearing them for ... I don't know, a long time. Then I see the blood oozing out next to his head. Like a snake.

"Oh, God. Fuck. Okay. We have to call an ambulance. Is there a car coming? Where's my phone? I need my phone. I'll get my phone and you look out for a car, okay? Flag the first one you see." My heart is racing and every inch of my body is shaking. I'm about to go into complete panic mode, I'm already hyperventilating, seconds away from hysteria.

"Katherine! Wait!"

She sounds as hysterical as I feel. I turn back to look at her. She's still crouched next to the man. Strands of her long, blond hair hiding the side of her face. She has pulled his scarf down and pressed two fingers against the side of his throat. I feel the bile rise up again. I don't know how she can do that. I couldn't touch him. Maybe it's because she's a volunteer. She must be good in times of crisis. She looks up at me. Her blue eyes fixed and staring right into mine.

"What?" I ask.

She waits a beat, it feels like a century, her fingers still on his throat, her eyes still drilling into mine, pleading.

"We have to go. We have to get out of here."

"What?"

"There's no heartbeat. I can't feel a heartbeat!" she cries.

I come closer. I still don't want to touch him, but I must. Because what Eve just said, it can't be true. I bend down and reach out, my arm shaking.

"Kat, stop, we have to go! He's dead!"

"Dead? How can he be dead?"

"Get in the car."

"No! I have to call an ambulance!"

The blood has stopped oozing and is settling into a puddle, slimy like a pool of snakes. It has reached her feet.

I throw up a second time, but nothing comes up.

"I have to get my phone," I say again, for what feels like the tenth time.

"Kat, please."

She's got a hand on one side of her chest, against her ribs. For a moment I'm afraid she's really hurt. That she's bleeding. That she's going to die, too.

"We have to leave," she says again. She sounds desperate.

"But we can't leave him here and just walk away, is that what you're suggesting?"

"Listen to me—"

"No. I mean it, Eve. Sorry, but we can't. Maybe you hit your head, too, I don't know, but it's not going to happen, okay? I can't believe you even—"

"I'm not going to jail!" she shouts.

I flinch. "Jail? Who the fuck said anything about jail!"

"And you're supposed to be the fucking genius? We're stoned, Kat! Up to our eyeballs! And I'm worse than you, I took a couple of pills—"

"You took some pills? What pills?"

"—and maybe I won't get locked up for possession, but you're definitely going to jail. You are way over the limit, and that's on top of the joint you've just smoked. How many drinks have you had?"

I shake my head. I don't know how many drinks, I've got no idea, time makes no sense right now, nothing makes sense right now.

"We can't just leave him here," I say again, but not so forcefully this time, because in the back of my mind, there's a little voice asking, *can we?*

Eve has taken hold of my arm and she's pulling me into the car. "Come on! Fuck, Katherine! Move!" She pushes me into the passenger seat and runs back around to the driver's side.

I keep repeating, over and over. "I don't understand. I didn't see him, did you see him? How could I not have seen him?"

She starts the engine and drives us down a side road that leads onto an empty lot. Another one. She turns off the ignition. She's still shaking. So am I.

"You're okay?" she asks with a hiccup.

"No, Eve, I'm not. Not okay. Not at all okay. How can you even ask me that?" I put my hand over my eyes. My entire body is vibrating. A mixture of adrenaline from the shock and the drugs I took earlier. I don't even know if any of this is real.

"We can't get caught for this. I'm sorry," she says again. "But I'm not going to jail. And you have to think about Abi, and your mother. They need you, Kat. There's nothing you can do for this guy back there. He's a junkie—"

"You don't know that."

"He sure looked it."

"So what if he is?"

She turns to look at me.

"Was, Kat, was."

But she's too shaken up to drive after all, so we swap places again. We don't speak at all on the journey home. I'm in shock. I can't believe what just happened. "Maybe you should take the car to a mechanic," she says. "In case anything needs to be fixed up."

"Like what?"

"Like any damage to the front of the car, where you hit—"

"Jesus, Eve, back up! It's not just me. Don't put this on me."

"I'm not, I'm just saying, where the *car* hit him, okay? Better?"

Somehow, we're on my street now. I pull up outside my house and turn off the ignition. Abigail has left the porch light on for me, but the upstairs windows are dark. It's after two in the morning.

"How will you get home?" I ask.

"I'll walk a bit, then I'll get an Uber. Get some sleep, Kat. I'll see you tomorrow, okay?"

I nod, knowing full well there's no way I'm getting any sleep now.

I'm about to put the key in the door, but I then turn back one last time. "Do you want to stay here?" I wipe tears with the back of my hand, tears of grief, exhaustion, and yes, gratitude.

She shakes her head. "I just want to get home." Then she adds, "We did the right thing, Katherine."

"Did we?" I wish she hadn't said that, because there's nothing right about what we just did. Not by any stretch of the imagination.

"Trust me," she says, and I watch her walk off down the street.

Later, with a couple of Valium to calm my nerves, I slip into my bed and immediately get into a fetal position. I think of Sasha, back in LA. I so desperately want to call her. *What have I done? What should I do?* But it's too late, and as the minutes, then the hours, tick by, I come to a conclusion. Eve is right. There's my daughter to think about, and my mother. I'd lose my job over this. I cannot lose my job. I'd lose everything. So yes, of course Eve is right. There's nothing we could have done for this man, and there's a part of me that blames him, too. A big part. What was he doing there? In the middle of the night, for Christ's sake! It was raining, it was dark! There's nothing down there. And I don't think we were going too fast. There was no traffic. I was stoned off my face. We were singing along with Miranda Lambert. I wasn't looking at the dashboard, I was looking at the road. I think. And for all I know, he's not dead. Eve said he didn't have a pulse, but what, is she a doctor all of the sudden? I bet he's fine. Someone found him and got him help. He'll be okay. I'm sure of it.

What was *I* even doing there? I don't go out with friends and get trashed like that. I haven't smoked a joint since college. I'm not even a big drinker.

Why was I there? I didn't want to bum my new friend, that's why. I wanted to show her that I'm not a sissy. I still know how to have fun.

How much fun are you having now, Katherine?

Chapter Eleven

The sound is so loud, so shrill, for a moment I think I'm in the car again, back on that road. Back in that crash. My heart feels like it exploded and has torn my chest in the process. I scramble out of the bed. It's my phone. I snatch it off the bedside table, answer it without looking.

"Where are you? Are you sick? You better be sick, Katherine," Mark says.

I sit up quickly.

"What?"

My head hurts so much. It's too bright in here. I put my hand over my eyes.

"I've been trying to call you all morning. We waited for you for over an hour." Then he hisses, "Where the fuck are you?"

I pull the phone away from my ear to check the time on the screen. Five past eleven. Shit. And I've missed four calls.

"I'm sorry," I say. "I think I slept in." The words are thick and blurry, like I've just come out of the dentist's chair.

"You think you slept in?" his voice has shifted up half an octave. Incredulous.

I spot a note on top of the bedside table. I pick it up and it shakes in my hand so much I can barely read it.

It's from Abigail.

Hi Mom, I hope you're okay, I let you sleep, you said you didn't have anything going on this morning. See you tonight. Love you xox.

"Sorry," I mumble. "What did I miss?"

"What do you mean, what did you miss? The SunCell Strategy meeting, Katherine! You organized it." Then in a lower voice he asks, "What's wrong? Are you ill?"

I swing my legs out of the bed. "Mark, the strategy meeting isn't until Tuesday."

"You moved it, Katherine, for this morning, nine am. What's the matter with you?"

Fuck. I did change it. I remember now. I wanted to move things along. No point in waiting, that's what I said.

I drop my head in my hand. "Oh, God. I'm sorry."

"For Christ's sake. Never mind, stay home. I'll see you Monday."

"No, I'll come now," I tell him, but he's already hung up, although not before I catch him mumble, "This is bullshit."

In the bathroom, my soiled clothes from last night are in a heap on the floor in the corner. Oh, God. They're still damp from the rain. I check them for blood. I can't see any. I shove them to the bottom of the laundry basket.

I stand under the shower for a few minutes and let the water hit my face with sharp, hot jets. Snatches of my nightmares are forcing themselves through the fog of my brain. Dreams of being lost in the woods, of Eve with blood on her hands. Of my father standing in front of my car as I press my foot down on the accelerator.

I push the visions away.

I pull out a dark grey suit from the wardrobe, with a white shirt. Not very original, but that's my go-to outfit when I don't want to think about it—slim, dark pants and matching tailored jacket.

I brush down my clothes quickly with the palm of my hand and run a hairbrush through my hair. I can't bear to think about anything, in case I think about last night, so I strive to keep my mind blank.

By the time I close the door behind me, it's eleven thirty-two.

Then I see my car. It's parked in the street, right where we left it last night. I don't usually park it out here since I have a garage. I get up close, quickly check the front, my pulse racing at the prospect of what I might find there.

There is something. A small piece of light, coarse fabric, caught on the edge of the license plate. I bend down and dislodge it, slowly, like it's a scary thing, like it might hurt me.

I'm going to be sick. There's a dent on the front of the car near the left headlight, like it's been pushed in. I wonder if Abi has noticed? Probably not. Why would she even look? It's not like she drives. God. This is already turning out to be such a shit day, after such a shit night.

Old Mr. Jones next door is peering at me from his window. I wave at him—not a wave exactly, more like a vague lift of the hand. He doesn't wave back. He pulls down his blinds instead.

I don't take the car. I couldn't even drive right now, anyway, let alone *that* car. I'm still shaky, groggy, out of place. I don't park it in the garage because I'm already late enough as it is. I'll do it when I get home. Hopefully someone will steal it before then. I leave the keys dangling in the ignition, just to make sure.

I take a taxi, and when I make it to work, a double espresso in one hand and a handful of Tylenol in my stomach, I spot Mark in his office, his back to me, talking to someone. Then I realize it's Eve. Okay, that's good. She's here. Good.

I push the door open and march straight in, but I pushed it harder than I intended so it bounces on its hinges and hits the wall with a clank.

"Shit. Sorry I'm late, let's go. Where is everybody?"

Funny, I never noticed that Mark's eyes are hazel. I thought they were brown, on the light side, sure, but—

"You're all right, Katherine?" he says, those hazel eyes now narrowed at me, but not in concern so much as annoyance, I note.

"I'm fine." I feel like I've already apologized a million times this morning, but clearly, it's not enough. "I'm sorry I'm late," I tell him. "It won't happen again. Hi, Eve. Let's go."

I've stepped outside, but neither of them is moving.

"We've had the meeting," Mark says. He flicks his wrist, checks his Fitbit. I hate that thing. He's always fiddling with it, checking his heartbeat, how many steps he's walked today.

"I said I was sorry, Mark, you don't have to make a big deal out of it. Jesus."

He winces at my outburst. Eve doesn't even look at me.

"You're sure you're okay?" he asks. "You don't look too good."

"I'm perfectly fine." They're both staring at the Styrofoam cup in my hand. I look down to see it's shaking uncontrollably. I make a point of pulling down my sleeve with my other hand, just to make it stop, but it's awkward, with all the things I'm carrying, my bag, my laptop.

"Let's go. Why are you wasting time?" I say.

"I just told you. We've had the meeting, Kat!" Mark's voice is unusually harsh, I think.

"You can't have the meeting without me, Mark. It's my strategy."

"Then you should have been here on time," he snaps.

"I know, you said that already, and I said I was sorry." I wish he'd stop. He's embarrassing me, in front of Eve.

"Eve filled us in. She stepped in for you."

"Oh?"

"And you can thank her because as you know, I don't like wasting time. I don't like wasting my staff's time. I had to move things around for this. If you couldn't manage it, then you shouldn't have rescheduled the meeting in the first place. Or at the very least you should have called to let me know."

Eve's face is a blank; she's looking at me, and I try to interpret the look in her eyes, but she doesn't give anything away. God, she's so cool! I don't know how she does it, but she's very calm, completely in control. And she's rested, too, I see that now. Or maybe she's very good with makeup. Either way, she looks good. Her eyes are clear, unlike mine, which looked so bloodshot earlier in my bathroom mirror, I had put on my largest sunglasses, a pair of mirrored Ray-Bans I found on a bus seat.

Which reminds me. I'm still wearing them.

I take them off and catch Eve's eye. She gives me a discrete shake of the head. *No.*

I slip them back on.

"I told you I was on my way," I say to Mark. "I was late, that's all, it's not the end of the world, is it? You could have served them coffee or something. Introduced the project. I would have turned up eventually."

"The meeting was at nine am, Katherine. It's now—" he does that wrist flick again, "—almost noon. Eve was here. She brought the team up to speed. What's up with the glasses, anyway?"

"Conjunctivitis," I say. "Eve, can I speak to you in my office?"

"Of course," she replies.

"Okay, how're we doing?" I whisper as I close the door. "You're okay? You seem to be coping, yes?"

I wish we had blinds. I should get some cheap drapes or something. A bed sheet. Just for a day like this.

I take my sunglasses off.

"Whoa, you don't look too good, Kat."

"Thanks, Eve, I really needed that. Thank you very much."

I put the Styrofoam cup on the desk, but I misjudge and it's too close to the edge—just by a smidgen, mind you —but enough for it to tilt and land on the floor.

There's coffee everywhere.

"Shit." I reach for the box of Kleenex and start mopping at it. I look up. "Can you help me out, please?"

She gives a quick shake of her head, but she crouches down next to me and does the same.

"Why are you so late?" she whispers.

"Why do you think? I've had a hell of a night. I took too many Valiums. Abigail took herself to school. She let me sleep."

I turn my head, look over my shoulder. Standing behind the glass of his office, Mark is watching us, arms crossed against his chest.

"You can't bring attention to yourself like that," she says. "You're supposed to act natural."

"I am," I snap. "This *is* natural. It's exactly the way I act whenever I run over someone and kill them. Oh, God." I bring the heel of my hands against my eyes and press hard. I can't lose it. Not now. No way.

"Kat, I'm begging you! Pull yourself together!" She looks behind her shoulder, and sure enough, plenty of eyes are on us, in our own personal fishbowl. She leans closer. "They found him. The last thing we want is for people to ask questions, put two and two—"

I freeze. "What did you just say?"

"We don't want anyone to suspect—"

"Before that?"

She dumps the sodden tissues into the waste paper basket and stands up.

"They found him. Why are you so surprised?"

I'm still on my knees, looking up at her.

"I think you should get up now, Katherine."

I look across reception. Mark isn't looking at us anymore. He's gone back to his desk. He's on the phone. Caroline, however, is lapping it up.

"Show's over!" I yell out.

Eve strides over to her own desk. "Take a look," she says, but in a low voice. She swivels the monitor toward me. I get up close. I'm looking at today's Herald in the browser window. I grip the back of her chair. I have to sit down for this.

Body Found in Hammond Pond Reservation

Brookline Police were called to Hammond Pond Parkway at 3:30am on Friday after an anonymous 911 call. The body of a man was found at the scene. Brookline Police say he was the victim of a hit-and-run and are asking for help in locating the driver. The vehicle should have front end damage. The victim is yet to be formally identified. Anyone with information should contact Brookline Police.

I wish we hadn't gone out. I didn't want to go, I wanted to stay home, hang out with Abi. Watch Netflix. Maybe have a single glass of red wine. I wish I could turn back the clock. All I can think now is that this man really is dead. Oh, God.

"I've spoken to my uncle Bill about this," she says, tapping on the screen to make her point.

"What?" I blurt. "You told your uncle? Are you out of your fucking mind?"

"I didn't tell him this! What do you take me for? I told him, I think I might—" she makes air quotes around the word 'might' "—know something about this, but I'd rather it stayed out of the news. Okay? At least for now. He said he'll see what he can do. I can't make any promises, Kat, you understand, but I'm his favorite niece and if he thinks this has anything to do with me, he'll make sure I'm safe. Christ, you really look like shit." She's shaking her head at me.

"He can do that? Your uncle?"

"Sure, he can. He's very high up. Maybe you should go home. I'm sure everyone will understand. I'll just tell them you've got the flu or something."

I want to go home. I want to go home and hug my daughter, but she's at school, and the last thing, the very last thing I want right now, is to be alone. I wave her words away.

"Thank you, about your uncle, you really think…?"

"Leave it with me."

"Okay. Thank you. That's good. I think." I stand up, I take a breath. I will myself to calm down. There's nothing I can do now. Okay. I'm good, I'm fine. Breathe.

"Tell me how the meeting went."

She shrugs. "Not much to tell." She's got a notebook on her lap, and she's tapping a pen on top of it. Tap, tap, tap.

I stare at her, unsure if I heard her correctly, but then I remember. She's going through the same thing I am. We're just dealing with it differently.

"Why don't you indulge me anyway," I say.

"Sure thing, Boss." She talks me through it, shows me the notes. There's nothing wrong with anything she says. I can't think of anything she left out.

"How did you know all this? About the strategy?"

She cocks her head at me. "I did a bunch of research for you, we discussed it. I know what's in the strategy paper. I'm the one who typed it up."

"Okay, great, good to know. Well, thank you for that. Sounds like you bailed us out of a tight spot there." But there's a part of me that wants to say, *Maybe next time, Eve, wait for me, okay?*

"No problem, Katherine. I enjoyed it," she says. She sounds so professional, chirpy even. Like we didn't leave some poor dead guy on the side of the road last night.

"God, I'll never take too many Valiums again, that's for sure."

Eve smiles at me. "Good," she says. Then she leans forward, and still smiling, she whispers, "For fuck's sake, Kat, pull yourself together."

Chapter Twelve

I pretend to do some work, but it's out of the question. My headache is killing me. I feel like someone is pushing a drill above my left eye. If I could I'd curl up right here on the floor and go to sleep. I don't want to take anything else because I've already lost my mind.

But I keep thinking about him. Will someone claim him? When? He did look ... alone, neglected. I wonder if anyone misses him right now. Does he have a wife? A brother? Is someone out there, making increasingly frantic calls? *Please, have you seen him? He's my brother. He's my son. He's my boyfriend.* Oh, God.

If I disappeared, how long would it take for someone to miss me? That one's easy. Judging by the number of missed calls this morning, I'd say twenty minutes, give or take.

At four o'clock I tell Eve she can go home. These are the first words I've said to her all afternoon.

"Go home, Eve. You've earned it."

She shrugs. "Sure, whatever you say, Boss." I wish she wouldn't call me *Boss*. It feels wrong to be joking around. I turn back to my screen while she gathers her things, retrieves her coat from the coatrack, puts it on, tightens the belt. She's taking her time. I pretend to be absorbed in what I'm doing, which is not very much at all, and I wonder if I'm even fooling her.

"You're okay now?" she asks, her head cocked at me. "We've had a hell of a shock, yeah? Take it easy. Relax. Everything is under control."

"Thanks Eve. And thanks for stepping in today."

"That's okay, I just wanted to make sure you wouldn't get in trouble."

"Right. I appreciate that."

"Have a good weekend, Katherine. I'll see you on Monday."

"You too, Eve."

Neither of us suggests we catch up over the weekend. We've had enough of each other for now, I suspect. I sure need a break from her. I bet she needs one from me. I wonder for the first time if she's mad at me. That would make sense. I think I would be, in her shoes. I was the one driving, after all. She may have goaded me on, but it was my responsibility. I'm terrible at responsibilities.

I expect her to saunter out the main doors and into the street, but instead she crosses the reception floor and walks right into Mark's office. That's a bit strange, but okay. She stands in front of his desk, says something to him. He nods, frowns, then they both turn to look at me.

The heat rises up my cheeks as I lower my eyes and move the mouse, click randomly. Then there's a sharp, single knock on my door even though it's open.

It's Liam.

"What happened to you?" he asks. He walks in, sits himself into Eve's chair, and swivels back and forth.

I shake my head. When I look back toward Mark's office, Eve is gone.

"Bad night," I tell him. "Real bad." I get up and close the door, then I cross my arms.

"How was Eve this morning? At the meeting?"

"In what way?" he asks.

"Was she nervous? Did she seem upset at all? That I wasn't there?"

"Not that I could tell. She was totally on top of it. She ran it like it was always meant to be her doing it, to be honest."

"Okay, good. That's good to hear." But it's not. Not at all. These people are supposed to miss me if I'm not here.

"Good call on your part, Kat."

"What does that mean?"

"To hire Eve, she's awesome."

"Oh, right. Good. I'm glad."

"You're okay? You look like shit."

Another hour and everyone is leaving for the day. No one works late on Fridays at Rue Capital—they're doing it enough during the week, myself included.

I watch them with envy. They're going home to their ordinary, quiet, boring lives. They don't have a care in the world. Not really. You don't know what stress is until you kill someone and leave them to rot by the side of the road. I find, anyway. Right now, there's a weight in the pit of my stomach that I can't get rid of. I'm fairly sure it will never go away.

Caroline bursts in and makes me jump. She laughs. "Hey, I didn't mean to startle you. You were sick this morning, you're all right now?"

"If one more person asks me that, I'm going to scream." I meant it to sound light but judging from the look of surprise on her face, I missed the mark.

"Sorry. Tough day. What can I do for you?"

"We're going to the bar downstairs for a cocktail, I thought Eve might want to join us?"

"She's already left."

"Oh." She looks disappointed. "You want to come?"

I'd rather have a tooth pulled out than have another drink right now, but I check my watch, just for show, then realize I'm not wearing it. "I've got visitors coming. I should go home, but thanks anyway, Caroline."

I just said that as an easy excuse but then it hits me. I do have visitors tonight. Shit. Hilary and Paige are coming for dinner. Shit. I have so much to do. I get up quickly and it makes me dizzy. I wonder if I'm dying.

I grab my things and go to see Mark to say goodbye, to apologize again.

"I'm going home," I tell him.

There's a look of worry in his eyes.

"Please don't ask me if I'm okay."

He smiles. Thank God. I manage a smile myself, from one side of my mouth only. A half smile.

"You're having a quiet weekend?" he asks.

I imagine telling him, *Something terrible happened, Mark. I killed somebody. I didn't mean to do it, but we went out and—*

"Yes, I am. I aim to be rid of this flu by Monday." I think that works. If everyone thinks I'm really ill, I may as well use it. "We have a lot on our plate next week, with the pitch and all," I add.

I'm about to say that it would be nice to catch up, maybe on Sunday, when he says, "It was good of Eve to offer to put together the pitch deck. How do you feel about that?"

"The pitch deck?" I smile, then I smile some more.

"You do remember about the presentation, right?" he asks. "You haven't forgotten about that, too?"

There's a certain levity to his tone. It's obviously meant to be a joke, but there's also a whiff of hesitation lurking under there, as if he's making sure, just in case.

"You can't be serious," I say. "Why on earth would Eve put the pitch deck together?"

"She offered, that's all." But his eyes linger on my face and he frowns. Then he says, "I think it's too early, don't you? She's not experienced enough yet."

"No! I mean yes, it's too early. She's only been here a week!" Then more softly I say, "This is way too important for us, Mark. There's no room for error on this one."

Why would he even suggest this? I am quietly freaking out here. SunCell is my ticket into becoming part owner of this company. We even talked about names for Christ's sake. *Rue & Nichols*. I'm the Nichols part. It would be simply careless for anyone but me to do the pitch deck.

He nods, a lot. "I know," he says. "I agree with you. One hundred percent. I just thought it would be good for her to learn. She offered, and she was terrific this morning. She presents very well. Impressive. You're doing a great job with her, Kat. Maybe next time let her have a shot, okay? Just think about it."

"I will," I lie. Then I smile and wave as if I'm a really happy person, and I leave.

A pitch deck is essentially a stack of slides to use for our presentation. It's fairly short—we use it as a visual clue, to keep reinforcing key points to our potential investors. Here's the product, this is why it's terrific, you do not want to miss out on this one.

It's a sales tool.

I always put the pitch deck together.

Always.

I'm good at it. Every presentation I've made has successfully met its funding target. My decks are short compared to some, which is good, I think. Twelve cards. I don't need to dress it up, I know how to put the numbers together, I know how to make projections that are both attractive and accurate.

So now, as I stand outside the office waiting for my Uber ride, I can't stop looping around everything Mark just said.

Eve! Let her have a shot some time. What do you think? She was terrific this morning!

And also, why didn't Eve mention anything to me? How could they discuss something like this during the meeting that I'm supposed to be chairing? And why does no one say a thing about it to me all day?

A glance at my phone tells me the driver is eight minutes away. It's busy. It's Friday. It's cold. People want to get home. I feel like they're staring at me. It's really strange. And then they're looking away. Like they know.

They know what I've done.

No, of course they don't. I'm just being paranoid.

Am I?

Chapter Thirteen

I considered calling Hilary and canceling this evening, but I know Abi will be disappointed. And anyway, I could use the distraction. I'll make pizza, that's what I'll do. I'll pretend everything is normal, and who knows, maybe I'll believe it.

When my ride turns onto my street, I see with a heavy heart that my little Honda Civic is still there, just where I left it. I also note that Eve is leaning against it, her arms crossed against her chest. As the Uber pulls up outside my house, she leans down and waves at me through the window. I get out and she greets me with a cheery "Hi!". She's all bright and happy, like she hasn't seen me in a long time and she really missed me. Then she dangles my car keys, and says, "Now, now, look who left the car unlocked and the keys in the ignition!"

She reminds me of my aunt Maud, the way she says it, with a sideways glance. I almost expect her to add a 'naughty, naughty' and wag a finger at me. "Thanks," I say, taking them from her.

"You're lucky it didn't get stolen. I know this is a nice

neighborhood and all, but that doesn't mean there aren't shady characters lurking around."

"Got it. I'll be more careful in the future."

I am torn between the urge to ask her what she's doing here, and concern that maybe I invited her and then forgot all about it.

"But the car looks good, kind of," she says now. She scans the hood and even runs her hand over it. "I mean, it's not too bad, right? Could be a hell of a lot worse."

"Do you want it?" I blurt. "I'll sell it to you at a good price."

"Me?" she laughs. "No! I'm not in the market for a car, but thanks."

I'm about to tell her I'll give it to her, but then she says, "Anyway, just checking if there was any damage, that's all. I couldn't see last night, being dark and all."

Her voice is too loud. I grab her by the elbow and at the same time look toward my front door.

"Jesus, Eve! Can you please keep your voice down? Abigail is home!" I think I'm going to be sick.

"Oh, sorry!" she whispers in that way people do when they're trying to whisper, but they think it's stupid. She even puts her hand over her lips.

"Do you want to come in?" I say finally, reluctantly.

"I thought you'd never ask." She slips her bag over her shoulder.

"Sorry," I say. "I'm overwrought. My nerves are shot. In fact, I'll probably go straight to bed."

I put the key in the door.

"Hello, I'm home!" I sing out, as I always do, although not quite as loudly or as brightly as usual. I hear the familiar sound of Abigail running down the stairs.

"Mom, guess what! I got in the—"

Then she sees Eve behind me and stops in her tracks.

"Oh, hi," she says.

"Abigail, this is Eve."

"Oh, my God! You're Eve?" Abigail turns to me, waiting for an answer to her silent questions. *Eve who saved Granny's life? Eve who works with you? Eve who you went out with last night?*

"This is Eve, who helped your grandmother, when she was ill."

"Hi, Abigail! It's really nice to meet you," Eve says.

"Hello, Mrs. Nichols," Paige says from the top of the stairs. I'm not *Mrs.* Nichols of course. That would be my mother. But I've never come up with a way of correcting these kids. *Please call me Ms.* doesn't quite cut it.

I introduce Paige to Eve and at the same time remove my coat and hang it up. I take Eve's and do the same.

"Abigail, Eve and I need to have a quick chat. Why don't you girls hang out upstairs for a while."

She shrugs. "Okay, we have homework anyway. Nice to meet you, Eve!"

"You too, Abigail," Eve says. Then she whispers to me, "Homework? On a Friday night?"

"She's conscientious," I reply.

Eve follows me through the living room, stopping to admire the framed photos on the wall. They're photos of Abi mostly; Abi at a Christmas party, Abi playing hockey, lots of those. Me holding Abi as a baby with my aunt Maud and uncle Trevor on either side of us. I look about twelve. She points to that one. "And who are these people? Relatives?"

I nod. "My aunt and uncle."

"That's nice. You're close?"

I shrug. "They died."

"Aww." She pouts. Then she points at another snap. "And who's this?"

It's a photo of Abi with her dad. She's beaming, her arms around his neck. They're on a beach somewhere. It was taken two summers ago.

"That's Harry, Abigail's father."

"Good-looking guy, I see where she gets her looks from." Then she bumps my shoulder lightly. "Kidding!"

"Do you want a soda?" I ask, moving her on toward the kitchen.

"Sure!"

I pour us both a glass. "So Mark said you offered to put the pitch deck together. For SunCell." Honestly, I don't know why I waited so long to say it. It's been buzzing around in my head ever since I found out. I should be asking if she's okay, I keep thinking that maybe she got hurt last night but she doesn't know it yet, and by the time her brain hemorrhages or a disc snaps in her spine it will be too late. But instead, I ask about my pitch deck.

She nods, sipping on her drink.

"Did Mark seem open to that suggestion?" I ask as nonchalantly as I know how.

I don't think I'm a jealous person. I think I am a loving person. Big difference. Although apparently that's open to interpretation. Like that time in college when I set fire to my boyfriend's dissertation because I caught him flirting with a first-year. He didn't think that was loving, I remember that. But anyway, the situation here is that Eve is gorgeous. No doubt about it. Then throw in that bubbly personality and certainly more than half a brain, and suddenly I'm getting a little nervous. To be fair, it's been a heck of a day. My brain is not working properly today, and neither are my emotions.

"I wouldn't say he was open to it. He said to ask you. I guess I forgot." She takes another sip then wipes her mouth delicately with one finger. "I was just trying to help. You weren't there. I was covering for you."

"Right. Of course. Thank you for that," I say.

She waves her hand. "It's no problem. We had a big night. I was happy to help. How are you feeling now—"

I instantly raise one hand, palm facing her. My eyes fly to the ceiling.

"Oh, sorry. Oops."

"Anyway, Eve, honestly, I'm beat, if there was something you wanted to discuss tonight?"

Neither of us says anything for a moment. She twirls her glass on the kitchen bench. It leaves a ring of moisture on the surface. I have to resist the urge to grab a paper towel. Then she says, "I need a favor."

"A favor?" I almost said, *another one?* Because I'm thinking, *I already gave you a job.*

"What kind of favor?"

"It's a little awkward. Normally, I wouldn't ask. But since we're friends now, you and me, I thought it would be okay."

"Right." I don't usually declare myself to be 'friends' like that so I wait to hear more.

"I mean, you and me, I feel like we bonded, you know? God, I'm going about this all wrong. I'm just embarrassed, to be honest."

"What do you mean? Embarrassed about what?"

"Well…" She looks away, as if struggling to formulate the words. She takes a big breath. "Okay. You know how I told you that I was staying with my friend, Allegra?"

"Yes, I remember."

"Well she's got a hot new guy in her life. Honestly, it's

stupid. They're at it all the time." She rolls her eyes. "Allegra wants her space back, like the sooner the better."

"Oh!" For a moment I'm dumbstruck. Here I was, worried that I'd have to ask her to stay for dinner and I didn't feel up to it. Turns out she wants to move in with me.

"Eve, I'm sorry, but you can't stay here. I just don't have the room."

"No! Kat, no! I wasn't going to ask that!"

I blink. Put a hand on my chest. "Phew! Sorry. I really thought you were going to!"

She twirls a lock of hair around her forefinger. "I was wondering if I could stay at your mom's house."

"My mother's house?"

"I wouldn't normally ask. But I'm in a bind. I really need a place to live. I don't have anyone else to ask. You said the house is empty, right?"

"Yes, but—"

Just then, I hear the front doorbell and Abi's footsteps running down the stairs. Then Hilary's voice singing out, "Hello! Where are you, Kat? Sorry I'm late! Hi, girls! I'm starving!"

Eve puts a hand on her hip and tilts her head. In a low voice, she says, "Really beat, hey? Going straight to bed?"

I roll my eyes. "We're in here," I call out.

"Ah, there you are!" Hilary says, unfurling her scarf. "Well, thank God it's Friday." She always says that on Fridays, which I always find funny because Hilary doesn't work.

I do the introductions. "This is Eve, Hilary."

Eve extends her hand, her face luminous, that smile again. "I'm so pleased to meet you," she says sweetly.

"Oh, hello!" Hilary replies, a little startled.

"Eve was just leaving," I say.

But Hilary has brought a bottle of Wayfarer Pinot Noir and she puts it on the kitchen table with a flourish.

"Do you have to go? Why don't you stay for a glass of wine, at least. I heard you ladies went out on the town last night. Abigail told Paige she couldn't get you out of bed this morning!" She directs that last part to me, with a chuckle.

I'm going to be sick.

"I'd love to stay for a drink," Eve says, then she winks at me and adds, "But only if it's okay with Kat."

And just like that, the very thing I didn't want to happen, is happening.

"Of course it's okay with me. Please stay for a drink." I pick up three wine glasses from the shelf. "But just a drop for me, please Hil, I think I overdid it last night."

Chapter Fourteen

When I tell Hilary that I have some frozen pizza bases and various jars full of things like olives or artichoke hearts, all still well within their use-by dates, I think, she looks sideways, raises an eyebrow and says, "Katherine please, don't go to any trouble for little old me," not meaning it, obviously.

"I got swamped at work. I forgot. Sorry," I say. I try not to dwell on the memory of the dinner parties she has invited me to. Lavish affairs with three courses and bowls of fresh flowers along the center of the table, real cloth napkins and different cutlery for each course.

Eve nudges Hilary with her elbow. "She didn't even make it to the morning meeting," she says, conspiratorially. It's clever of Eve, actually. Hilary could be threatened by beautiful Eve, but she's not, because Eve is her ally. Eve and Hilary are going to gang up on me, and it's going to be super fun. Hilary laps up this unexpected camaraderie.

The girls have come back downstairs and they're setting the table. Hilary wants to know where Eve and I went, what we did.

"Let me show you," Eve says.

"What?" I blurt, snapping my head around.

Eve has pulled out her cell and has one finger scrolling on the screen. I crane my neck to take a better look.

"We went dancing. Check this out." She holds the phone right up to Hilary's face. I stop chopping the garlic and race around the table to see. We all are. Hilary, me, the girls, but not Eve because she's holding the phone with a funny smile that makes my stomach flip.

Hilary frowns. "What's this? Oh it's a video." Then she screeches and points at the screen. "Kat! That's you!"

Fuck. It is me. It's me dancing at that stupid club, the name of which I can't even remember. I'm swaying, my arms up, my eyes half closed. Now I run my hands through my hair so it falls onto my face, and I do that over and over with my head swinging left and right. I actually remember this part, sort of. I thought I was languid, sexy. I thought I looked like a mythical creature from the sea, part siren, part French model straight out of the sixties. Instead I look like an octopus that's gotten caught in a drain.

"Give me that," I snap, reaching for it.

"Oh, Mom," Abi wails. I can tell by her tone she's mortified. No kidding. So am I. But Eve is holding the phone out of my reach and Hilary is laughing so much she's screaming. And then the video zooms in and I watch myself part my hair away from my face, just a little, and with my eyes closed, still swaying like some rotting bit of seaweed, I slip the tip of my index finger into my mouth.

I snatch the phone from Eve's grip.

"I can't believe you filmed that!" I swipe the app shut and drop the phone on the table.

Abi has both hands over her gaping mouth and to my relief she's trying not to laugh. As opposed to trying not to gag. Paige, however, is staring at the floor, wide-eyed. Like she's about to throw up all over it.

"Jeez, Kat, you can dance!" Hilary hoots.

"She takes over the dance floor, let me tell you!" Eve says with another one of her elbow nudges.

Hilary is still in hysterics. "You have *got* to give me a copy of that! I'll pay anything! Anything, I tell you!"

I point the tip of my very long, very sharp knife in Eve's direction. "Don't you dare, I swear."

"No need, it's all over YouTube," Eve says.

She takes one look at my face, my mouth opened wide, and bumps my shoulder again, in what I realize is a thing she does, and says, "Kidding!"

"You better delete that, I mean it," I say, returning to chopping garlic.

"Oh, come on, lighten up," Hilary says, wiping the last tears from her eyes. "Let's get these pizzas on the way. You're staying for dinner, Eve?"

Fact: I was bullied as a child. Just a little. No big deal. And not because I was fat (I wasn't), or because I wore thick glasses (I didn't), or even because I was good at math (okay, maybe a little).

No. I was bullied because I was nice. That's right. You heard it here first: Nice people get bullied for being nice. We're an easy target. Low hanging fruit. So when Mary Cooney in second grade peered into my lunch box and said, "Yours looks nicer than mine, can I have it?" I gave her my cheeseburger and blueberry yogurt, or whatever it was. Just like that. After the third or fourth time she stopped asking, and I just gave it to her, anyway. Then I carried other kids' bags. *Kat, will you take my bag? It's really heavy*! I did other people's homework. *Here, Kat, and it's due tomorrow*. I guess I just didn't know how to say *no*. I was too nice. I still am.

The strange thing about this moment, when Eve is laughing and teasing me about the video—other than it reminding me of being bullied as a child—is that she finds anything about last night funny at all. Me, I'm a mess. I am jagged and foggy at the same time. I'm heavy. Frightened, too. I never want to be reminded of it, ever again, and Eve thinks it's hilarious.

But somehow, the evening goes on and Eve is sweet and charming, and particularly attentive to me. When Hilary teases me about the video for the umpteenth time, Eve steps in. "Come on Hilary, stop being so mean." At one point she announces that I am *an amazing career woman. An inspiration*. "She's the smartest person I ever met! And what do you do for a living, Hilary?" and I begin to wonder whether it's me who's overreacting.

I relax. I tell myself that if the man died at the scene, then there really was nothing we could have done for him. Does that work? I don't know. We'll see.

When the evening comes to an end, I call a taxi for Eve, and I retrieve her coat from the rack.

I stand with her outside on the porch.

"What about the house?" she whispers.

My mouth tightens. Magically, over the past couple of hours, I'd forgotten about all that.

"I'm desperate. I really need a place to live. I don't know who else to ask." And I think, why not? It is empty, after all. Why wouldn't I help her out for a few days?

"Okay. I'll take you there on the weekend," I tell her.

"Oh, Kat, thank you! You're the best!" she throws her

arms around me. When she releases me, I glance over my shoulder and catch Hilary watching us.

I pull the door behind me, leaving just a gap, and I ask conspiratorially,

"How do you do it, Eve? You're so … together, in control. You've been like that all day. It's as if nothing happened last night."

She cocks her head, her eyes searching my face. "That's because nothing happened last night," she says.

And for a moment, the world brightens, the shadows lift, the stars twinkle, and I actually believe that I'm waking up from a horrible nightmare, and that just maybe, *nothing* happened last night. Then she bumps my shoulder lightly, and I know what's coming next.

"Kidding."

She registers the look on my face. "Sorry. Bad joke. Yes, obviously, something happened last night."

She glances around quickly then leans forward, her mouth so close I can feel her breath next to my ear, like a feather, and just as I think she's going to kiss my cheek, she cups her hand over the side of her mouth, she says, "You killed someone."

Chapter Fifteen

On Saturday I wake up late, bleary-eyed and exhausted from nightlong nightmares. Abigail thinks I'm ill. Of course, she does. I have dark, bluish rings under my eyes.

"You should go to the doctor, Mom," she says.

"You're right, I'll go this afternoon," I lie.

"Is it because of the drugs?" she asks, her sweet face strained with worry.

I prop myself up quickly. "What drugs?"

"The ones you took. Eve said that's what made you weird in that video. You shouldn't do drugs, Mom, not at your age."

"You shouldn't do drugs period, you hear me? Anyway, no I didn't take drugs." Not then, anyway. "I just had one drink too many. No big deal." My head still hurts. Everything hurts. Especially my heart.

It occurs to me that I did feel unusually euphoric at the club. Is it possible that Eve spiked my drink? Does that even make sense? Why would she do that?

. . .

87

"Here we are," I say, flattening myself against the door so that Eve can see into the narrow hallway. "Welcome to my mother's house."

"It's a lot smaller than I expected," Eve says, hands on hips.

"Is it?"

"Considering the address and all."

"Oh, I see. Yes well, we're the smallest house on Kirkland Place. But I'm sure you'll have plenty of room."

She drags a large pink suitcase into the hall with both hands. It looks incredibly heavy, and as far as I can tell, it doesn't have wheels. I'm already getting nervous about the floorboards. I'm already wishing I'd said no.

But it's too late for that, so I give her the tour of the place, which doesn't take long; it's a narrow, two-bedroom house. We begin upstairs where both bedrooms are, although the one that was mine is now filled with cardboard boxes, old Christmas decorations, and a vacuum cleaner that no longer works.

I push open one door. "This is the main bedroom."

"Oh, has someone been staying here?"

I realize with a start that the bed is unmade and the sheets entangled. I pull them off quickly, feeling the color rising on my neck, and I dump the bundle in the corner. "No, just a friend. There's fresh linen in the hall closet."

"I see," she says. Then she smiles, taps the side of her nose. "Married lover. Love nest. Away from the prying eyes of the Mrs. I get it."

My face burns. She pats my arm. "Don't worry, Kat. Your secret is safe with me."

There's a pause between us, which strikes me as good a moment as any. "How long were you thinking of staying?"

She shrugs. "I don't know, as long it takes, I guess."

"Oh?"

She opens the linen closet and brings a towel up to her nose. "These smell a bit musty, don't you think?" she says, pushing a towel in my face.

I take it from her. "They probably just need a wash."

"Can you bring some fresh ones over?" she asks, as if I hadn't spoken.

I relent. "Okay."

She wanders around the room slowly, running her hand over surfaces, checking the springiness of the bed.

"I'll show you downstairs," I say quickly. More out of a desire to get her out of this room.

Downstairs is straightforward. A combined living and dining room, the kitchen, and my father's study, which I show her now.

It's a small room and like the rest of the house, I've kept it just the way it was. I open the door to show her and I don't mean for her to walk in, but she does anyway, sliding past me in the doorway. "I'd rather you didn't use this room, if you don't mind."

She picks up a paperweight from the desk. It's a scarab trapped in resin. She holds it up to the light. "Why not?" she asks. "This isn't Blue Beard's den, is it?"

"I just … I'd rather you didn't. That's all."

"What's this?" She has lifted an ornamental abacus from the shelf and turns it around in her hands.

"Please don't touch that. It's very fragile."

"Sheesh! Excuse me for living!"

"Sorry. It's just that, it's an antique Chinese abacus. Very rare." I take it from her and quickly slide it in a drawer. "It's mine, actually. It was a gift from my father."

"So why is it here, and not at your own place?"

I shrug. "I don't want it. It was a stupid gift for a twelve-year-old."

I touch the beads softly before locking it away, remembering that part of my life. Such a long time ago. My father always said I knew how to count before I could talk. That I'd hold up the right number of chubby fingers when asked, *How many apples are in the bowl, Katherine? How many windows in the room, Katherine?*

I doubt any of that is true.

"What did he do? Your father?" She scans the bookshelf, pulls out books at random.

"He was a professor of mathematics." I align the books back after her. Blow off a bit of dust.

"So Eve about you staying here…"

"Mmm?"

"I was thinking, more like a few days maybe."

Her head snaps around. "Excuse me?"

"It's just that, I'm not really emotionally equipped to have someone in the house right now. It's a really personal space for me, and I'm happy to help you out, but I just thought I should mention it, about the timeframe. Just a few days would be totally fine. Until this Friday, how about that? Is that okay? I wouldn't charge any rent or anything, of course. You can stay for free. Goes without saying."

She stares at me with big round eyes and in her most incredulous tone she says, "Not emotionally equipped?" which is funny because I feel like I said that ages ago.

"Right, maybe I didn't make myself clear—"

"Do you think you would be emotionally equipped right now if it wasn't for me?"

I wince. "I'm sorry?"

"Let me spell it out for you. You would be in jail, at this very moment, if it wasn't for me. How does that sound, emotionally? You'd be arrested for murder. That's right. Look it up if you don't believe me."

I can't believe what I'm hearing. Then her words from last night echo in my mind.

Of course something happened. You killed someone.

I point a finger at her, my eyes narrowed in fury. "You listen to me!" My mouth is so tight I can barely speak. "I didn't even want to drive us home, but *you* kept goading me. And when I hit that man, you were right there with me. It was *you* who insisted we should leave. *You* who said you didn't want to get arrested. So don't pin this on me now, Eve, it's your fault just as much as mine. Maybe even more so, if I'm honest."

She studies me, calmly, one hand on her hip.

"Kat, I'm sorry but I wasn't driving the car, you were. I am not responsible for your poor judgment. And I certainly don't remember *insisting* that we leave that poor man behind. And why would I get arrested? I was a passenger in the car! I was hurt, Kat! *You* hurt me, with your negligence! And all I've done since is try to help you!"

I can't do it. I can't deal with this.

"You know what? I changed my mind. This isn't going to work out. You need to leave. Right now." I point to the door. I'm shaking with anger.

"Really?" Her mouth hangs open. Like she's astonished. Like I'm the one who's being completely unreasonable.

She shakes her head. "Kat, the reason you can wax lyrical about your emotional state of mind is because I'm keeping you out of prison. One phone call from me to Uncle Bill and the cops will be at your house to take a look at your car, and that's after they've reviewed CCTV footage that shows *you* clearly driving toward the scene of the accident, at the right time. The footage on the other side will show that you didn't drive out directly. And when you did, you had that nasty little bump on the front of the car. Then there'll also be plenty of evidence of how drunk you were, including some handy video footage, courtesy of yours truly. I'm a witness. Let's not forget. Don't look at me like that, Kat. So here's how we're doing this. I'm going to stay here as long as I like. That's right. And if you're not emotionally equipped to deal with that, then I don't know, take a fucking mental health day. And can you please get the fuck out of my face?"

I can barely breathe. I'm going to be sick. I'm going to faint. Then I say it out loud, the unthinkable realization that is dawning on me. "You— you're blackmailing me?"

She clicks her tongue. "Blackmail is a very hostile word, don't you think? I'm thinking more of sharing in your good fortune. Catching the tail wind. Basking in all that glow. You're a very selfish person, Katherine. I shouldn't have to use such tactics for you to be nice to me. You should have just done it anyway, let me stay here. That would have been the right thing to do. The *friendly* thing to do."

My whole face is tense, it makes my jaw hurt. I'm doing everything I can not to cry.

"And you know something else I noticed?" she says. "You didn't even thank me for saving your ass."

I'm too stunned. My chin wobbles and my eyes fill with tears until a single one falls. I wipe it quickly with one hand.

"Right," I say.

"So? Do you want to do that now? Maybe?"

"Do what?"

She sighs, looks away, like she's had enough, like this is

all too much. Finally she spreads her arms out and says, "Thank me, Kat! Jesus!"

"Oh." I nod, like I'm considering it, but the fact is I just want to get out of here and away from her. "Thank you," I mumble.

"Okay, not the most convincing display of gratitude I've ever seen, but it'll do."

She moves past me and holds the front door wide open. For me.

"I'll see you Monday, then. Oh, and don't forget about the clean towels."

Chapter Sixteen

I'm in hell. And I have to pretend in front of my daughter that everything is fine and dandy, while carrying a horrible secret, a soul-destroying burden and I'm scared. It's pure, unadulterated fear. It takes hold inside my gut, then it twists it. It stops me from taking a breath, from falling into a slumber. I can't even talk properly anymore. Everything I say comes out like I have a mouth full of hot soup. This fear, it's weighing me down every minute, every second. And fear has friends, too, called Guilt and Shame. They're like a crew, the three of them. They hang out together, causing mayhem inside my head.

Now it's Sunday morning and I have not slept at all. Not one minute. Abigail has hockey practice today, and I call Hilary and with a stupid sick-not-sick voice I ask her to take Abi. "Since Paige's going too, would you mind?"

"Okay, but I hope Abigail isn't sick, is she? She's not a carrier, is she?"

"No! She's totally not sick. Not a carrier. Just me."

"Because I don't want to catch anything. Henry is taking me to the gala next Saturday."

"You won't catch anything. I promise."

"All right. I'll come by at 10 am."

Another reason I don't want to take Abi myself is because I don't want to get into that car. I don't want her to get into that car, either. I will, however, drive it inside my garage. I've left it in the street ever since the accident, and yesterday old Mr. Jones next door told me I was blocking his driveway, even though I'm parked a good ten feet away from it. Then he chided me for leaving the keys in the ignition. "Someone will steal it, if you're not careful," he growled.

As soon as Abi's gone, I call Sasha. She picks up on the first ring, and the sound of her voice is like a raft in a storm.

"How are you doing?" she asks. "You still coming home for Easter?"

Home. Easter? That's weeks away, how can she be thinking of Easter? "Yes," I reply. "Absolutely. We are absolutely going home for Easter. I can't wait."

"Okay, good to hear. You sound funny. Is everything all right?"

I spot a loose thread on the cushion I'm hugging. It comes loose surprisingly easily. "I need to ask you something."

"Sure! Hit me with it. What have you done?" she says, breezily. To be fair, this is a running joke between us. And until now, it was funny. I don't tell her what I've done. I'm not crazy.

"What if…"

When I was a kid, we used to play that game.

What if you found a million dollars by the side of the road, would you keep it?

What if you found out you were adopted, would you still love your little brother?

What if I died, would you cry?

What if I did something really bad, would you still love me?

"I'm asking in your capacity as a lawyer. Sort of." Fuck. It's already coming out all wrong. "Do you ever deal with hit-and-runs in your work?" I blurt.

"Sometimes, why?"

"There's someone I work with, she got herself into some trouble."

"Then she needs to talk to a lawyer."

"Right."

"*You're* not in trouble, are you?"

"Me? God, no!" I laugh. Shit. This is the problem with Sasha. She's really astute and she's really smart and she's my friend. She gets me.

"Why would you ask that?" I say anyway.

"Because you sound funny."

"Well no, like I said, I'm asking for a friend."

"You said it was a colleague at work."

"Who happens to be a friend. A new friend. She's gotten herself into some trouble, apparently. A hit-and-run, I believe. I'm not sure. The thing is…"

"Yes?"

"She may have drunk a little bit too much. Hence the 'run' part."

There's silence on the line for a moment. I'm about to ask if she's still there when she says, "Don't say anything, hon, okay? Just listen to me. If you've done something wrong, you need to talk to a lawyer. So tell your friend, your coworker, whatever, to get one. Hit-and-run is a very serious offense."

"Can she go to jail for it?"

"Highly likely. It's vehicular homicide. And if she was driving recklessly, then it's a felony. So yes, I'd tell your friend to pack a toothbrush."

I hold back a sob.

"You stay away, Kat. I know you. Don't get sucked into someone else's shit, okay? Your friend could be in a lot of trouble. Don't make it your problem. Tell her to get herself a lawyer. That's the best thing she can do at this stage."

She's right of course. I should have done that days ago. I don't know what's wrong with me, but that's okay. I know what to do now. I'm going to get a lawyer, and I'm going to tell Eve and she'll have nothing on me then, and everything is going to be okay. I hang up and promise to call soon. When my phone pings I assume it's Sasha again, that maybe she forgot to mention something. But it's a text. From Eve.

Towels???

I use my key to get in my mother's house. I have with me a bag of freshly laundered towels and I leave it on the floor by the console table. I'm very quiet. Like I'm the hired help. I'm also heavy with dread, and when Eve's head pops over the banister at the top of the stairs, my heart drops.

"Hi, Kat!" she sings out, friendly and bright. She runs downstairs. "I was going to put coffee on. You want some?"

"No," I stutter. "Thanks, I should probably go home. Still not feeling a hundred percent … you know…"

"Yeah, you don't look too good. Maybe you should rest."

"Right."

She picks up the bag and peers inside. "Thanks for bringing those. I really appreciate it."

I nod, thinking I should back away slowly or something because clearly, this woman is completely crazy.

"Well, I'll be out of your hair then," I mutter.

"Sure, I'll see you tomorrow, Kat."

She holds the door open for me, and when I'm outside she says, "And next time, Kat, ring the bell, okay? I'm not very comfortable with people just letting themselves in like you just did. Personal space and all that."

The walk home isn't very long but when you're shell-shocked it takes no time at all, and by the time I reach my own house I don't remember how I got there. Then Mark calls and I want to cry.

"Hey," I say through my tears. I think I really want him to know something is wrong. Then I want him to wrestle it out of me. Instead he whispers, "I miss you. Usual place? In one hour?"

"I can't, I … I have someone staying there."

"Who?"

"It's a tenant."

"You're joking."

"No. Sorry, long story."

"I'm disappointed, I won't lie." He sighs and says, "Oh well, I'll see you tomorrow then."

Chapter Seventeen

I manage to disperse the fog that's settled in my brain long enough to think. I need a strategy. I can't go on like this, obviously. It's only been two days, and already I think I will die. I decide to take the bull by the horns. I'm just going to ask Eve straight out: what do you want? A place to stay? What, like, forever?

There's also the possibility that I'm overreacting. Very, *very* remote possibility. I'm probably grasping at straws, but what I'm thinking here, is that maybe the whole thing is one elaborate joke, because one thing I've noticed about Eve is that she has a strange sense of humor. And it can be abrasive. And often, not funny at all. The other possibility is that she hit her head. This could even be the most likely explanation. I looked up *concussion* on the internet, and it's amazing. People behave in the most extraordinary ways after a head injury. While I don't remember Eve hitting her head on anything, I do know that she was hurt.

I've started to bite my nails. I'm doing it now, at my desk, thinking about Eve and all this, and also about SunCell, because I absolutely must not screw up SunCell no matter what, and I'm worried that this stress is going to affect my handling of SunCell. So yes, there's a lot going on in my brain this morning. Also, it's nine thirty. She's half an hour late when she finally walks in.

"Katherine, hello! Did you have a nice day yesterday? You look better, I'm glad," she chirps.

She hasn't even glanced my way. I could be wearing a paper bag over my head and she wouldn't have noticed.

"Thanks, Eve," I reply in my most professional tone. She drops her bag on her desk and sits heavily in her chair.

"Listen," I say. "Can we have a chat?"

"Of course! Is it a serious chat? Is something wrong? Anything I can do? Do you want to go and grab a coffee?"

At this point I honestly can't tell if she's pretending to be normal, even friendly, or if she is being genuine. I get up and close the door for privacy then sit back down and swing my chair so that I'm facing her. I cross my legs and rest one elbow on my knee, and one finger lightly against my chin. I hope to convey that I am relaxed but nevertheless mean business.

"Okay," I begin. "So, you and me, we've been through something really traumatic together. And I was thinking —" but I can't remember what I was thinking, because while I was speaking just now, she pulled out her cell from her bag, tapped on the screen, brought the phone to her ear, and now she brings up one finger, as if to say, 'hold that thought' and she's on a call.

"Hi!" she squeals. Not to me, obviously. I wait.

"I know!" she screeches. "How awesome was that!"

She goes on like this, her side of the conversation peppered with *I know! I love that! Awesome!* for quite a while. Maybe ten minutes. Then she hangs up, puts the phone back in her bag, and now she's doing something on her computer. From my vantage point it looks like it's something to do with emails.

I, on the other hand, am still sitting in the same position, legs crossed, elbow on knee, chin on curled fingers, ready to have a serious chat.

"Eve?"

"Mmm?"

"I really think we should talk about this."

She swivels back and looks at me now. "About what?"

"You know what."

"Kat, sorry but you're going to have to be more specific. I don't know what you're saying. Maybe it's because I'm not smart like you. After all, I can't even balance a checkbook, as you know. What are you trying to say?"

"That I …" I was going to say *'scared, I am scared of you. Isn't that ridiculous?'*

But Caroline's head pops up around the door, and I don't finish the sentence.

"You guys ready for the staff meeting?" she says.

"Be right there," Eve and I reply at the same time.

"Eve?"

"Yes, Kat?"

"What do you want?"

"Hey, take a look this," she says.

Maybe she's hard of hearing, I don't know. It's like she hears me, but she doesn't. I'm here, but I 'm not here.

She taps her nail against her computer screen. I recognize the masthead of the Herald and realize with a start that it's another news item.

I jump to take a closer look.

Brookline Police have renewed their appeal for information into the Hammond Pond Parkway hit-and-run. Victim identified. Shortly after 3:30am on Friday emergency services were called to Hammond Pond Parkway after a thirty-five-year-old man was found deceased on the side of the road. The victim has been identified and was known to police due to previous drug related offenses. Police are still searching for the next of kin. Police are urging anyone with information in connection to the accident to contact Brookline Police station or Crime Stoppers.

Eve's screen is facing out, because of the way she's positioned it to show it to me. Anyone could see it. I swing it back quickly and check over my shoulder just as Liam walks past. He gives me a low wave. I nod back. *Go away.*

According to the clock on the main wall of reception, the meeting has been under way for nineteen minutes.

I hate that clock. It's one of those showy, pseudo-retro digital clocks with square numbers and blinking dots between the hours and the minutes, which so far sounds ordinary enough, except it's made out of blue neon tube and it's huge. It must be at least three feet high and twice as wide. Obviously, it's meant to be bold and quirky, young and optimistic, just like the company.

Mark doesn't like people to be late. He says that, barring any exceptional circumstances, tardiness can only be attributed to one of two personality traits: laziness or narcissism, neither of which have any place in his firm. Hence the twitch in his left eyelid. The one he gets when he's irritated. When I join the others he doesn't skip a beat, doesn't even look up. You'd never know he noticed I was late, except for that twitch.

He's in the middle of a sentence when I sit down. "Let's not forget that perception, in the marketplace, is everything." That's the sentence. It does not make a lot of sense. In fact, it rates as a pretty inane, useless sentence, but I see that Eve is studiously writing it down. She's already here because she left me back there to read the article and without saying a single word she walked out of the office and went to take her place at the meeting. Now she looks up, with just the right amount of concern clouding her pretty face, and mouths, *everything okay?* as if my being late had nothing to do with her.

"New business," Mark says now. "What have we got?"

This is when we propose companies that might be looking for some capital investment. Maybe they've contacted us, which happens more and more. Maybe we came across them through specialist publications, or just from picking up some chatter on the grapevine.

"I have one," I say, still flustered from being late. I always have at least one. After all it's my thing, it's what I'm good at, and I know that Mark will like this one. I'm flicking through my iPad, trying to locate the right document, all set to give my spiel when Mark says, "I'd like to hear what Eve has to say." I look up and realize she had her hand up and an eager expression on her face. I put my own hands in my lap.

"Thank you, Mark," Eve begins. "So I took the liberty of going through recent FDA applications, to see if anything stood out. Anything that might be a good fit for us, and I was pleased to come across what I hope could be promising: a company called PellisTech has filed an application for, wait for it: artificial skin grown from fiber. According to my notes, it's very advanced, huge potential in medicine, skin grafts, that sort of thing. Never been done before. Could have anti-aging applications even. I'm no expert, and I'll leave to others to decide whether the tech stacks up." She nods in my direction as she says this.

"But on paper, it looks extremely promising. I'd say we should take a look."

I stare at her, mouth open, heart in throat, as she reads *my* idea from *my* notes, the very notes she typed for me, as if they were hers.

"I don't know," Aaron the legal guy says. "Products like these are very difficult to get investment for. They have to go through an obstacle course of testing and approvals. We should at least wait until after we hear from the FDA."

Which makes sense. The government has to approve the product and deem it safe, so that it can be used in the way it is intended. That, in a nutshell, is the FDA process. Without FDA approval the product is worthless.

"Absolutely," Eve says. "I'm so glad you brought that up, Aaron. Thank you." Aaron colors and lights up like he's a Christmas tree. "But if I may," and here she checks her notes again, meaning my notes, "this one has already done a lot of the ground work. They're very advanced in the process, with FDA approval to be granted any minute. Isn't that right, Katherine? Katherine did a bit of research for me on this one, by the way."

Mark looks at me now. They all do, waiting to hear what the bit of research I did for Eve yielded.

Research—for me, not for Eve—may be overstating things a bit, but what I wrote down in my notes was *FDA: looks good*.

"It's looking good," I say now, aware that the corners of my mouth are drooping. "I think it will go through."

"We don't know that officially, though," Aaron says.

"We'll know any day, and if we wait until it's official, we won't get the investment at that price," Eve says. "Every other firm out there will be wanting to get on board. They're all bigger and badder than we are. We won't withstand the competition. We'll get pushed out of the way. I say we do it now."

Mark nods his approval. "That's terrific, Eve! I like the sound of that. And thank you for taking the initiative. Great idea to look through FDA applications." He turns to the rest of us and adds, "Take note, people. It's that kind of enterprise I want to see more of around here."

I've been doing that for months, checking FDA applications. And patent applications, and all sorts of initiative taking. Mark knows that. So why is Eve the fucking genius all of sudden?

She drops her gaze and blushes prettily, coy and grateful. I take it back. She is a fucking genius. If she were to put all that *enterprise* and *initiative* to do good instead of evil, there's no telling how far she could go.

"Katherine? What have you got for us?" Mark asks now.

I shake my head. "Never mind, it was a mistake."

Chapter Eighteen

I let a psychopath into my life. No, it's worse than that. I *invited* a psychopath into my life. Then I gave the psychopath a job, right in my office. After that, I set up the psychopath in my mother's house, made sure she was comfortable, and gave the psychopath a set of keys.

Can I disinvite the psychopath from my life? As Eve pointed out, there's bound to be plenty of CCTV footage around showing me driving into the park. Although there is no footage of me actually at the scene of the accident. That's because there's no CCTV at that exact spot. I know that, because I looked it up on that helpful website that shows exactly where all the CCTV cameras are around Boston. So that's one thing in my favor.

The other thing in my favor is that the man, the victim, is dead, and I'm very, very sorry about that, but as a result, he can't testify about me. So what have we got that points to me? Eve's word. That's all. Is that enough?

When we're alone in the office, I say to Eve, in a voice so low she has to lean in to hear me, "I'm going to get a lawyer, and I'm going to go to the police."

I'm not going to the police, obviously. I'm not crazy. But a lawyer, why not? Sasha's right. At least, that way, I'll know if there is any chance I could avoid jail. Anyway, I'm right out of ideas. "And you won't need to be involved at all," I add. "I'll tell them I was on my own when the accident happened. They won't hear about you at all. Definitely not from me."

"And that's great, Katherine," she hisses. "You'll go to jail for a long time, but hey, whatever works for you."

I wait for more, I don't know what exactly, but there is not more.

"Why me?" I ask, my bottom lip wobbling.

"Oh, Kat! Don't cry! It's nothing personal! I'm being entrepreneurial, that's all. I was presented with an opportunity, and I'm taking it. You have a lot to offer, Katherine. You have money, a good job, pay's okay, isn't it? You're smart, so you keep pointing out anyway. You've inherited a nice house, on the small side but nice, no mortgage. You're lucky. I just want some of that luck. That's all. What's wrong with that?"

I nod, like any of that makes any sense, but I'm scared. She terrifies me.

That night I call Mark. I want to tell him that I have made a terrible, terrible mistake in hiring Eve. He needs to fire her, but he can't say it's me who asked. No, no, no. Definitely not. Then this crazy thought comes into my head.

Let's run away. You, me, and Abi. Let's go and make a life together somewhere else. In a new country. I hear New Zealand is attractive. I'll sell the house, I'll take care of my mother's care, and then let's begin a new adventure.

What do you say?

I imagine saying that on the phone.

But it's Sonya who picks up his cell phone, and I'm so unprepared for the sound of her voice that I end the call.

I check the car again. I consider taking it to have the front bumper fixed, but I am concerned the mechanic will feel compelled to report it.

Remember that hit-and-run, officer? Well I've got a car here with just the kind of damage only explained by hitting a pedestrian. I thought you'd want to take a look, officer.

I don't dare take the car. Maybe later. In a month. Or ten years.

Later, I write a letter to Sasha. Sasha is the person I trust most in the world, and I ask her to take Abigail in, in case I'm arrested. I tell her how very sorry I am. I screwed up, totally, completely, utterly. But I know she will love and care for Abigail like her own daughter. Abi will be safe with her, and it's probably a very good thing if Abi were back in LA where we were all happy once and where she has many friends.

I seal the letter, write Sasha's name on it, and leave it in the drawer of the nightstand. If they come for me, I'll tell Abi where the letter is, but not before.

"Hey, Kat, there's no washing machine in the house, can you get one in?" Eve asks the next day. If she said *hello* this morning, I didn't hear it.

"There's a laundromat around the corner on Kirkland," I reply without looking up.

She laughs. "A laundromat? Don't be silly. What would I do with a laundromat?"

I'm still typing but my fingers are trembling and my email turns to gibberish. I sigh. "I'll need to measure the space first. In the laundry."

"Great! You can come and do that this evening. I'm going over to visit Allegra after work. Her new boyfriend dumped her. Can you believe it? What a jerk. She's in pieces, poor thing. So sad." She shakes her head. "Anyway, I'll stay over there tonight. Allegra needs a friend. So the place is all yours, babe. Measure to your heart's content!"

She won't be there tonight. My heart speeds up. I wait for as long as I can, fifteen minutes maybe, then I go to the bathroom with my phone in my pocket and lock myself in a stall.

I text Mark.

Can I see you tonight? The usual place? 6pm?

I wait, tapping my foot on the floor, then I see the tell-tale dots pulsing.

What about tenant?

No tenant, I reply, feeling a bit disappointed at the abruptness of his message. Someone opens the door outside. I hold my breath. *Come on, Mark!* But there are no pulsing dots. Nothing. Minutes tick by. I'm about to give up when finally, it comes.

Okay. 6pm.

I close my eyes. The thought of being with Mark makes me feel light, hopeful. I should talk to him. Explain what happened. Maybe he can help me. I'm sure he can. I can feel my shoulders relax and when I walk out of the stall and back to the office, it's like a weight has lifted. I chide myself for not thinking of this sooner. Of course, Mark is the answer. Mark loves me. We're a team. He'll understand. I know he will. He'll know what to do.

Mark has pulled up in a brand-new red Tesla. I didn't

recognize the car at first and for a moment I thought it was a friend of Eve's.

"Nice," I say, my fingers tracing along the side of the car.

"It's better than nice," he replies, tapping the side of the car. "It's true love. State of the art, baby." He grins. "Want a ride?"

"Not that kind of ride," I reply before pulling him inside the house.

"I've missed you so much," I whisper in his ear. I'm sitting on his lap with my arms around his neck. He smells of rain. He needs a shave.

"Me too." He puts his hand under my shirt, unclasps my bra. I want to rip the clothes off his body, but I'm finding it difficult to relax. I wish we hadn't come here. I'm not thinking straight. Why didn't I suggest a hotel? It's not as if this is the only place we can be together, it just happens to be the only place we *have* been together, intimately. But it's a mess. I gasped when I walked in. Eve's things are strewn every which way. She's only been here four days, but she hasn't done any cleaning, let alone taken out the trash. And yet we're sitting in the kitchen because the living room, which is where I imagined us naked, on the couch, making love, is full of her stuff. Clothes, mainly. But I don't want to move anything.

Suddenly Mark pulls away.

"I forgot to ask, did you have a chance to take a look at Eve's suggestion? PellisTech?"

I blink. "What?"

"The artificial skin startup. The FDA application. I

want to setup a meeting. Is there anything I should look at? Any regulations?"

"There's always regulations…"

He kisses me again, on the neck this time. His breath is warm and makes my spine tingle.

"What's your instinct, we go for it?" he says, his voice languid, sexy, the tip of his tongue teasing my earlobe. "It's such a good idea, PellisTech. She's a real smart cookie, Eve," he whispers.

I snort, pull away.

"You really think *she* came up with it? You must be joking."

"What does that mean?"

"PellisTech was my idea! In fact, I've been dying to tell you since yesterday. Eve stole my notes. God! Just the memory of it makes my blood boil." I rearrange a lock of his hair, but he moves my hand away.

"What are you talking about? What notes?"

"I gave Eve my notes to type up, about PellisTech, but then she used those notes in the meeting. She made it look like it was her idea. And please promise me you won't say anything to her about this, okay? I mean it."

He frowns at me, confused.

"Promise me, Mark."

"Sure, okay."

"Something's not right with that girl," I whisper.

"But why would she do that?"

"To make herself look good, what else?"

"Why didn't you say anything? At the meeting?"

This is my cue. It's the perfect moment to tell him. I play with the buttons on his shirt, undoing and redoing them while psyching myself up for a confession. *He'll understand. He'll help you. He'll know what to do.*

"There's something I need to tell you. Something happened, Mark. I—"

"JESUS!" He gets up so fast that I fall to the floor. When I see Eve standing there my heart explodes. She has one hand clasped over her mouth, eyes wide.

I scramble to get up. "For Christ's sake! What are you doing here?"

"Katherine, I am *so* sorry. I had a change of plans. I had no idea you—the two of you—I apologize. I should have rung the bell but I didn't expect…"

My face burns.

"Is that your car out there, Mark? It's gorgeous!"

"I should go," Mark says. He runs both hands through his hair and straightens his shirt. The buttons don't match the buttonholes. I want to reach out and fix it.

Eve lifts a hand to stop him. "No, please. I'll go. I'm so sorry. It's my fault." She's already turning on her heels, but Mark just shakes his head and snatches his jacket from the back of the chair. In two strides he's at the door. He turns to Eve and says, "I didn't know you were—" he gestures vaguely around the room—"staying here." Seconds later I hear the front door shut. He didn't even look at me on the way out.

Eve throws her head back and laughs. "Oh, my God! This is priceless! You and Mark? Mark is your married lover? Oh, Kat! What a scream! And you think he's going to leave his wife for you because you dropped your panties? You are killing me!"

"Shut up."

She makes a show of wiping tears of laughter from her eyes. "No wonder you're so good at your job! And here I was, thinking it was all on merit."

"This is my house. I thought you were out tonight?"

"And I thought you were going to measure the space in the laundry, so there you go. Hey, do you give good head? Asking for a friend."

"Eve I swear…" My arms are by my side but my hands are closed tight into fists.

"What? You swear … what?"

My whole body is vibrating. I ignore her and turn to retrieve my bag from the floor.

"What do you swear, Katherine? You swear that you're a slut? I know that already! That's why your daddy threw you out on the street! I guess you just can't get it out of your system, can you?" Her eyes narrow and a shadow comes over her face.

"I don't give a fuck that it's your house. I'm here now. At your invitation, I might add. Go turn tricks somewhere else, okay? I don't want you bringing people here. What if they take my stuff? Who's going to pay for it? You? Just don't do it again, okay?"

I push past her and before I get to the door she calls out, "I don't think I'm being unreasonable!"

I'm in the street with bile in my throat and tears on my face that I wipe with both hands. Of course she did it on purpose. That little story about going to her friend's house for the night? She was setting a trap for me. She knew I'd used the house to meet with Mark, although she didn't know who it was then. She wanted to find out. She threw the bait and reeled me in. I'm an idiot. Like I said, low hanging fruit.

Chapter Nineteen

I call Mark later that evening, but each time it goes to voicemail and I don't leave a message. That night I can't sleep. I can't stop thinking about the way Eve behaved after Mark left, the look on her face when she berated me.

Pure evil.

Now I'm running late because I didn't hear the alarm. I feel off balance and not at my best. I run up the stairs and when I reach the landing, I see Eve. She's in his office, talking animatedly, her back to me, but Mark sees me and gets up immediately.

"Can you come in here please Katherine?"

Eve is sitting in the only guest chair, on the other side of Mark's desk. She looks up at me with big round eyes and a timid smile.

"Good morning," she says shyly.

I look around for somewhere to sit, then drag Caroline's chair across. Mark has closed the door and sat back down and now puts both hands flat on his desk. "Okay, let's clear this up once and for all," he says. I give him a pleading look. *Don't say it, you promised, remember?*

"Mark was just telling me," Eve begins, and my heart sinks because I know I'm too late. "—that you're unhappy about PellisTech? About the way I handled it?"

I narrow my eyes at him. *Fuck you, Mark. You promised*.

He puts one hand up. "Let's get this sorted out, ladies."

Ladies? You patronizing prick.

"Who first came across PellisTech and thought it was a good prospect?" Mark looks at me for an answer.

"I guess—"

"I don't know what to say," Eve interrupts with a shake of her head. "I went through recent patent applications, as I mentioned at the meeting. It was an idea I had and when I saw PellisTech, I got excited. I thought it looked like a good prospect. I asked you what your thoughts were, Katherine, do you remember? We were chatting about my uncle Bill, and then I showed you the PellisTech patent, and you agreed it was very promising and that you'd look into it. You remember?"

Nice touch, bringing up Uncle Bill. I don't reply. I don't even nod.

"I just didn't realize you wanted to bring it up yourself," she continues. "I'm terribly sorry. It's a misunderstanding on my part about how things work around here, and Mark, I only meant to contribute to the new business meeting. I thought it was the best way to learn. If I stepped on anyone's toes, then I apologize profusely."

Mark smiles, his face a picture of benign understanding. Then he turns to me. "Katherine?"

My face burns. "I guess… I made a mistake."

"But you said something about notes, that Eve used your notes? What was that about?"

"What notes?" Eve asks. "Katherine did kindly look into the FDA prospects for me, and I'm very grateful. Are those the notes you mean, Katherine? Although I did acknowledge your help, I believe."

Mark nods. "You did. I remember."

"Thank you, Mark," she says, then turns back to me. "Should I have let you present this new prospect? I guess I'm still learning what my role is, I did assume that since I identified this new possible opportunity, it was all right for me to bring it up. I see now that it was wrong. There's clearly a hierarchy, and a protocol at Rue Capital that I need to follow. I shouldn't have spoken up like that. It won't happen again."

"No, Eve," Mark scoffs. "There's no protocol or hierarchy at Rue Capital! We welcome everyone's contribution. We're a team here."

"Well that's what I thought, but…"

Now they're both looking at me. My heart is pounding in my ears. "Like I said, it was my mistake. There's no problem."

"Are you sure?" Eve asks, one hand on my arm. "Because I'd hate to think…"

"No," I say quickly. "No problem whatsoever. I don't even know why we're talking about this."

"Oh good!" she says, one hand on her chest. "I'm so relieved!" she laughs.

"Okay, well I'm glad we've cleared that up. Thank you for your time, Eve."

"It's no problem at all, Mark. Thank *you*."

She walks out and I'm about to follow. "Don't go yet," he says, and I sit back down.

He closes the door after she leaves. "You want to tell me what the fuck that was all about?" he asks.

I flinch.

"She's trying really hard to fit in," he says, pointing in

her general direction. "So she comes up with a good idea and suddenly you can't handle it? Are you really that threatened by an intelligent young woman like Eve? I expected more from you, Kat."

"I made a mistake," I say, finally, because I know I'm screwed. Eve has all the cards. She can make my life as miserable as she likes, and I'll just have to suck it up and keep out of her way.

"I don't have time for this shit, Katherine. I'm not going to act as referee every time you feel eclipsed by a talented young woman. Next time, sort yourself out, okay? Now go and do your job."

We never mention it again, Eve and I. It's like a silent understanding between us. *You won.* But over the next few days I do everything I can to get away from her. I can't bear the sound of her voice. It gives me heartburn. I hate everything about her. I hate her. I even hate the way she says my name. *'Kat'. 'Hey, Kat'.* It makes my stomach clench because I don't know what comes next, but I know it will be really awful. But I can't get away from her because she's like glue. No, she's worse than that. She's like Velcro.

Hey, Kat, shall we have lunch now?

Hey, Kat, Liam wants updated details for the website, what should I tell him?

Hey, Kat, you know that file you gave me the other day, do you know where it is?

By the way, Kat, the hot water runs out really quickly in your place, do you think you could get a plumber? This afternoon? Yes?

At home, Abigail swings between worry and frustration. She complains that I'm constantly distracted. I tell her it's because of work, it's only temporary, I assure her.

I spend sleepless nights trying to decide if I should get a lawyer or not. I'm scared they'll convince me to turn myself in, so I keep putting it off. It's more important that I get Eve out of the office, somehow. And I mean completely out. Out of the building. I could complain to Mark that she's always late, and her work is not up to par. I could ask him to fire her.

But that's not going to work. Not with her type. She'd sue Rue Capital if he did that. She'll say she got fired because she stumbled upon her married boss screwing an eager employee. *I caught them in the act, so he fired me.* And if she found out it came from me, I don't know what she'd do, but I can't imagine it would be pleasant.

Chapter Twenty

Two weeks today. I'm really nervous, but also excited. Mark and I can put all this ridiculous PellisTech business behind us. I've considered having a go at him, for betraying me like that, but he hasn't brought it up again so I thought, hey, let sleeping dogs lie and all that. Still, it will be a relief to move forward. And I don't know why, but I feel like when we get together finally, officially, I'll be free from Eve. It won't be that easy, obviously, but it feels like I won't be so alone, at least.

I'm wearing the grey woolen dress I know Mark likes, with black knee-high boots and a wide belt. I look good. Tired, sure, but nothing a bit of makeup won't fix. I imagine we'll go out after work to celebrate somewhere, quietly, just the two of us, with a glass of champagne, perhaps.

I watch him all morning, with butterflies in my stomach and a ray of light in my heart. I'm waiting for a sign. Which means I'm not doing any work. I clock Eve walk past his office, pop her head round the door and say something. Mark laughs. So does Caroline, who gets up and walks to Eve and hugs her. What the fuck? Suddenly I'm desperate to know what she said that made them laugh. Was it something about me?

I got this idea last night that Eve could work somewhere else if it were a better job. Better pay, better perks, better job title. I figured maybe I could give her a top reference, fake, obviously, and even invent an entire work history. I'll find the perfect job then give it to her. Like a present. Like I'm doing something for her. So that's what I'm doing right now. Going through online employment ads when she comes out of Mark's office and he's right behind her. He has his jacket on. He's carrying his laptop in the black Burberry leather bag I bought for him last Christmas. My heart is beating too hard. I don't understand what's happening, but they go down the stairs without looking my way and a moment later they're out of the building.

In two strides I'm in his office.

"Where did Mark go?" I ask quickly.

"PellisTech meeting," Caroline replies without looking up.

"PellisTech?"

"That's right."

"With Eve?"

She looks at me now. "Why? What's wrong with that?"

"N—nothing," I stammer. "I didn't know, that's all."

"Didn't you?" she asks, with a small smile.

I can't concentrate after that. Back at my desk, I sit there, my legs bouncing, biting my nails. It's at least two hours before they return, and I just stare through the glass to the staircase until finally I watch them come up the steps. They seem in high spirits. She's laughing, one hand on his arm. I want to snatch that arm away. Rip it out of her shoulder.

He goes right to his office and she comes to ours.

"Well!" she says. "That was *very* interesting. I can see why you love your job so much. And Mark is such a cool guy."

I don't answer. I'm already out the door and heading straight to Mark. He's still removing his jacket when I enter. Caroline isn't there, and I close the door behind me.

"You took Eve to a client meeting?" I blurt out.

"That's right."

"Why didn't you ask me to go with you?"

He frowns. "I didn't need to ask you. You have plenty of work, I thought I'd take Eve, it's good training for her. After all, she's the one who came up with the PellisTech project."

He narrows his eyes at me, daring me to contradict him. I want to grab him by the lapels of his shirt and scream it into his face. *She didn't come up with it, I did! She stole my idea! She's an awful human being, can't you see?*

"I'm just surprised you took her, that's all. I come with you to all of our initial meetings. What about the projections? Did Eve do those?" I snort.

"Of course not. I did those. I didn't expect Eve to handle that yet."

"So why not ask me, for fuck's sake?"

He flinches. "What's the matter with you? It's not a big deal, I don't understand why you're so upset. And I don't take you to all meetings."

"It would have been better if I'd gone with you. That's all."

"I thought we resolved this issue you have with Eve. Or are we going to have this conversation every time I involve her in something? I've got work to do here." I'm about to argue but he rests his arms on his desk and says, "Katherine, what's going on? You're distracted. Your work is getting sloppy. Is it something at home? Is Abigail okay?"

"Yes! I mean, no! There's nothing happening with me, whatever the fuck that means!" I bite the inside of my mouth. A part of me knows that deep down, I look like I'm overreacting. Mark doesn't know what Eve's really like. He doesn't know she's the devil.

"You haven't asked how she did."

For Christ's sake. Why would he even say that?

"I don't need to. I already know she was perfect."

He rubs the side of his nose. "I wouldn't say *perfect*, but she was terrific. A real talent. I can definitely see a future for Eve at Rue Capital. She'll need your guidance though. With you as mentor, she could really learn."

I suspect he thinks this is some kind of olive branch. I think I'm going to be sick.

"Good to hear. Look, Mark, I don't want to argue with you today, of all days." I pull up a chair and sit down. "On another topic," I say, softer now.

"Yes?"

I wait for him to catch up.

"Remember our conversation?" I prompt.

He cocks his head and frowns. "What conversation?"

I have an urge to tell him that no matter what, he should never, ever, take up acting. Because he is very bad at it.

But I play along.

"Two weeks, Mark. Remember?"

Something crosses over his face. Something weak and powerless. My heart drops with the weight of disappointment.

"You promised."

"I know. It's not that easy," he says.

"You said two weeks."

"It's her illness—"

"I know. I remember. Chronic fatigue. You said she was getting better."

"It's not that easy. I need more time."

"I don't have more time."

"What?" He jerks his head in confusion. "You're … not…"

"Pregnant? God, no! that's not—" But as I watch the relief flood over him, a prickle of tears bites at the back of my eyes.

"You're an asshole," I snap, getting up.

"Katherine, don't," he pleads. "I'm sorry. Next time I'll take you to the meeting, okay?"

I'd actually forgotten all about that.

"No. Take Eve from now on. I don't care."

Chapter Twenty-One

As the days go by, turning into weeks, Eve settles nicely into her role as my torturer. She gets me to do things for her. Lots of them, mostly little things. Pick up her laundry, bring her coffee, book her manicure. She says that when she comes into the office, I should take her coat and hang it up for her. It's a very expensive coat. Chanel. Very nice. So, I've started to chew gum which I then stick somewhere on the coat. So far I've managed to put one under the collar, and another under the pocket flap. Although not in the pocket itself. I'm not crazy. She hasn't noticed yet, maybe she never will, but I know, and it's the kind of small gesture that makes me feel good. You take what you can get.

Then there are bigger things. I now do her work as well as my own, so I work longer hours. I'm in by seven in the morning, and I leave at seven at night. Abi is really getting worried, needless to say. Sasha is calling me from LA. She leaves messages: *I miss you guys! Talk to me!* I don't return the calls. Or when I do, they're quick chats. *I'm so busy, I need a break already. Can't wait for the big presentation to be over! Chat soon, okay?*

I call Hilary. *Can you pick up Abi from hockey practice? I'm sorry, I know it's the third time this week. I'll make it up to you, I swear.*

I'm exhausted. I can't remember the last time I slept. I'm at the point where I forget what I'm doing, and I don't know how much time has passed. This happens a lot, especially when I catch myself watching her, which I do often now, but slyly, just over the rim of my monitor. I'll glare at the back of her head, without thinking, sometimes for hours at a time, until my eyes hurt. Then at some point she'll say something like, "You're doing my work, Katherine? I'm not hearing any typing!" And I go back to pretending to work.

I have a notepad on my desk where I'll jot quick notes if I'm on the phone. I picked it up yesterday and I was shocked to discover pages covered with black, dense scribbles.

Eve. Evil. Evil Eve. Manipulative Eve. ManipulatEve.

Pages. Lots of them. At first, I didn't believe I'd done them, but it is my handwriting. In some parts I've pressed so hard on the paper that the pen scratched the words through to the next page.

I'm going crazy.

I used to love coming to work. Now I dread it. I can't stand the sound of her voice, especially when she laughs. It makes me want to break something. And every time I try to resist one of her stupid demands (*Hey Kat, seeing you're a math genius and I can't add two numbers together, can you do my taxes for me?*), she says that when she came for dinner to our house that day, the day after the accident, she took photos of the damage on the car while waiting outside. She mentions her uncle. *My uncle the cop, you know the one.* She says he keeps asking her if she knows anything about the hit-and-run on the Parkway, but it's okay, she says, because she tells him not to worry. Just keep it off the books, she tells him. Whatever the fuck that means.

"Hi, Katherine, can I speak to you for a minute?"

I jump. Mark is standing just outside the door.

"Of course."

I follow him into his office with eager anticipation. It's an idea I had yesterday. I emailed him and said we should get Eve her own office. We don't have a lot of room left downstairs, actually we don't have any room. All offices are occupied. But upstairs is a different story. It'll be a bit odd, sure, to have my so-called Executive Assistant up there with the IT guys, but we're too cramped down here. Hell, I'll go upstairs. With Liam and the other IT guy who never says anything. My Executive Assistant can have my office. I don't care.

Mark closes the door and indicates the chair for me to sit down. There's a black Montblanc fountain pen in front of him. Expensive. I don't remember seeing it before. I wonder when he got it.

He picks it up and beings to play with it, clicking the cap off and on.

"How are you, Katherine?"

I rub a finger on my forehead. Between the eyes. Hard. "I'm okay, you?"

He smiles. "I want to talk about you." My left leg is bouncing. I grip my knee to make it stop.

"I'm good. Tired, lots going on, God! Right? But it's all good. I'm not worried." I bite my nail on my left index finger. I never used to do that, ever, but now I can't stop. So much so that there's hardly any nail left to bite. Sometimes I even draw blood.

"I'm sorry I haven't been in touch," I whisper.

He tilts his head slightly. "In touch?"

"You know … we haven't spoken or texted for ages, let alone … you know. I'm just so busy. God, I miss you."

His eyes dart around and he makes a small gesture with his hand, low over the desk, hovering. It takes me a moment to figure out what it means. Ah okay, it's a warning of some kind, I believe.

"I don't think anyone can hear us," I whisper.

"Never mind. Look, I—"

"Can we talk about Eve's position now?" I blurt.

"Yes, good. Let's do that." He swivels the screen around so that I can see it.

"Have you seen this?" he asks.

This is the pitch deck. For SunCell. I have indeed seen it, because I wrote up the fucker. Eve put a hand up to do it, *I don't mind Mark, really, it's not a bother. I'd like to learn,* and later she told me, "I'll be honest with you, Kat. I have no idea what I'm doing. I don't even know what a pitch deck looks like. I don't care, either."

You already know how this part ends. I did the pitch, she gave it to Mark pretending it was her work. Just another day at the office.

"It's awesome, Kat. It's really brilliant," Mark gushes. I roll my eyes, I can't help it.

"Take a look at it when you get a chance. If you haven't already, I know you've been busy. But Katherine, I am so impressed with Eve. I can't thank you enough for bringing her to us and helping her learn the ropes. She is such an asset to our little company. She must be a great help to you. I'm glad you're not carrying all this on your own."

"All this what?"

"The responsibilities you've taken on. It was a lot, I realize that now. I put a lot on you Kat, crazy smart Kat, hey?" He winks. Then, in the manner of an afterthought that fools no one, certainly not me, he adds, "I think she should do the client presentation next week."

I put a finger in my ear and shake it, because I don't think I'm hearing him right.

"What do you think?"

I cock my head at him. "The SunCell client presentation?"

"Yes."

"I always do the client presentation, Mark. And SunCell, it's … it's mine!"

"Jesus, Katherine, please! Not this again!"

"What do you mean, *this again*? Eve can't do it, period! She doesn't have the skills. She doesn't know how."

He points at the screen. "She did a fantastic job with the pitch deck."

"No, I—"

"What?"

It's like running into a door. Every time I want to blurt it out, *No! It's me! Don't you see? I did it! And PellisTech! And everything else she claims credit for! I do it all!* But then, whack I go against the door. *Don't. Keep your mouth shut. She'll make your life even more miserable, if that's even possible.*

"We cannot screw this up, it's what we've been waiting for, Mark. It's the big one."

He crosses his arms. "I agree with you. Which is why I don't think you're the right person for it right now."

"*I'm* not the right person?"

"You're not very well."

"What are you talking about? I'm fine!"

"No, Kat, you're not. You look awful. Your hair, it's …"

My hair? What the fuck does my hair have to do with anything? Sure, normally I invest some time and product grooming. I have dark hair, almost black. I wear it down to my shoulders, layered. Nice and easy, but flattering. Okay, maybe now it doesn't look its shiny best. I bring up a hand to touch it. It does feel a bit greasy.

"You're talking to yourself all the time," Mark says now. "Everyone has noticed, you know. Look at you. You're biting your nails—"

I quickly get my fingers out of my mouth and pull my sleeves over my hands.

"You know what Caroline said to me this morning?" he asks.

I don't answer. I know a rhetorical question when I hear one.

"You smell, Katherine."

"Jesus, Mark?"

"I'm sorry, but it's true. You do."

"Of what? For fuck's sake!"

His eyes won't meet mine. "Body odor."

The way he says it, I crack up laughing. I can't help it.

"Well, that's a relief," I say, wryly.

"You've come to work all week with the same clothes. Look at you. You're a mess. Take a look in the mirror, Katherine, for Christ's sake. Maybe you should go home."

My jaw tightens. I can feel a vein throbbing on my temple. It's me now, who crosses my arms on the desk. But I'm sitting too low and it doesn't have the same effect.

"SunCell, that's mine. I'm doing the presentation." I

raise one hand to ward off his protests. "I'll clean up, I'll take a shower. I didn't realize you were such a stickler for stuff like that," I mumble.

He moves things around on his desk, meaningless things. Yellow Post-it Notes. A small cactus that Caroline gave him for his birthday and no one has ever watered. And I mean, ever. It's shriveled and the color of compost.

When he's run out of things to fiddle around with, just so he doesn't have to look at me, he says, "Eve will be doing the SunCell presentation."

"Why? Because she smells nice?"

He turns his head, looks out across the office to where she's sitting. I follow his gaze. She's on the phone, smiling, nodding, making notes, then she laughs prettily, throwing her head back with one hand lazily fingering her pretty white throat, and I wonder if she knows we're watching her. I turn back to face Mark and that's when I know, beyond a shadow of a doubt, as clear as day, that he's been fucking her.

Chapter Twenty-Two

Everyone has their limit, and it seems like mine has finally showed up. I should be a mess right now. I should be, I don't know, sobbing. Pleading? Devastated. Instead I'm just really, really angry and really, really disappointed.

"So, we're good?" Mark says. I stare at the dead cactus on his desk, imagine myself picking it up and smashing it over his head. Then I replace the image with the Montblanc pen, snatching it from him and stabbing his hand with it. Repeatedly.

Yeah. We're good.

Seeing it's already after four, and Eve never works past four (I don't need to, I'm a very fast worker, she said to Mark), she has left for the day. There's a pink Post-it Note stuck to my computer screen instructing me to finish some work of hers. I crunch it up and throw it over my shoulder. I don't know where it lands.

"Hey."

I look up to see Liam leaning against the doorjamb. I ignore him and grab my jacket.

"How's things?" he says.

"Why?"

I expect him to shrug, but instead he walks in and puts a cup of coffee on my desk. Then he pulls up Eve's chair.

"Caroline says you're having a nervous breakdown."

"Fuck Caroline." I push the coffee away. "Why would she say that?"

I don't expect him to reply, but he does anyway. "Apparently, that's what Eve told her."

"Really?"

"You have to admit, you're MIA lately. Holed up in here all the time. It's like you're hiding."

I didn't expect Liam to be so perceptive. Or so concerned, actually. I'm kind of touched by that.

"What else did Caroline say?" I ask, trying to zip up my jacket but my fingers are shaking and I can't get it done.

"That you're training Eve to do your job because you're leaving soon." That one makes my head snap up.

"She said that?"

"I overheard Mark talk about you. So I asked her."

"What did Mark say?"

"He's not sure you're up to the job anymore. I'm sorry. I wasn't there, exactly. I just overheard him."

"Who was he talking to?"

"Eve," he replies, with reddening cheeks.

I shove my chair hard against the desk.

"Don't listen to office gossip, Liam."

"Okay, well, good to hear. I hope you're staying, for what it's worth."

"Thank you. I appreciate that." I fiddle with my bag, and without looking at him I ask, "Don't you think she's weird? Eve, I mean."

"I don't know, not really. I mean, she's friendly."

Right. Like that means something. Because nobody ever said that about any psychopath ever.

"To be honest, Kat, you're the one who's being weird."

"Yes, I know."

"You're going to be okay?"

The question brings tears to my eyes. I can't control them. I snatch a Kleenex from the desk and pretend to blow my nose.

"I don't know, Liam. I sure hope so." I haul my bag onto my shoulder and walk out, jacket unzipped.

"Don't you want your coffee?" he calls out after me. I raise a hand without looking back.

I have noticed, because how could I not, that Eve and Caroline have become office buddies, so to speak. They go to lunch together. I see them at the kitchen bar whispering to each other. Sometimes they cast furtive glances my way. I've stopped caring. Caroline never liked me, and I still have no idea why. I guess Eve sniffed that out and now she's engaging her in some kind of character assassination. It occurs to me that people in the office have been avoiding me. I should tell them that a nervous breakdown is not contagious.

It's been snowing and my high-top Converse sneakers are totally wrong for this weather. This is what happens when you stop paying attention to what you're wearing. I just pull out whatever is closest to me at the time, which often happens to be the clothes I wore the day before. This morning, it was high-top, dark red, Converse sneakers. I walk and scrunch my toes at the same time, trying to warm them up.

As the Kirkland Place house comes into view, the front

door opens and Eve steps outside. But she's not alone. There's a man with her. Her uncle the cop, maybe? He doesn't look like an uncle. He seems too ... un-uncle like. I stop and retreat just enough around the corner so as not to be seen. She puts her arms around his neck. He encircles her waist and they kiss tenderly on the lips. Not the uncle the cop, then. He puts on a motorcycle helmet and I clock the blue motorbike parked just outside. She rubs her arms as if she's cold, which she most likely is, considering how little she's got on, and goes back inside. I wait until he starts the bike and takes off in a roar of engine noise.

So Eve had a visitor. Interesting. A boyfriend, by the looks of it. I should tell Mark. No, actually, let him find out for himself.

I stamp my feet on the mat outside. Eve said something the other day about me not letting myself in. That I should ring the bell. I use my key. It goes without saying.

"Katherine!" I've startled her. Her eyes dart quickly around the room. I wonder what she's looking for. Something I shouldn't see?

"I'll make this quick," I tell her. "You have to leave. Find somewhere else to live."

She's changed into a pair of old jeans, ripped in all the right places, and a T-shirt that falls off one shoulder. Her blond hair loose down her back. Her feet are bare. There's a glow in her cheeks. She looks especially radiant.

I think she's just had sex.

She cocks her head and stands with one hand on her hip, but it feels posed. "Is that right?" she says, shifting her features back into mock defiance.

She follows me to the kitchen. I retrieve a plastic garbage bag, the type you unroll and tear off, and begin randomly picking up her things and drop them into it. A single sock. A copy of this month's Vanity Fair magazine. A packet of slimming tea.

"That guy just now, outside, is that your boyfriend?"

"None of your business. Hey! What are you doing?"

"I told you. You're leaving."

I don't know what's wrong with me, but I'm not thinking of the consequences. I'm just going with the flow, and the flow is very angry. The flow has had enough. The flow does not want to put up with this shit anymore. I'm so furious I want to bite her.

"Cut it out!" She grabs hold of the garbage bag, but it rips, and its contents tumble out.

I pick up the roll and proceed to tear off another.

"Katherine! Stop! Why are you so mad?"

The question is so stupid, so bizarre, that it makes me stop.

"You're insane," I tell her. "And you're going."

"You can't make me," she says. "I'll call Uncle Bill."

I stand so close to her that I can smell her breath. "So call Uncle Bill. I don't give a shit." I pull out my cell and shove it against her chest. "Do it."

It's only for a second, but I'm hypersensitive right now and my antenna is picking up everything. Something in her face. A hesitation. She recovers so quickly that I'm not sure if I imagined it.

She pushes me away with both hands and retrieves her phone from the back pocket of her jeans.

"Fine. Let's do it your way." I watch her tap the screen. It makes my pulse race. I didn't actually mean for her to call Uncle Bill. That was the flow. She turns slightly away from me, and I reach to her, slowly, ready to snatch the phone away from her ear.

"Uncle Bill, it's me. Can you call me back please?"

I pull my hand back as she lifts the phone to show me. As if that means anything to me. "Voicemail," she says, and shoves it back into her pocket. I close my eyes. What have I done?

She takes the bag from my hand. "As a matter of fact, I have found a place to live. I was going to tell you tomorrow. I'm moving out."

I wait for the punchline. It doesn't come. "You are?"

Unbelievable. She knew she was leaving, and she didn't say anything, and now I'm screwed because fucking Uncle Bill is going to call her back and I don't know what she's going to tell him.

"Where is it?"

"Fort Point."

"Oh nice! Fort Point is nice." Now I'm trying to sound like we're two friends having a nice chat, and I really like her after all.

"I'm glad you approve. Actually, I was going to ask you. I have a bit of a problem."

"Oh?"

"Normally, I wouldn't ask…"

Oh, God. Okay. Here we go.

"… but I thought to myself, Eve, if you can't rely on your friends, then who?"

"What is it?" I ask, the familiar weight of dread settling in the pit of my stomach.

"They want first and last month's, and a security deposit. It's a bit rich, frankly, but there you have it. And I'm a bit short."

"How short?"

"Ten thousand dollars."

I laugh. It sounds like I'm barking. "You can't be serious!"

She cocks her head at me. "Why can't I be serious, Kat?"

"Okay, you really are serious. That's a lot of money. How much is the rent?"

"Even if that was any of your business, what difference would *that* make? I'm not asking for your financial analysis of the rental market, I'm asking for a helping hand."

"You want me to lend you the whole ten thousand dollars?"

"No. I want you to give me a neck massage. Yes, Kat. I'm asking you to give me ten grand."

"I don't have that kind of money lying around."

"Kat, like I said I wouldn't normally ask. But I signed on the apartment because I really thought you wanted me out of your mother's house. I hate to say this, but I can feel the vibe coming from you, Katherine. I'm not joking. Loud and clear. And I thought the sooner I'm out, the happier you'll be. But the market, the way it is at the moment … well I'm not one to call in favors, you know that, but seeing that I was there for Nancy and then I was there for you when you crashed and killed—"

"Shut up!" I hiss.

She twirls a lock of hair around her finger. "It's up to you, Kat. Uncle Bill will call me back any minute. I can tell him about you, and what you did, or I can just say I was calling to say hi. Your call."

I bite the side of my thumb, gnaw at the bit of skin. It's starting to hurt.

"Will you take a check?"

"A check will be just fine."

Chapter Twenty-Three

Then there's Abigail. Sometimes I feel like she's the last thing I have, the last link keeping me tethered to the world. Everything else I thought I was—a woman in love, a woman with a career path, a woman about to launch into the next phase of her life—has dissolved into nothing. There's nothing of me left, except for Abi. My baby.

Sometimes I'm afraid I'm going to lose her, too. At first, she watched my descent into catatonic anxiety with panic in her eyes. She'd ask me constantly if I'd been to the doctor. "Yes, baby, and I'm fine. Really." She thinks I have a terminal illness and I'm lying to her. I swore to her that I don't. On my life, I said. I'm just a little stressed, that's all. Nothing to worry about.

Abi says I'm chewing my own mouth. "You'll get wrinkles, Mom. People will think you're smoking. You're not smoking, are you?"

"No, baby, I'm not."

She's beyond frustrated with me. She says I'm not trying. That if I really cared about her, at least I'd get out of bed on weekends. And I wouldn't sit there every night, still as a statue with a dead stare. She says sometimes I drool without realizing, and it's gross.

"That's ridiculous. I've never drooled in my life."

"Yeah, right," she scoffs.

She barely speaks to me now. She spends as much time out of the house as she possibly can, or that's how it feels. Every afternoon after school she goes to her drama club. She spends hours at Paige's house rehearsing for the play. I have a vague recollection that it's going to be in the State Drama Festival and it's a huge deal, but I could be wrong. At least it gives Abi a hobby. I don't know where she gets the energy.

She asked me this morning if I had menopause. Not if I was going *through* it, if I *had* it. She's so young. I put my hand on her soft cheek, but she removed it. "I'm being serious Mom!" Apparently, that's what Paige told her. She said her mom was the same when she 'had' it. They talk as if menopause is an infectious disease. Like measles. Still, I made a mental promise never to tell Hilary about that conversation.

"I'm not going through menopause."

"Well that's a shame, Mom!" she snapped. "At least we could have done something about that! Get you some hormones!" She slammed the door on the way out.

I wanted to tell her, I know it's hard, I know we can't go on like this, but I don't know how to break free.

I had a dream last night, and I sure hope it's a premonition, because I dreamed that it was me who was blackmailing her. I woke up with a start. Could I? Is there some chink in her armor, waiting to be discovered? What about the motorbike guy? The boyfriend? Could I possibly use that? Threaten to tell Mark? I can't possibly imagine that would scare Eve. She'd probably laugh at me if I said that. But there's got to be something. Everyone has *something*. I just need to start looking.

Chapter Twenty-Four

Eve moves out today. While I wouldn't say my heart is *singing* exactly, I won't lie, it sure feels a little lighter. She got the day off, of course. "Take all the time you need," Mark said. "You deserve it," he added, and I wanted to puke all over his nice brown leather shoes.

I expected her to be gone when I got to Kirkland Place —after work, since I don't deserve a day off—but no such luck.

"Hello, Kat. I'm almost done! I'm so excited! How are you feeling? Better?" She lays a hand on my arm. I stare at her pretty pink fingernails, nicely buffed, a bit long for my taste, but then again if I should carry a pair of pliers in my back pocket … never mind.

She's folding some towels into her suitcase. I'm about to point out they're mine, but I change my mind. I don't want anything to come between her and the front door.

On impulse I go to my father's study. Everything looks the same, nothing out of place. Except the abacus of course, since I put it in the drawer for safekeeping that day. Except it's not. I've opened the drawer, and it's not there. I check the other drawers, even though I know I put it in the first one. No abacus.

I run back out. "Eve?"

She's got her coat on. She's closing the clasps on her case.

"Yes, Katherine?"

"Do you know where the abacus is?"

"The what?"

"The Chinese abacus, it was in the study, I put it in the drawer. You were there."

"Then that's where it is. Have you checked?"

"Yes! That's why I'm asking you!"

She puts her hands on her hips and faces me squarely. "Ah. So that's why you're here. You've come to count the silverware."

"Do you know where it is? Yes or no?"

"I have no idea where your fucking abacus is, Katherine. I couldn't care less either, okay? Now if you'll excuse me." She picks up her suitcase and walks past me. She makes a show of puffing with the effort of pulling her luggage. I'm surprised she hasn't asked me to carry it for her. She drags it on the floorboards, leaving long, pale streaks that I already know will never come off, then heads right out the front door and into her ride. She doesn't even look at me. She hasn't thanked me, either, for letting her stay here. That goes without saying.

I check the rest of the house, inch by inch. The other thing missing is the small Gaudi bronze. That's been on the mantelpiece in the living room since I can remember. But not anymore.

I don't even know how to handle the theft, and it's driving me nuts. If I confront Eve about it, she'll deny it, but if I say nothing, she's going to get away with it. She's like some albatross around my neck, always dragging me down.

That's all I can think about when I get home. I'm beginning to obsess with finding a solution to Eve. That's how I think of her now, as a problem, in need of a solution. And these things she took from me, I want them back. And I want to be rid of her. I hate her.

It consumes me.

Chapter Twenty-Five

Ten am. I've been here since seven. It's the day of the SunCell presentation, the big client presentation that Eve is going to give, apparently, because according to Mark she's ready but then he also says I have to help her prepare. It makes no difference to me. I do all her work, anyway.

Maybe she's not coming. Maybe she got cold feet and I'll get to do it in her place, save the day and all that. That would be nice. Mark would have to acknowledge that I am reliable. That I am the best. That he loves me more than her.

And then she comes in.

I stand up immediately, expecting to be handed her coat, the way she does, but she shakes her head and hangs it up herself. I sit back down, a little disappointed, it must be said. I was going to be bolder today. I was going to stick the chewing gum into the wool fringes at the hem and scrunch it in. I take the gum out of my mouth and drop it in the wastepaper basket.

"I'm so nervous," she says. "I have butterflies in my stomach. What if I screw up? It feels like such a responsibility. I wouldn't want to let Mark down, what's your advice, Kat?"

"Don't screw up."

"You're going to be like that the whole time?" she snaps. "Because Mark says you have to help me."

"You can handle it." Then I perk up. "Think of this as an opportunity, Eve. This will propel you in this business, trust me. There are people queuing up to get a chance at that kind of exposure. You're being fast-tracked. You'll be able to get a job with the big guys soon. Big investment companies. Think about that. Big salary plus perks. Lots of them."

She laughs and squeezes my hand. "Thank you. You're so right. Rolling stone gathers no moss, right?"

This has nothing to do with what I just said. It's like she just pulls out random sentences from some databank somewhere in her brain. Like she's compiled a list of 'Things Normal People Say' but she doesn't always nail the context.

"All right," I tell her. "Come on, let's go."

"Whatever you say, Boss," she replies. She shuts the laptop and unplugs it, picks it up. I scoop up the folders, and we make our way upstairs to the presentation room.

The presentation room is a small auditorium. It's very modern, like everything else in this place. The seating is made up of rows of tall steps with colorful cushions for people to sit on. I don't think it's the best design for our purposes, but like I said, it's trendy, edgy, and all those buzzwords. And with one wall of glass, it's bright.

Not everyone gets invited to our presentations, and I think that's where we have set ourselves aside from the competition. People want to be invited, but they have to work for it. We only bring in investors we have a reasonable prospect of signing up, and they need a minimum of $100k to buy in. SunCell being the golden child at the moment, there's a lot of interest. We expect around forty to fifty people to attend.

Caroline is already here. I hand her the folders. She sets them down along with notepads, pens, and carafes of water on every sitting space.

"Hi, babe!" she chirps to Eve. *Babe?* She says nothing to me. I consider walking up to her and raising my armpit in her face.

This okay? It's deodorant. Dove. I slapped on gallons of the stuff. Just for you. Which would be doubly funny because in fact, I forgot to put on deodorant. I can't remember if I showered.

"You're coming Saturday, Caroline?" Eve says.

"You bet, I can't wait."

Then Eve turns to me. "I'm having a little party, nothing fancy, over at my condo on Saturday. A house warming, you might say. Are you free? Saturday evening?"

I stare at her for a full minute, waiting for a punch line that doesn't come. "Are you inviting me to your party?"

"No, dummy! I need someone to serve canapés." Then laughing, she adds, "Kidding!" and bumps me lightly on the shoulder. From the corner of my eye, I spot Caroline smirking. "Eve! You're so funny!" I say, patting her on the back, even though I'm not sure she didn't mean it.

Then Liam arrives on the stage and does something with cables. Eve springs up to join him and offers to help. He smiles shyly, a red glow creeping up his neck. What is it with everyone around here? He takes the laptop from Eve without a word, plugs it in and turns it on. The screen overhead comes to life, mirroring the laptop.

She claps once. "Oh wow, Liam! How did you do that?

That's incredible!" Liam looks down, grinning. He lets his long fringe fall and obscure most of his face and traces something on the floor with his toe.

Jesus wept.

Minutes later we are ready to do a quick rehearsal, and while at first Eve is a bit nervous, she finds her rhythm pretty quickly. She'll do all right. Of course. By the time the first clients arrive to take their seat, she's got her groove.

Mark greets everyone personally. Then he saunters to the stage, introduces the project, then Eve. She flashes the smile and I can tell from the nodding heads around me that everyone is smiling back at her.

When Mark is done with the introductions, he joins me in the back and sits next to me. I can't tell if it's some kind of gesture, a peace offering, or if he wants to stay close in case I try to sabotage the event.

We sit through slides of pie charts and number graphs and images of lab benches, all of which I put together, obviously. Eve is walking the length of the stage, back and forth, as she tells the story of SunCell and why you really, *really* want to get in on this one. There's a touch of Marissa Mayer in her. It's nicely done.

"By now, I bet you're all dying to see what it looks like, am I right? Well, wonder no more." She walks up to the lectern and picks up a small box, the size of a standard iPhone, with a cable attached to it. She lifts it up and shows it to everyone, like a magician displaying her props before pulling out a rabbit. By now there's epic music swelling and a laser show above the stage. The screen above is bright and multicolored, like an explosion of fireworks.

She pulls out the cable, and the entire building, which seconds ago was pulsing with electrical energy, goes out with the whirr of a dying motor. No projection, no screen, no lights, no epic music. It's the middle of the day so it's still bright in here—I would have pulled the drapes if that had been me.

"That's right. This little box here supplies all the energy required for us to operate here. That means lights, computers, the fridge upstairs, not to mention the coffee machine (titters of laughter), and the air conditioning. One of these, fully charged, allows us to operate off the grid for over a week. That's right. Eight days at least, most likely ten. And it takes about four hours of sunshine to charge it."

She connects the cable again, and everything whirrs back to life with much color and movement. Cue thunderous applause.

"I think it's going well, don't you?" Mark whispers. Then, staring straight ahead, with a wistful look on his stupid face, he says, "God, she's fantastic."

If I didn't passionately hate this woman, I would have to admit that she is shining. She makes jokes, and they land well. People are laughing in all the right places. They're listening, too, you can tell. All in all, it's gone better than I'd expected, and by the time the presentation is over, everyone claps. That's actually unusual, in this context. I can't tell if they're excited about SunCell or about the delivery.

Then everyone is invited to come back downstairs to the reception area where we are serving drinks and closing deals. She slides up next to me as I reach the last step, and she is beaming.

"What did you think?" Her tone is urgent. She's pulling at my shirt, almost bouncing on her toes, her face flushed with the buzz of it all. I know that buzz. That's my buzz. But I note she asked loudly enough for people nearby to hear, to show how modest she is, even though it's clear the disciple has outperformed the teacher.

You want to know what I think? I think you're crazy, lady.

"Look, I don't know how to say this, but frankly, I'm a little disappointed," I tell her. I don't know why those words have come out of my mouth because it's not what I was going to say, right up until the moment I said it.

She bursts into a peel of laughter, and I turn my back to her and walk toward the exit. I can see her face reflected into the glass pane in front of me, and the word that comes to mind is, crestfallen.

Good.

Downstairs quickly feels like a party. We're serving champagne, always a good lubricant to the closing of a deal, but this time there's no need. We can't sign them fast enough.

I clock Mark standing next to the conference table, Eve having magically materialized by his side. She was way behind me moments ago, now she's right up front. How does that work?

She's quite a bit shorter than he is, so he's bending down to speak to her. I join them quickly, breaking through a tight group of potential investors. I want to remind them that we're not here to exchange pleasantries with each other. She spots me coming across and searches my face with a frown.

"Hey, you! Well done, congratulations," I tell her. I even kiss her on the cheek. There. Two can play that game. She waits a moment, as if to check, then she says, "Do you mean that?"

"Of course, I mean that."

She closes her eyes and puts a hand on her chest and

says, "Oh, God, thank you. Thank you. I was so worried just now."

"Don't be silly, you were—what's the word you used, Mark? Fantastic! That's it. Well done, Eve. Truly. I couldn't be more proud."

"But before, you said—"

"Kidding!" I clap my hand over my mouth. "Oh, Eve, honey. Sorry, did I make you feel bad? Oh, so sorry. Silly me. Honestly, me and my wacky sense of humor, haha." I lay my hand on her shoulder, and in a more serious tone I say, "You were brilliant. Really. I mean that. Thank you, Eve. Really."

Mark isn't listening to us anymore. He's chatting with Vlad, our biggest client. His name is really Alex Matei, but he calls himself Vlad. I want to remind Mark that I brought Vlad in. I'd heard through the grapevine that he had a lot of money, and I mean *a lot* of money, and was looking for some exciting projects to invest in. I invited him for a meeting, he showed us some documents—maybe forged, who knows—about the funds having cleared money-laundering checks. I did some research, made some calls. Other industry people thought he was too much of a risk. Aaron the legal guy said we should stay clear. Sometimes I wonder why we employ Aaron if we never listen to him.

I pointed out to Mark that Vlad and his friends are drowning in money that needs a home, and why wouldn't we welcome them in? We're a broad church. They invested millions of dollars, and now Mark likes Vlad.

Vlad says hello, shakes my hand, then turns to Eve and says in his slightly scary accent, "I have bought in, the maximum allowed. Ten million dollars. It's a good investment for me. Just don't let me down, young lady. I'm trusting you." He puts one arm around her shoulder in a somewhat paternal way, but I detect a tinge of menace as well, or maybe that's just me. Vlad has a scar that runs along the top of his hand and wrist and it's clearly visible right now. A scary scar. Then he laughs, a big belly laugh that shows his gold tooth in the back of his mouth. Who puts gold at the back of their teeth? People like Vlad, that's who.

And this is where things start to get even more irritating, if that's possible. Mark's focus has returned to our little group, and Eve begins to wax lyrical about why SunCell is an amazing opportunity, and how honored we are to have been tasked with raising its capital. Melanie, cofounder of SunCell, is here, too. Eve is crapping on, albeit animatedly, about how this is the future, the missing link in the green energy revolution, the product the world has been waiting for to ditch fossil fuels, and what it's going to do for third-world countries, for health and infrastructure projects that would be impossible to finance otherwise. Basically, all the material I carefully researched, distilled, and wrote up for the marketing department and for our presentation, and all the material I included in press releases and articles and pitches and all the rest, and Eve—who is a fast worker, that's established—is parroting my work to one and all, and now she's talking about the war in Africa (which one?) shaking her head in disgust at the state of the modern world (why can't we all love each other! Isn't there an app for that? There should be!), ending poverty, (imagine being able to pump clean water over thousands of kilometers! How awesome for those people!) and they all think she walks on water while I stand there, pulling my lips away from my teeth in what I hope looks like a smile. Nobody, and I mean nobody, mentions me, or my contribution, which is everything, or the fact that if it weren't for me, we wouldn't be having a SunCell funding round right now.

"Awesome work, Eve," Mark says.

"Yeah, awesome work, Eve," I parrot. Mark shoots me a disapproving look. I wonder when exactly they started fucking. I watch him now, with his puppy eyes lingering on Eve's bosom. Like a lovestruck teenager. Then they smile at each other and she even blushes. Two cute red circles on her alabaster cheeks spreading slowly. Honestly, it's unbearable. Everything is unbearable. I bet he leaves Sonya right now for her. None of this two weeks bullshit, because I can tell this is different. This is true lust.

I catch Eve's eye, and I point to my lip.

What? she mouths.

I point again. Tap tap, on my top lip. She keeps wiping it off with one finger. I shake my head. She comes closer, eyebrows drawn together. "What?"

"Something on your mouth, what is it?" Then a little louder, "Oh, it's herpes!"

There. Now whenever Mark thinks of kissing those sweet, plump lips, there will be a little voice whispering in his ear.

Herpes...

Like I said. You take what you can get.

Chapter Twenty-Six

I wonder whether Eve has ever been diagnosed as a psychopath. There is a diagnostic tool to evaluate whether someone is a psychopath or not. It's called the Hare Psychopathy Checklist. Essentially, you score a person's attributes, like whether they exhibit delusions of grandeur (check), whether they lack any remorse or guilt (check), if they are pathological liars (probably check).

So maybe she had been seeing a shrink, and the shrink had assessed her using the Hare checklist, and the results are in her house somewhere.

Okay, long shot. Also, I don't think psychopaths voluntarily submit themselves to the Hare checklist. I think that happens if they've been arrested for some horrible crime. But maybe there's the name of a psychologist lying around. A bill, a business card, something I can use to find out more about her. Maybe she's been locked up in the past, she's crazy enough for it. That's the kind of thing I could use. Then even if she went to the cops I could point to her unreliability as a witness.

She's crazy, but you don't have to take my word for it, officer; it's well documented. By the way, she was the one driving the car that night.

I wasn't going to go to her stupid party. I'd rather get my teeth pulled out. But then I remembered the dream, and I thought, when will I get such an opportunity again to snoop? So when Hilary called to say she was taking Paige to the movies over at the Apple Cinema and would Abi and I like to join them, I asked her to take Abi instead.

"I'll make it up to you, I swear." I could tell she wasn't happy about it. I didn't remind her of all the times I ran errands for her, or took the girls somewhere because she was going out with Henry. There are other things I've done for her, but I can't remember them.

"I suppose it's your incredibly important work again, is it? Tell me Katherine, this business about having it all, a career, a child, a home, how is it working out for you?"

It's a nasty barb, even for Hilary, and it makes me gasp. I don't know what's gotten into her. She mumbles something I don't catch.

"What did you say?" I ask, coldly.

"I said I'll do it."

I want to tell her to get lost. But I can't. I need her, and that's the truth.

When I tell Abi she's going out with Paige and Hilary, but not me, she raises her eyes under her eyelids. I catch a glint of reflected light at her throat.

"That's pretty." I sit on the bed and reach to finger the necklace, a simple gold chain with a multicolored round glass pendant. She wraps her hand around it, but her cheeks turn pink and she won't look at me. Oh, I see, that's really sweet. I think maybe Abigail has a boyfriend.

"Hilary says you can stay over there tonight," I tell her,

hoping to diffuse the tension. She nods, once, but doesn't reply.

She goes to her dresser and takes out a T-shirt and a pair of pajamas. She crunches them into a ball and into her backpack. I reach across to take them out to fold them properly, but she snatches the bag away from my grasp.

"What movie are you seeing?" I ask.

"It's called *A Simple Favor*. It's about a woman who goes missing. Just like you, Mom." Then she walks out, slamming the door after her.

So yes. I'm going to Eve's stupid party, and I'm going to go through her place and I'm not leaving until I find something about that bitch.

And now I'm here.

Of course, the condo is stunning. It's like something out of an interior decoration magazine. An architect's showcase. My eyes slide up and down every surface, fascinated. It's very industrial, which is not necessarily my taste, but I appreciate the style. It's a bit like our office actually, that same aesthetic of exposed wood and steel beams and exposed brick. Personally, I wouldn't like it. I'd feel like I was still at work but without the people.

The kitchen however, is different. It's huge, all steel and marble. I note there's absolutely nothing on any surface. I wonder if she has a cleaning lady. Overall, the condo is a bit bare, suggesting that she hasn't invested into much furniture yet.

I wonder how much that'll set me back.

"You're here! Great!" she says. "Could you run to the store for me?" She needs some tonic water. She rummages through a kitchen drawer. "Here, take these." She hands me a set of keys. "Just put them back before you leave."

On the way out, I run into Caroline. She looks nice in her dark blue dress and a chunky ruby necklace.

"Katherine! I didn't expect to see you here!"

"You didn't? Why not?"

She cups her hand over her mouth and says, softly. "Your mental health problems. Eve told me." Her eyes scan me up and down, then slide off, in search of other, more interesting people to talk to.

I wonder if Caroline is Eve's new plaything. I should warn her. *Stay away from her, she's Evil. Eve-l. Evil Eve.*

By the time I get back with tonic water, there are only a dozen people or so, ten of which are my colleagues, plus two or three people I've never met.

I sit down on the couch and help myself to a glass of cheap sparkling wine, which I fill to the brim·and knock back immediately. Then I do it again. Eve materializes by my side. "You might want to take it easy there, Katherine."

"Why?"

"You're sitting on the coats."

"Oh!" I stand up and indeed, she's right. I was sitting on a pile of coats. "Why don't I take these to the bedroom?" I suggest.

"Great!" she says. She's very chirpy. I gather them up into my arms and bump into a potted palm tree on the way out. "Oops, sorry," I say to the palm tree. Which is silly, of course. It's not even a real palm tree.

The bedroom is very messy, with a stack of clothes dumped onto the bed, as if she tried on a hundred outfits this morning. I dump the coats on top of the pile and turn to inspect the room. The built-ins with their mirrored doors take up the whole back wall. At first, I don't recognize myself in full-length like that. My clothes are hanging off me. I take a closer look at my reflection. I knew I looked awful, but I did not know *how* awful exactly, because I have successfully avoided looking at myself as much as humanly possible. If I'd known there was a mirror, I'm not sure I would have walked in here.

My eyes are bloodshot. There are dark, purplish rings below them, where the skin is so thin, so tired, it's like the texture of a scrunched-up paper bag. The rest of my face is somewhere between pale green and grey, pasty. Except for a redness on either side of my nose. I'm not wearing any makeup because frankly, I don't have the energy.

I make sure the bedroom door is closed and slide open the built-ins. More clothes spill out from the top shelf. Silk shirts, camisoles, scarves. Still on the shelf is a large, flat, red box—like one of those office storage boxes. I pick it up and open the flap.

Twenty Up and Coming Boutique VC Firms to Watch This Year.

The article from Forbes Magazine. I remember telling Eve about that piece the very first day I met her. She must have searched for it and printed it. She has circled my name, too. *Katherine Nichols, Rue Capital's secret weapon!* I suppose that makes sense, I'd just offered her a job, hadn't I?

God. What I wouldn't give to go back to that day, to tell her no, I don't have time for a bite to eat at the Italian place around the corner, thanks all the same. I look closer and see that she's scribbled something in the corner: *The Salon 2pm Jan 10 cut + color Maureen.*

I know that place. That's where I get my hair done, too. Although not anymore, as of right this moment.

The door opens, making me jump. A woman stumbles

inside. "Oops, sorry," she says. "Wrong door." I pretend to be checking my face in the mirror, still holding the red box. She's gone in a flash, and I shove everything back on the shelf, hold the pile of clothes back with one hand, and slide the door closed, probably just the way she would have done. Seems like a lot of effort just to take something in and out of a closet. I wonder if she has considered hanging her clothes? Tidying up her drawers? Best not ask, or she'll make me do it.

Someone turns the music up. Grace Jones, I think. Someone—Eve it sounds like—laughs. Maybe this drag of a party is finally getting started. I'm about to open the other side of the built-ins when the door opens again.

"What are you doing?" Eve asks, hands on hips.

My heart is racing. I pinch my cheeks, facing the mirror. "Nothing, trying to look nice."

"Yes well, good luck with that."

We return to the living room together. Eve ups the volume, and now she's moving her arms around with some whoop whoop noises, like she's having so much fun she can't help herself, she really *has to dance right now*. She throws her head back, her pearly laugh bouncing around the room, so irritating it's making my teeth hurt.

"Hi, Kat!"

I turn. It's Amy from reception.

"Hey, Amy, how are you?"

"Good, thanks!" Then her features rearrange themselves into concerned look. "I'm sorry about your breakdown," she says. "I hope everything works out." I thank her for her kind words, because why not, and ask, "What breakdown?"

She nods. "Eve said we're not supposed to talk to you about it. Or about your dementia."

"Dementia?"

"Eve told us about the diagnosis. Early onset. I'm really sorry. But it might seem like we're all ignoring you, and it just doesn't feel right. I hope I haven't upset you by bringing it up."

"It's fine, really." But Eve has spotted us and before I have time to say *wrong diagnosis, actually,* she's by our side, hooking her arm into Amy's before taking her away. *Let me show you...*

Ah. So that explains why everyone at the office turns away, embarrassed, whenever I catch their eye. *Just terrible ... nervous breakdown ... early menopause, that's what I heard ... history of dementia in the family ... then there's the drug abuse...*

I continue my snooping around the place, pretend I'm admiring the walls, the door knobs, helping myself along the way to a glass of that nice Shiraz that someone brought. And that's when the doorbell rings.

Chapter Twenty-Seven

Mark looks both surprised and a little embarrassed to see me standing there, but he recovers quickly.

"Katherine!"

"That's me!" My heart is beating so fast it hurts. I want to take his face in my hands and kiss him. I want to lick his earlobe. I want to whisper in his ear. *I love you.*

"How are you?" he says briskly. But it's not really a question, because he walks right past me and into the party without waiting for an answer.

I lean against the wall and watch Eve's face light up at the sight of him. He kisses her on the cheek. There's a glow to him. I know that glow. It's the glow of someone in love. I used to have that glow.

He puts his hand on the small of her back, where her dress is cut out in the shape of a lozenge. I feel like my heart is breaking. He rubs her skin with his thumb. I lift a bottle of Jack Daniels from the bar and retreat to the kitchen. I lean against the sink, grab hold of my hair in one fist and pull hard. Some woman comes in and opens a cupboard, finds a glass and walks out, barely looking my way. I take a swig of whiskey, then another, and by the time I've gone through about a third of it, Jack and I decide that it's time I stopped behaving like a sissy and take matters into my own hands.

I return to the living room where, I am happy to report, the party is about as exciting as watching paint dry. There's a small group of guests in the middle of the room chatting awkwardly. Mark is standing next to Eve, still doing that stupid thumb-on-her-back thing. She sees me and smiles, but it's not a nice smile. It doesn't reach her eyes, for one thing. It's more of a 'gotcha' kind of smile, and I know in that moment why she has invited me: for this. She wanted me to see her and Mark together. Well fuck them both then. I grab his arm and twist him to face me, which makes him spill some of his drink onto Eve's pretty dress.

"What the—"

"Who do you think you are!" I slur.

"Now that's enough!" Caroline says, rather sternly I think. I tell her to shut up.

"I think you should leave now," Mark says.

"And I think you're an asshole!" I take hold of his hand and pull him toward the kitchen. Eve shouts something but Mark says, "It's okay, I've got this!" just as I slam the door shut after us.

"What's going on, Mark? What are you doing?"

He lets out a sigh and looks sideways.

"Mark?"

"I should have said something earlier."

"Said what?" I ask.

He turns to look at me. "It's over Katherine, between us. I'm sorry."

"Over?" I knew that was coming, I suppose. But still, it really hurts. It saps my breath away. "Why?"

The door creaks open, just a bit. "Fuck off!" I shout, kicking it shut. Mark flinches.

He rubs a hand through his hair. "It's not you, it's—"

"Damn right, it's not me! It's her!" I yell, pointing toward the living room. "Don't get sucked in Mark, please! She's a bitch—"

He winces. "There's no need to—"

"I mean it! Really! She doesn't even like you! She's a psycho!"

"Now that's enough, Katherine!"

"I'm telling you the truth! She's—" But he's taken my wrist and his fingernails are digging into my skin.

"Listen to me. It's over between us. I'm seeing Eve now. I know it's not what you wanted, and I swear, I never meant to hurt you. Neither did Eve. But that's how it is."

I pull my wrist away from his grip. "Does Sonya know?"

His mouth tightens, and he does that little twitch of the eyelid.

I cock my head at him. "She doesn't."

"I'm going to tell her. Soon."

"Right."

"She's getting better, almost—"

"Right."

"Don't you dare—" he snarls.

"What, you're worried I might tell her myself?"

"Don't you dare interfere. Not if you want to keep your job."

I scoff. "You must be joking." But then it occurs to me I need that job. I don't have another one, and I need that money. I have bills. Lots of them. Our little house, Abi loved it so much that I took on the lease even though it was more money than I wanted to pay. Way more. Then there's Atwood House… I can't lose this job.

"If you want to resign, I would understand," he says now.

"And what would you do then, Mark? I'm the one who brings in the business, who has all the ideas, who gets the investors in. It's me who makes you money! I may as well have bought you that Tesla!"

"Don't be ridiculous. There's a whole company behind me, it's not just you, Kat. No one is irreplaceable. I think Eve is doing rather well, or maybe you didn't notice? Or no wait, you did. That's why you're behaving like you are."

"Like what?"

"Like a jealous woman. You can't stand the fact that you're no longer the smartest woman in the room."

I let out a laugh. "Mark, I *am* the smartest person in the room. You have no idea. So thank you very much for your offer, but no. I'm not going to resign." I cross my arms. "I want a raise."

He points a finger right into my face. "I'll let you keep your job, in memory of what you and I once had, but only if you behave. You understand? There will be no raise. You take one step out of line and I'll fire you. Are we clear?"

I could have said more, done more, but Eve opens the door. "Everything all right you guys?" she coos, all girly-flirty, and takes Mark's arm. He kisses her on the top of her head. I grab the bottle and walk out to a room full of people gawking at me.

I am so upset, so wired, and yes, so drunk, that after I stumbled through the front door, I tiptoe upstairs, my shoes dangling from my fingers, and pop my head into Abi's room to check on her. I sway inside, holding onto the door, and pat my way to the edge of her bed where I sit down gently.

"Hey, baby," I slur in the darkness, running the palm of my hand onto the covers. "I love you, so, so much." I sigh. "Mommy loves you more than life itself. And Mommy did a bad, bad thing. And Mommy is paying for it. That's right, baby. Mommy is being punished." I start to cry, then wipe the snot on my sleeve. "I'm *so very* sorry. I love you so much. Can you *ever* forgive me, sweetheart?" She won't answer me, so I pat the covers and make my way farther across the bed until I get to the other side, and that's when I remember. She's not here.

Thank God for that. There's only so much that kid can take from her mother.

I spend Sunday morning wandering about the house like a hospital patient. I cry into my pillow, into my pajama top, into the cushions on the couch. I listen to Carrie Underwood and Ashley Monroe singing sad songs. Mark lent me a scarf once, which I've never returned. I have it with me now. I bury my face in it, go over every moment I've had with him, every scene, every kiss, every smile. Like a show reel playing in my mind.

The Best of Mark and Loser Kat, brought to you by Jack Daniels Single Barrel.

If it weren't for Abigail or my mother, that show reel would be sponsored by Smith & Wesson.

I think I can safely say the evening was a complete failure. A disaster in every respect, except for that bottle of Jack Daniels I stole.

I peel myself off the couch and go visit my mother. We spend the afternoon together, her asleep, me sitting by her side, watching the snow outside. They've moved her chair to be near the window, which is nice, she likes looking at the world outside. I lay my head on her shoulder, gently, so as not to wake her up. I'm so spent, and tears well up in my eyes. I don't try to stop them. They fall onto my cheeks. I wipe them off with the back of my hand.

"I've done a terrible thing, Mom. Something really bad. Something I can't undo." I rest my cheek against her chest. "I have ruined everything. I don't know what I'm going to do."

And my mother does something she has not done since I was a child. She lays a hand softly, gently, on my head. "Shh," she whispers. "It will be all right."

I don't even breathe. I'm frightened that if I do, I'll lose her. But she caresses my hair, and it's like I'm ten years old again. We sit like this for a long time—me crying, her consoling me with such tenderness, I sink in it.

"You'll find a way," she murmurs.

Chapter Twenty-Eight

That Monday, I call in sick. "When will you be back?" Caroline asks.

"When I'm well again," I tell her, then I hang up.

Of course, I'm going to tell Sonya. I'm going to tell her everything. I wonder if she knows about Mark and me? She must know *something*. He must have broached the subject at some point. It's not like they're together anymore, not for a long time. It's just because she's not well.

But she doesn't know about Eve. Well, she's about to. Mark will hate me for telling her, but he should have thought of that before breaking my heart and taking up with the psychopath.

Mark lives in one of the most expensive neighborhoods of Boston. I picked him up outside his place once, I can't remember why or where we were going, but as I waited in the car, admiring the building, I remember thinking how rich he must be to live in an apartment here. I vaguely wondered what floor they lived on. Whether they had a view of the park. Now as I stand at the door, looking at the single, unmarked buzzer, I am shocked to realize they own *the whole townhouse*. Needless to say, my resolve gets a beating. I am more than a little intimidated. But then, what do I have to lose? Absolutely nothing, that's what.

I press the buzzer with all the bluster of a local politician on the campaign trail. It's immediately opened by a young man in a grey suit and I wonder if I have the wrong house.

"Is Sonya home?" I ask sweetly. I deliberately use her first name so that he thinks we're friends. He quickly appraises me. "I'm afraid not. Are you expected?" His gaze slides up to the top of my head and his left nostril twitches. I remember, too late, that I forgot, again, to wash my hair. I really must start using mirrors again.

"Expecting me? Not exactly. I was in the neighborhood. When will she be back?"

"I don't know. Can I leave your name?"

"It's K— Kara. Kara. With a K." I'm not completely sure how she feels about me, even though they're separated. Best to do the introductions face to face, I think.

Young man in suit stares at me with one raised eyebrow. "Kara…?"

I stamp my feet on the ground and rub my hands together. My fingertips are so cold I can't feel them anymore. "Kara Frost," I say.

Then I find a bench in the park and I wait, vaguely aware of the damp seeping into my jeans, but not enough to do anything about it.

By the time a red Lexus pulls up outside the building I can't feel my feet anymore. The passenger door opens and a young blond woman steps out. She walks briskly around to the driver's side. The tinted window comes down and I get a view of the driver, a woman wearing a black beret spotted with gold beads. Then the other woman, the blond one, tucks a strand of hair behind her ear, revealing the glint of a diamond earing. She bends to say something to the black beret, her cute yoga-pants-clad bottom proudly sticking out. I suppose they've come from an exercise class, which would explain the white floral trainers. Adorable, but not suited for this weather.

She stands up again and pulls her green puffer coat tighter around her. Then she trots up to the front door of Mark's house, opens it, just like that, without having to ring the bell, and as she turns back to wave at her friend, I finally see her face properly. She's very pretty, her cheeks pink from the cold. She smiles. I bet she's got pretty white teeth. Small and perfectly aligned. It's only when her friend shouts, "Bye, Sonya!" that I realize with a shock who she is. And the first thought that comes to me is, *she sure doesn't look tired*.

I'm stunned. I've always pictured Sonya as a thin, worn-out woman, her face pale and drawn. I thought she'd be, I don't know, austere, clutching a set of pearls. I know she's an interior designer, so I'd assumed she'd be dealing in antiques. But this person, just now, is not Sonya. She couldn't be. She's too happy, for one thing. Too pretty.

She's too fucking healthy.

I'm standing with a hand on my chest and I'm about to cross the road, because I'm going in there, I'm going to ring that bell and shove that pompous guy in the grey suit out of my way and I'm going to demand an explanation. Because she is supposed to have chronic fatigue syndrome, and that means she is very, very tired. And tired people don't skip around the place in their designer puffer jackets with faux-fur trim. Tired people don't laugh like they don't have a care in the world. They don't go to the gym, they don't have friends, and they look ugly.

I should know. I'm so fucking tired.

"What are you doing here? You're all right?"

For a moment I'm confused but then I see that it's Hilary. She takes my arm, but I shake it off.

"I have to go," I say.

"Where? What's going on?"

"I have to go and talk to her!" I point to the door behind which Sonya has just disappeared.

"I don't think you should talk to anyone right now. What's the matter, anyway? You're very upset, Katherine."

"She's supposed to be tired!" I wail, still pointing. Hilary takes a closer look at me.

"Jesus, Kat. You look awful."

"Fuck off, Hilary!"

"Okay. I understand. I see that you're distraught. Come on. I'll buy you a drink and you can calm down." She takes my arm again and pulls.

"A drink? It's not even lunchtime."

"So have a warm milk then," she says. And because I'm so fucking tired, I let her drag me away.

She's right, of course. And the G&T does help, as do the next two. The way she keeps knocking hers back and immediately ordering another makes me think this is a regular occurrence for Hilary, this lunchtime drinking thing. It occurs to me I've been entrusting my daughter to her care quite a lot lately. Maybe I should reconsider.

"All men are pigs!" she declares. "It's just a fact."

It's the first time I've spoken to anyone about Mark.

Other than Eve, I mean, and even then, I didn't actually say it was Mark. But now I can't shut up. I told her everything. About Mark, I mean. Not about my psychopath. That goes without saying.

"And you know what? I got headhunted!" I wail. "That's right! The big boys at DMC—"

"—DMC the band? Really?"

"What? No! DMC the venture capital firm."

"Oh, right," she says, before knocking back the rest of her glass. "I was thinking Run DMC. The band."

"Jesus, you're showing your age, Hil. Anyway, what was I saying? Ah yes, I was headhunted! Big bucks! Health insurance! Better than the crap deal they dish out at Rue Capital ladidah. This one had dental for fuck's sake."

"You passed up on dental?"

"Yep, I did. That's right. And you know why? For love. For fucking Denver, that's why. We went to Denver, we made love—oh, God." I start to cry again. Hilary clicks her fingers and the waiter arrives immediately with two more G&Ts.

Hilary hands me my fresh drink. "I've never been to Denver," she says.

I sip a little then spin my glass on its coaster, studying its contents. "Count yourself lucky then. It all starts in Denver, believe me."

She shakes her head. "It's not Denver, Kat, it's men that's the problem. They're all pigs."

"Not all men. Your Henry is sweet. He loves you. Anyone can see that."

"Yeah, right," she sneers. "That, he does."

"Oh, stop it, Hil. He's a nice husband. And he's a nice dad to Paige. You're really lucky."

She bops her head, up and down and sideways, it's pretty funny actually.

"Okay, I'll give you that," she says. "He is a good father. That's true. He loves Paige."

I put my hand on her arm. "Thank you for looking after Abigail these past weeks. I can't thank you enough. I'll make it up to you, I swear."

She nods. "I'm worried about you, Kat."

"Yeah, well, take a ticket."

"No, really, and so is Abi. You need to pull yourself together, for Abigail. You can't keep doing this to her. It's neglectful."

Tears roll down my cheek. I rub my nose on my sleeve. "I know," I say, between sniffles. "You're right."

She pats my wrist, just at the spot wet with snot. She makes a grimace, holds up her fingers. I laugh. "Here," I say, giving her a paper napkin. "Speaking of Paige," she says, wiping her fingers. "She wants to have her sixteenth at Barolo. She had so much fun at Abi's party."

"Ha!" I shriek. "I told you so! And *you* said it was inappropriate or something, remember?"

"Fine. I don't think I said inappropriate, but okay. I did want to host Paige's birthday at our house. I had something quite a bit more elaborate in mind, I even talked to a party planner, Cloth & Sparkles, you know them? White themed, it was— Ouch!"

I've taken hold of her wrist. A little too hard by the sound of things. "Stop talking," I blurt out. She pulls her arm away and rubs at the spot where I've squeezed. "What the heck?"

"Abi's birthday party. Oh my God!"

"What about it?"

"I have to go." I quickly gather my things and bend to kiss her on the cheek.

"I'll call you later, Hil. Thank you. I love you."

It must be the gin. I've never said that to Hilary before. But I sure mean it right now.

Chapter Twenty-Nine

Fact: I have not been inside my car since *that* night. Sometimes I don't think I'll ever get back behind the wheel. Instead, I choose to spend money I can no longer spare on Ubers and taxis, so this is why now I'm running, my arm stretched high waiving for a cab that hasn't come yet.

It's the date, January 10, the hair cut appointment scrawled hurriedly on the corner of the printout. The article that Eve printed and stored in her red box, on the shelf of her wardrobe. *Twenty VC Firms to Watch.* I thought she printed it because I'd mentioned it to her, the very first day I met her.

January 10, that was two days before Abi's birthday party at Barolo.

I hadn't met Eve then.

I can hear my own breath. Ragged, a little panicky. I'm trying to understand the implications of this realization because what this means is that Eve printed the article about Rue Capital at least three days before meeting me. Not only that, but she circled my name.

There's also another possibility: that my memory is

failing me here, like everything else about me. I am broken, after all. It could be that I read the date wrong. The more I think about that, the more I conclude that it's the only explanation. Except I don't think I did. I can see it in my mind's eye. I vaguely recalled at the time how close it was to Abi's birthday. A couple of days before. I hadn't connected the dots then, but it gave me a strange feeling. A sensation that something wasn't quite right. I remember that.

I pull out my cell. I know the place, the hair salon. I get my hair cut there, too.

I manage to locate their number. God, I hope they're open. It's Monday, some places close on Mondays, don't they? I have to know. I pray that they're open, and my heart beats too fast as I listen to the phone ring at the other end, once, twice, I close my eyes and—

"Hello, The Salon, Robyn speaking, how can I help you?"

Thank you, God. Thank you.

"Yes, hello, it's—" I stop. I was going to say it was me, Katherine Nichols, but I change my mind. I definitely do not want someone there ever mentioning Eve and me in the same sentence. Ever.

"Oh, hi, um, a friend of mine, Eve Howinski is her name, she visited your salon a few weeks ago, and I really like her cut. Could I make an appointment?"

She's very happy to help me out, asks for my name. I blurt out *Kara Frost*. I might be a liar, but at least I'm consistent. Still, I feel bad. I'm not a natural liar.

"I just want to check who did my friend's hair. She mentioned a name, but I forgot. I'm pretty sure she said she came in on January 10."

There's a rustle of paper, the sound of pages being turned.

"January... 10... let me see.... Ah yes, that's right, Eve, I have her here. Thursday January 10, 2pm. Maureen did her hair. I'll check when Maureen is available if you like."

I knew it. I fucking knew it. I feel dizzy. I can taste bile at the back of my throat. "That's okay, I'll call back." I end the call.

I'm in the cab now, going home. The driver wants to know if I watched Nigella Lawson's cooking show the night before. "She cooks like a Greek goddess," he assures me. "I should know, I am Greek. She cooks like my mother."

Whether that implies his mother is a Greek goddess, I don't know. But I point out that Nigella Lawson is English. He insists I've got it wrong. "Greek!" he argues. "Only Greeks can cook like that!" And I know that I will not win this battle so I end up agreeing with him.

After that I zone out, because I am trying to remember where I left Eve's spare keys after Saturday night. I'm pretty sure I still have them. I didn't put them back in the kitchen drawer. The truth is, I just forgot, then I fought with Mark, then I walked out with a bottle of Jack Daniels.

I empty the contents of my bag onto the seat next to me, but they're not there. I remember I was wearing a leather jacket.

I get home, promising the driver that I'll watch Nigella Lawson, Greek goddess, from now on, and run upstairs. My leather jacket is still on the bedroom chair, where I left it Saturday night. I go through the pockets and Bingo. Found them!

My heart is racing. It's a little after two, so I have at least two hours before Eve gets home from work. I should have asked the driver to wait. I shove the keys in the pocket of my coat and run to the subway station and get on the red line because it's just as fast to get to her place.

I want to know why she has that article about me. I want to see if there's anything else in that red box that would explain why she has it. I feel a bit overwhelmed by all the people around me. It's amazing how many there are, walking around, waiting around, doing stuff, going places. Doesn't anybody have to be anywhere? What are they all doing? Where are they going?

I get off at Broadway and walk quickly across to Eve's condo. It occurs to me that it's also possible Eve scribbled that note on that article *after* she met me. As in, *I must not forget that I had my hair done a few days ago, that it was 2pm and that Maureen cut it. I better write all this down.*

I think not, somehow.

Downstairs, I press the buzzer to her condo, just like burglars do in the movies, then I wait. I press it again. I even put my ear against the intercom just to make sure. No answer.

I take the elevator to her floor. A door closes somewhere. It makes my heart stop. But it's not from her apartment.

I knock on her door, twice. Then, when I'm reasonably certain that there is no one inside, I slip in, checking both sides of the corridor. Like a thief.

It's deadly quiet, and even messier than last time I was here, which was only a couple of days ago but feels strangely longer. I walk into her bedroom and open her closet. The clothes fall out, just as they did before, and there's the red box. I pull it out and sit cross-legged on the carpeted floor to examine its contents.

I pull out the first page. It's trembling like a leaf in my hand. And there it is. Jan 10. The date is correct. But then I already knew that since it was confirmed by the hair salon. The following page in the pile makes my breath catch in my throat.

It's a copy of my father's obituary, cut out from the Boston Herald. It's just a paragraph. I've seen it before, of course. It's an acknowledgement of his teaching work at Harvard, and that he leaves one daughter, me, and his wife, Nancy Nichols, née Hayden, of the elite Hayden family. It mentions that in recent years my father had retired to help care for his wife who suffers from acute dementia.

I pull out my phone and take a photo of each page. Then I flick quickly through the rest. None of the other printouts are about me, but they are about other people. Copies of insurance policies. An article about a defamation case. A newspaper photograph of a woman wearing sunglasses, one hand lifted to shield herself from the camera. The caption mentions a divorce. I lay the sheets down on the floor to take photos of those, too, when something catches my eye from the other side of the closet. That side is also opened, only by a foot or so, but I can just make out the edge of something, and before I slide the door open as far as it will go and push the hanging clothes apart, I already know what it is. I'm staring at the Gaudi bronze statuette, the one that went missing from my mother's house.

I pivot onto my knees and rummage through the items thrown every which way. More clothes, a box that once contained a set of Dior beauty products but is now used for cheap costume jewelry. A baseball cap. More shoes, lots of them. A white paper bag. It's heavier than it looks. I open it and pull out a necklace. Gold and jade. That necklace was a gift from my father to my mother. He brought it back from a trip to China. I wonder what else is missing from my mother's house. Because there must be more, and she must have sold some. This isn't just to spite me. This is business. Then I spot the abacus, peeking out from under a rolled-up yoga mat. I pick it up, make sure it's not broken, and I'm relieved to see it's intact. Then for some reason that I can't explain, I lift it high and bring it down hard so that the porcelain edge hits the rail at the bottom of the closet. A chip flies off and I do it again, harder this time. The porcelain frame breaks into a hundred pieces. I'm still not sure why I did that. Maybe because it was a gift from my father and it reminded me of an earlier, easier time, when I was still the apple of his eye. Maybe because seeing it here, out of place, it felt allowed. Maybe because I'm angry today. I must be, because I'm clenching my jaw so hard my teeth hurt.

I am still on my knees when I hear the door close.

The front door of the apartment.

Chapter Thirty

I am fifteen years old. It's the middle of the night and something has woken me. For a moment I assume it's Abi wanting her feed, and I raise myself on one elbow and wait, listening. A car drives by and throws its headlights through the blinds and onto the ceiling of my bedroom.

Then I smell it. The cheap drugstore cologne he wears all the time. My eyes adjust to the darkness and I make out his bulk. He is standing, motionless and silent, in front of the closed door of my bedroom. Incredibly, I still don't know what he wants and I'm about to ask him if everything is all right, but I'm frightened. Something about the way he doesn't move. Abi makes a sound in her crib, somewhere between a moan and a sigh, and he moves now, quickly, and he is by my bed and pulls off the covers in one slow motion. I'm shaking. Suddenly he is on top of me, one hand over my mouth, the other lifting up my nightie.

Meet Uncle Trevor.

I am remembering this scene because after that first time, I would tie a length of cotton thread to the doorknob and another to my wrist, so that when he opened the door, the tension of the thread would wake me up and I would quickly crawl inside the closet and tie the doors together from the inside. He couldn't get me out without waking up Aunt Maud and eventually he'd leave, and I'd fall asleep in there until Abi's next feed.

So yes, hiding in closets is not usually a pleasant experience for me, and this time is no exception. I managed to quickly gather the papers into the red box and pull it inside with me. The shoes on the floor are making it uncomfortable but I don't dare move. Something is wedged against my hip. I feel for it and gently nudge it out of the way. I think it's the Gaudi. The door is not quite closed and slowly, silently, I reach with the tips of my fingers and press sideways but it's cheap furniture after all, and the edge resists in the rail.

There's the sound of footsteps, the door of the fridge opening. Why is she here, anyway? She's supposed to be at work.

My heart is thumping so hard I'm afraid she'll hear it. The door gives and I manage to close it another inch, but there's still a gap, and it won't budge. Something crashes in the sink, a glass maybe. I think I am having a heart attack. Now I can hear her in the hallway.

She's going to walk into the bedroom.

She's going to open the door to the closet.

She's going to see me.

I am going to die.

I'm holding my knees to my chest, trying to hide amongst her coats and dresses. The edge of a scarf tickles my nose but I don't dare move. My eyes are squeezed shut praying to a God I didn't know I believed in, and that's when my phone pings.

I stop breathing. Very slowly, I reach in my pocket and

feel for the switch to silence my phone. I'm shaking so much, I can't tell if I've put it on vibrate or not. I keep flicking it back and forth, looking for a clue, and then I give up.

There's movement out there, the rustling of someone moving around, soft footsteps on the floorboards. I bury my face in my hands but leave enough of a gap between my fingers to see the door of the bedroom open wider.

She stands there, one hand resting on the door handle.

Except it's not her.

Because of the clothes hanging in front of me, I can only see the bottom part of him through the gap at the edge of the door. He's wearing black jeans, loose and worn. Boots. Heavy boots. Motorcycle boots. The edge of a brown leather jacket. His hand on the door handle. There's something— Oh, God. I can hear him breathing. Through his nose. Does that mean he can hear me, too? I've retreated as far back as I can, my spine against the wall, so I can't see him fully, just pieces of him. I shove the knuckle of my forefinger in my mouth and bite it.

Help me, God. I know who this is. It's that guy from the other day. Her *other* boyfriend. At least it's not her uncle the cop. He is going to see the broken abacus in front of the wardrobe, and the bundle of clothes that tumbled out earlier, on the floor in a messy pile. He must be wondering what happened. He's going to come and take a closer look, maybe put the clothes back in, even. That's if he hadn't heard my phone. Because for all I know, maybe he already knows there's a burglar crouching at the back of the closet.

I'm so scared right now I actually raise my forearms to my head to ward off the blow that's bound to come any minute. Images of Abi fly through my mind. Abi as a baby. Abi dressed up as a fairy. Abi's left dimple. Abi's first day of school, turning back to wave at me, smiling. Abi playing ice hockey.

I'm sorry, baby, I love you so much.

He walks farther inside the room, and I wait for the door to open and for the inevitable brutality.

But he walks past. Now he's in the ensuite bathroom. I hear him urinating in the toilet. For a moment I consider running out of the condo, but I don't. I don't dare move.

He's back. He didn't flush. He didn't even wash his hands. So they're both slobs, then.

Footsteps. Rustling. And then, like a miracle, the sound of the front door opening, soon followed by a soft click. I don't move. I let the air fill my lungs. I listen with my eyes closed.

He's gone.

I wait a few more minutes, letting my heartbeat find its normal rhythm, sort of, and shakily, slowly, I crawl out of my hiding place. With trembling hands, I rearrange the papers back in the box, trying to remember what order they were in, and failing. I stick the box back on the shelf and push the pile of clothes on top of it, then close the sliding doors. I pick up the pieces of the abacus and put them in the bag with the necklace, which I take with me. Finally, I return her keys to the kitchen drawer.

Then I run the hell out of there.

Chapter Thirty-One

I'm here. I'm home, I'm alive. Thank you, God. I love my house. House, I love you. I've never loved a house as much as this one right now.

I close my eyes. Try to remember what little I saw of the man, which wasn't much. I wonder if he was at her party? Without Mark realizing the competition was in the same room? After all, this is Eve we're talking about. Psycho, weirdo, evil Eve. Mentally, I go through the people who were there, try to jog a memory, but it's no use. And anyway, I wasn't paying attention.

What do I know about him? That he has a set of keys, that he is very comfortable in her place, comfortable enough to urinate in the ensuite bathroom. And I bet he left the seat up.

I take off my coat and lay it on the back of the couch. My laptop is on the coffee table in front of me. I connect my phone to it and transfer the photos I took earlier. I save them in a folder on my computer which I name 'receipts-travel' and hide among other tax related documents.

But I am frightened. I tell myself it's because of what

just happened back at the condo, but there's something else. The feeling of being watched, like a prickle on my skin. I stand up and check outside the window but there's no one there of course. It's just me being paranoid.

I return to my place on the couch and zoom in on the first sheet, the article from Forbes. Nothing I hadn't already seen there. Next, I look at the obituary. Same thing. Nothing that explains why she has a copy of it. I bring up the next image. It's of a printout from a legal blog, or that's what it looks like to me. It's titled *Case Law, A. Walters vs. Delta Insurance*. There's a date in a small font in the footer. It's almost three years old.

It's about a workplace defamation case brought on by an employee. The employee in question, A. Walters, had been making complaints about the company's practices of assessing insurance payouts. Seems like A. Walters had been asked to deny claims A. Walters knew were legitimately payable.

The company then fired the employee and sent a general email to everyone to say A. Walters had been dismissed because of fraud. A. Walters took the company to court and successfully argued that the company's actions amounted to defamation of character.

What seems to have attracted Eve's eye, and I say this because she circled that part, was that the defamation claim was successful, and A. Walters pocketed around two million dollars.

Under the circle, she has scribbled a name.

Alison

Below that, a New York phone number.

(212) 555-0187.

I may as well. I have nothing to lose here. I make the call.

"Hello?"

I hadn't actually expected anyone to answer. I was ready for a recorded message telling me the number had been disconnected. But it's a real person at the other end. A woman. An older woman, judging from the quality of her tone. And she's waiting.

"Oh, hello, this is..."

I don't know what to say. I have not thought this through.

"Who is this?" she asks.

"Is this Mrs. Walters?" I stammer.

"Yes, it is. Who are you? What do you want?"

I have to say something. She's not going to stay on the phone forever waiting for me.

"I'm looking for Alison. Alison Walters."

I hear her gasp.

"Who is this?"

"My name is Katherine Nichols, Mrs. Walters. I was hoping to speak to Alison." I thought about giving my fake name, but it didn't feel right this time. And I don't think *she* is Alison, somehow, and because of the way she reacted when I mentioned the name, I decide to take a chance. "Are you Mrs. Walters? Alison's mother?"

Silence.

"Mrs. Walters?"

"Who are you?" she asks again, although not quite as strongly as before.

"I'm a friend of Alison's."

"If you were a friend of hers, you'd know she's dead."

Now it's my breath that catches. I stare at the date of the printout.

"I am so very sorry, Mrs. Walters. I really had no idea. Can I ask what happened?"

"My daughter killed herself. What did you say your name was?"

"Katherine," I whisper. "Katherine Nichols. I am so very sorry to hear that. It's very sad news. Very sad."

"And you're a friend of Alison? Nichols did you say? I don't remember you. I have to go now."

"Wait—"

She's still there. I can hear her breathing, short sharp breaths through her nose.

"Did Alison know someone called Eve? Does the name mean anything to you? Eve Howinski?"

There's a beat of silence.

"Hello?"

"How dare you," she hisses. She is so full of spite that I want to pull the phone away from my ear.

"I'm sorry Mrs. Walters, but it's very important."

"Don't ever call this number again. You hear?"

"Mrs. Walters—" But she's gone. I put the phone down next to me and it rings almost immediately. I pick it up, thinking Mrs. Walters has had a change of heart but it's my psychopath.

"Hey, Kat, how are you holding up?"

I swear, the sound of that voice makes me break out in hives. I close my eyes, wonder what she wants now. Can I not have one day off? Please? Just one? For a mad moment, I'm tempted to ask her. *Ever heard of Alison Walters? Her mother has heard of you.*

"What do you want?" I ask instead.

"That's not very friendly! Did you get up on the wrong side of the bed or something?"

"Sorry," I say, not because I am but because it's easier, essentially. "I just had some bad news."

"Oh, that's too bad." She doesn't ask what the news is.

If she had, I would have said, *Someone died. A woman. She killed herself. I just found out.*

Then a thought occurs to me. It makes my stomach lurch. Is she at home? Does she know I was there?

"Are you at work?" I ask.

"Of course I'm at work, dummy! Where else would I be?"

"Right." The tension in my body releases a little. Just a little. "So what can I do for you?"

"Well, I was wondering if you would like..." she waits.

I sit up, my body stiffens.

"Would like what?"

"To be my maid of honor! At the wedding!" she squeals.

I bury my face in my hand. "What wedding?"

"Kidding!" she says now. "We haven't set a date. Actually Mark hasn't proposed. But when he does, I really hope you'll be there for me. Anyway, the reason I called is, when are you coming back to work?"

I don't know why I let her get to me like this. It's like she has superpowers over me. Every conversation with this woman feels like I have to back away slowly. It's really exhausting.

"I'm not sure," I reply. "In a few days. Mark insisted," I add. Which is a lie.

"Really? Aww, he's such a nice boss. If it was me, I'm not sure I'd want to pay you for doing nothing, but there you go."

I close my hand into a fist and feel the nails dig into my palm.

"I have work to do, Katherine," she hisses suddenly. She sounds like she's put the phone right against her mouth. "You need to be here. *You*, have work to do. I expect you here tomorrow."

Something makes me look up. A sound outside, like a rustle in the branches. Again, that creepy feeling of being watched prickles up my spine. I wonder if she's really at work, and not standing outside, spying on me.

I stand up and check out the window again. I look down the corridor to the front door, through the frosted glass at the door.

"Katherine?"

"Yes! I'll be there tomorrow!"

"Okay. That's all I wanted to know."

The moment she hangs up I rush to open the front door in case she's out there. Across the road, the Ackermans walk out of their front gate with their two small dogs. They wave at me, smile. They don't look worried. I wave back. I can hear my phone ringing again inside and I wonder if it's her, trying to lure me back in before I catch her, or him, because maybe it's the guy from the condo. Maybe he followed me. That thought makes my stomach lurch. I quickly peer down the side of the house, where the living room window is, but there's no one. Just me and my paranoia.

I go back inside. The ringing has stopped. I close the door and lean against it, waiting for my pulse to slow down. Then I walk around making sure all the windows and doors are locked.

Chapter Thirty-Two

I should have spent more time at the condo to make sure everything was left as it should be. Except I panicked, and now I'm worried I left a trace. She might not miss the abacus or the necklace right away, but she'll notice the shards of porcelain on the floor. Now I wish I'd made sure I picked them all up.

Then Abigail walks in. She stops in the hallway to take her coat off.

"Hi, honey!" I sing out.

"Jesus, Mom! You scared the shit out of me! What are you doing home?"

"Sorry, baby. I'm working at home today. Did you have a nice day at school?" Why I'm speaking to her like she's a ten-year-old, I don't know.

"Like you care," she replies, before running upstairs to her room.

I follow her up the stairs. She's turned her music on and blasted the house with electronic beats. I walk in and turn the volume down.

"I don't want to worry you, but Mr. Jones said there are

burglars in the area." I just hope she doesn't ask him about it.

"Seriously?"

"Yes. Seriously. It's probably nothing to worry about but from now on I want you to set the alarm at all times. Set it to the Home mode when you're inside, you remember how to do that?"

She rolls her eyes at me. To be fair, we never set it when we're home. "Alarm on, whether you're in or not, okay?" I repeat.

She shrugs, but she heard me. I leave her to it and go back downstairs. The music comes back up.

I return to my task with renewed vigor. I bring up the photos again on the computer, and an hour later, I'm no closer than when I started. There are two people who I have no idea how to contact. One of them is the woman in the photo that was taken outside a courthouse in Tennessee after divorce proceedings were concluded. It looks like she was handed a heck of a lot of money by her now ex-husband, but there's no scribbled phone number this time, and her name, Jane White, is unfortunately too generic.

The next one is Luciana Rodriguez, the surviving daughter of a couple who were killed in a car crash. Her name is circled in their obituary, but that's it. No contact details, nothing. I can't find her, either.

Then I do have one small success. A woman—and they're all women, as far as I can see—whose name is Adley Fowler. How do I know Adley is a woman? Because I've heard of her. She was granted a patent for a technological invention that improved Wi-Fi transmission speeds. It went on to make millions for its creator. I remember reading about this before I started working with Rue Capital. If this had happened today, I would have put my hand up to manage her funding round.

She sold her company but remained as one of the managing directors. And it's easy to find a phone number for the company.

When the receptionist asks me who's calling, I give my real name, just as I told Mrs. Walters. After all, we are bonded together, and we're all vulnerable. All of us caught up in Eve's mysterious little scheme. I believe it's unfair for me not to show my cards, so to speak, if I expect her to do so. Then I say I'm calling from Rue Capital and they put me through to Adley right away.

"I know this is going to sound strange," I begin. "But I have reasons to believe you and I know someone in common. Are you familiar with the name Eve Howinski?"

I don't hear the short gasp I expected. Instead she lets out a low, soft wail. Almost inaudible. But I heard it.

"Please don't hang up," I say quickly.

"I don't know who you are—"

"I told you my name. Katherine—"

"—but I don't want to talk to you. I don't care what you're selling, or what you want from me."

"Adley, listen. I don't know what she's done to you, but I think she's doing it to me, too."

There's a short pause, then she says, "I doubt that very much." And there is such sadness in her voice that it makes my heart ache. Like a stitch.

"I have to go now," she says. "Don't call me again."

"Just take down my number, please. In case you change your mind." I reel off my cell number. I repeat it. "You have it? Call me, anytime. Please."

But she's already hung up.

And that's it. That was the last photo I took. I don't have anyone else to call. I don't have anyone else to ask.

But that's not true. Is it?

I tell Abigail that I'm going out but will be back to make us dinner. She's sitting at her desk with school books opened. I don't understand how she can do homework with this noise. "Whatev," she says, without turning around. I stand behind her and put my arms around her, bend down to kiss her cheek. "I love you," I tell her. "I'll make it up to you. It's all going to be okay, I promise you." She doesn't answer, but at least she doesn't push me away, so that's something. I set the house alarm on the way out and check the sides of the house for burglars, or strange men in leather jackets, or psychopaths, but it seems we are safe.

Inside Atwood House, which is where I am now, I go through the double doors downstairs. I wave at the nurse at the front desk, who gives me a quick smile, then I pull out my pass so that I can get up the elevator.

Upstairs, I don't go straight to see my mother, the way I usually do. Instead, I stop at the nurses' station.

"Is Fiona here?" I ask.

Fiona walks up the hall and sees me.

"Hey there, Katherine, what can I do for you?" she says brightly. Then she frowns.

"You're all right, Kat? You look a wee bit under the weather, if you don't mind me saying. Are you working too hard?"

"I'm fine, thank you, can we go into your office?"

"If you'd like."

I wait until she closes the door after us. I sit down, take my time, try to seem calmer than I actually am.

"What can I do for you, Katherine?"

"Can I ask you about Eve?"

"Oh, Eve." She shakes her head. "She left, you know, such a shame. We were all so fond of her."

"So she hasn't been back lately?"

"Afraid not. She hasn't been here for a long time. Some of the residents still ask when she'll be back."

She taps a few keys on her keyboard, moves the mouse around. "She called in the middle of January and told us she wouldn't be coming in anymore. She got a job, you see. A full time job."

Don't remind me.

"But she wasn't here long, then."

She frowns. "Two weeks. Almost." She swivels in her chair to face me. "But that's not that unusual, volunteers come and go in this place."

"But two weeks? That seems really short to me."

She shrugs. "I suppose it is. They usually stay for a couple of months, at least. I wish we could retain volunteers, but what can you do?"

She glances at her watch. "I don't mean to rush you Katherine, but was there anything else?"

I stand up. "No. Thank you."

"Do you want me to pass on a message if she contacts us again?"

"I just wanted to thank her again, don't worry about it, Fiona."

But I want to ask her, *Do you really think that my mother choked? Or is it possible that Eve made that up? No one saw it happen, did they? Other than Eve? Whoever did see something, they only saw Eve helping my mother, right? They saw her slapping her back, something like that, but that's it, isn't it?*

Did it even happen at all?

But I can't ask that. As a theory, it's too strange to throw that out there, without any preparation. She'll think I'm questioning the security in this place. That I'm pointing out that anyone can walk up and call themselves 'volunteers' and put residents in harm's way. If the volunteers slipped into a resident's room and stole from them, would you know? What if they hurt them?

Or pretend a patient is choking when no one's watching?

Fiona has one hand on the door handle when I remember to ask.

"Did she have family here? Is that why she volunteered?"

"You mean among the staff?"

"No. I mean a patient. An elderly relative. A grandmother, maybe?"

"No. No one."

But of course, I knew that already.

I walk home and when my phone buzzes in my pocket I'm tempted to ignore it in case it's my psychopath. But then I wonder if maybe it's Adley, and when I see it's a number I don't recognize, I'm sure it's her. She's changed her mind.

"Hello?"

"Is this Katherine Nichols?" But not Adley. It's a male voice.

"Yes?"

"My name is Richard Walters. You spoke to my mother earlier. Alison Walters was my sister."

I freeze.

"My mother told me you called," he says. "You asked about Eve."

"Yes. Yes, I did."

"Do you know Eve Howinski?" he asks.

"Yes. I do," I reply. "Do you?"

"I've met her. Twice. Is she a friend of yours?"

"Not exactly."

"Let me rephrase that." There's a pause and then he asks, "Do you *like* Eve Howinski?" and I know that we are on the same page. It's instant. A recognition of shared pain. A common enemy.

"No. No, I don't."

"Then maybe we should talk."

"I'd like that. Thank you. I really would like that very much."

"We could meet somewhere. I'm in New York—"

"Oh, of course you are." I can't hide the disappointment in my voice. "I'm in Boston, Cambridge to be precise." I feel myself deflate. How the fuck am I going to get to New York?

"—but I could come to you. There's lot that I need to understand about Eve Howinski, and what happened to my sister. Because I'm sure she had something to do with Alison's death. And I want to find out what it is. I could get on a flight early tomorrow morning, meet you somewhere, wherever you like. Would that be convenient?"

"Yes, it would," I tell him. Very convenient. We agree to meet for lunch the next day.

It's impossible to describe the sensation that comes over me after we end that call. But the closest emotion I can come up with is, *hope*.

Chapter Thirty-Three

That night, I sleep. For the first time in ages, I sleep properly. That's what hope does, it's amazing. It helps you sleep. I wouldn't say I wake up refreshed, but at least I'm feeling like one day, I *might* be refreshed. I wake up without the thud of too many thoughts fighting it out in my head and too many pills to shut them up.

I even make breakfast for Abi and me. She looks at it with suspicion, but she eats it.

I'm out of the house now, and the world feels … kind of normal. Upright. I wonder if I'm going normal. That's got to be the opposite of going crazy, right? I've been going crazy for weeks, could I be going normal now?

I get in to work right at 9:00 on the dot. Today, I'm wearing my nice blue suit— a pencil skirt and a cute little matching jacket that goes just down to my waist. I'm also wearing my hiking boots because they happened to be the closest to me when I reached in the bottom of the closet. I'm not going hiking, but I thought, fuck it. Why should I make the effort to look farther in the shoe closet? I wish I were going hiking. But I'm not, and let's face it, who gives a shit.

I'm astonished to find Eve is already here. Not so surprisingly, so is Mark. They're standing together in the foyer and as soon as they see me they stop talking. I wish Mark wasn't here. He glares at me when I walk in and curls his lips in disgust. Like I'm the one who deserves being glared at. I used to love those lips. Now I want to bite them off. In two strides, he's standing in front of me. "Listen to me, Katherine, I want to make one thing clear here. Behave yourself and we'll be fine. But if you harass Eve, or any of my staff, or you do anything to discredit this organization, you're out. We're clear?"

I smile, then lean forward so I can speak into his ear, and in a low voice I say, "You're an asshole, Mark. We're clear?"

I walk away with barely a brisk nod. Eve immediately follows me into our office and closes the door after her.

"Hello, Eve." I remove my jacket and hang it on the back of my chair. My mouth is dry. It's the nerves I think. I'm scared she knows I've been in her house.

She clicks her tongue. "That wasn't very friendly back there, Kat. Mark is your boss. There's no need to be rude."

I turn on my computer without replying.

"You see? That's exactly the kind of attitude that's holding you back. I mean, look at me, I've only been here a few weeks and already I'm managing client presentations. Meanwhile you just look like doom and gloom personified. Nobody wants to be around that, Katherine."

I quickly flick through the Post-it Notes she's stuck all over my desk, when suddenly she taps my head with her knuckles. "Hello? Anybody home in there?"

I turn around, rubbing the spot. "Sorry, I was thinking, about what you said."

"Right, well, do think about it. Frankly, at this point, you're a bit of an embarrassment to Rue Capital. Hey, speaking of which, I've been telling Mark he should add an 'e' at the end of 'capital', Rue Capitale! What do you think? Very French, 'La Rue Capitale,' get it? You know 'rue' is 'street' in French."

I shake my head.

"You didn't? Huh! And yet I'm the one who can't balance my checkbook. Go figure. Anyway, here we are."

I'm trying to process what she says, but it's difficult. Mostly because she jumps around and makes no sense. So Eve wants to change the name to, what was it? Street Capitale? That sounds like some underground communist organization to me. I can't imagine investors flocking, not that it matters to me anymore. They can call it Donald Duck, for all I care.

"You're not very happy, are you?" I'm about to protest, but she raises her hand.

"No that's okay. I understand. I really do. In fact, I've been thinking of ways to help you."

"You have?"

"I'll be honest with you, Kat. Working here, it's all very well, but it's not like this job is unbelievably fascinating, is it." She puts a hand up again, as if to stop me from interrupting, even though I wasn't going to.

"I know, I know. You love it, you're a nerd, it's your thing. But look at me, Kat, do I look like a nerd to you?"

She turns her head this way and that, still looking at me and raising her eyebrows.

"No?" *You look like a total wacko, but never mind.*

"That's right. Nerd work is not what I had in mind for

myself. But I did a wonderful job last week for SunCell, even you'd have to agree, Katherine, and Mark wants me to get a lot more involved in those—what do you call them again? Pitches? No offense, Kat, but it just isn't me."

"So what did you have in mind?" I ask this not because I want to know, but because I can tell she wants to tell me. She wants me to ask twenty questions until we get there.

"What I had in mind, Kat, is essentially nothing. By that I mean, not working at all. But—" she sighs, rearranges papers on her desk— "one has to make a living. That's the way of the world."

I nod.

"So I have a proposition for you. Would you like to hear it?"

Probably not, I think, but I say yes anyway.

"One million dollars, that's all. You give me one million dollars, and I consider us even. It's a bargain, when you think about it. I mean, you still have plenty of working years ahead of you, you can save money later. You're what — forty-eight? Fifty years old?"

"Thirty-one," I mutter.

"No! You're only five years older than me? Really? Wow, you have not aged well, Katherine. You might consider getting some work done on yourself. I mean, look at me, I'm twenty-six. Guess how old people think I am?"

"I ... I don't know."

"Come on! Have a guess!" she does it again, turning her head so that I'm seeing her in profile.

"I don't know. Twenty-five?"

"Twenty-two. I kid you not. Men in particular, always think I'm younger than I am."

She checks over her shoulder, then leans closer to me, inviting me to do the same. "Mark thought I was twenty. I'm not kidding." She leans back in her chair, raises one satisfied eyebrow. "You're all right? Because you've gone all white there, Katherine. Anyway. What was I saying? Ah, yes. Mark thought I was twenty years old! I swear to God! I haven't told him the truth, if he wants to think I'm twenty … I'm not complaining. He says I make him feel young again. You don't need to feel young, baby, I said to him. You're so hot! And he is so hot, right? You know that, of course. Although he wouldn't have said that to you, the bit about feeling young again, I mean. Don't look so put out, Kat. It's unattractive. I don't know what he was like with you—" she checks over her shoulder again, "—but with us, the sex, it's fucking spectacular. Like, really. I get tingly just thinking about it."

Then she swivels back to face her desk. "You should think about getting some work done. You still have time. Have a collagen facial, at least. I usually do one once a month. You let yourself go now, it's all over, red rover. Trust me. You'll thank me later."

"Eve?"

She sighs. "What is it, Kat?"

"I'm sorry, but I don't have a million dollars."

"Sure, you do. You have your mother's house, right?"

"I know. But it's the collateral security, for my mother's long-term care, at Atwood House."

"What does that mean?"

"Well, to secure a place you have to commit long term, you see? You are required to provide some kind of collateral. So that if you can't afford to pay anymore, they don't have to evict the residents, you see? Instead they call in the collateral."

"Oh, that! Okay. How much is the house worth?"

"I believe the last appraisal came to one-point-one-million."

"So? What's the problem?" she asks.

"Well, as I said, if I give you one million, then there won't be enough for my mother's care."

"So? Nancy can go and live with you. Have you thought of that, Einstein?"

I nod frantically, as if I think that's an excellent idea, then I say, "Actually no, you see, my mother requires twenty-four-hour care, as you know. Her living with me is, unfortunately, not an option."

"Katherine, think. Come on. There must be something you can do. Don't you have an investment portfolio? Didn't your folks leave any cash? Anything you can use to pay for her loony bin?"

"I don't think so, no."

She sighs. "You know, I didn't want things to get this tense between us."

I look around the room to check if there's anyone else here, because this sentence makes absolutely no sense. "You've stolen my job, my boyfriend, my money, but you don't want any hard feelings between us?"

She nods a few times without looking at me. Like she's understanding something. Like I just confirmed her suspicions. "Did you come to my house yesterday?"

I die. "No, of course not." I do my best to sound puzzled by the question but my heart throbs in my ears.

She looks at her nails, then reaches behind her to the pencil cup, pulls out a slim, pink emery board, and proceeds to file her nails.

"I was talking to Uncle Bill, you know the one, my uncle the cop?"

Uncle Bill gets wheeled out so much lately, I begin to

wonder if maybe he's all the family she has. Maybe she's an orphan. Maybe that's why she's so fucked up.

"He's such a nice uncle, to do this for me. Don't you think, Katherine? You don't have an uncle, is that right?"

"I had one. He's dead."

"Ah yes. I remember. Well, you don't know what you're missing. Uncles are awesome. Anyway, my point is that I could, if I wanted, tell him that I changed my mind, and if he wants to investigate who is behind that hit-and-run case, he can go right ahead."

She leans closer to me and says, quietly, as if anyone was listening. "I could have been much greedier. One million, for what you did? You're getting off cheap, Katherine, so don't push me."

Chapter Thirty-Four

Richard Walters and I have agreed to meet for lunch at a Cafe in Somerville, near his hotel.

"I'll be the guy eating a waffle, reading the paper," he'd said.

"This place is known for its waffles. You're sure that's going to narrow it down?"

He chuckled softly then proceeded to give me a full description. "Well, let's see. I have brown hair, I wear glasses, I'm pretty average in every respect, to be honest. I tell you what, I'll bring the book I'm reading. *House of Spies*, by Daniel Silva. Paperback. Black and yellow cover."

I watched the clock all morning. Not a real wall clock, but the one in the corner of my computer screen. I willed it to go faster.

Then Eve asked when she could get the PellisTech projections. "I told Mark I'd have them to him by end of this week, but I want to surprise him and give them to him sooner. Even tomorrow morning. I think he'll be really impressed, don't you?"

I told her they were almost done even though I hadn't

started. Finally, at noon exactly, I stood up, casually, got my things and walked out.

"Going to lunch already?" Eve said behind me.

"Back soon," I replied.

I'm so excited I could burst. This is it, I know it is. He'll know something about Eve, something I can use. I thought about this all night, and I've come to the conclusion that Richard Walters believes Eve killed his sister, but made it look like suicide. Do I think Eve capable of murder? Absolutely. Actually, I believe everyone is capable of murder, given the circumstances. She just has different triggers than most people.

My theory is that Richard wants to prove Alison didn't kill herself. He needs my help, and he'll get it. I can already picture myself telling Eve that it's over, this little game of hers. I'll tell her that I know she killed Alison Walters, and how about *I* call Uncle Bill and tell him all about it? Hey? How would she like that? I'm a bit nervous as well, because if Eve killed Alison Walters, what's to stop her from killing me?

Christ. Just thinking about it makes my skin tingle with fear. I brush the thought away. And now here I am and he's easy to spot. He's got his earbuds in and pulls them out as I approach.

"Katherine?"

"Hello, Richard." He's wearing a dark green V-neck sweater. He has a nice, open face. Brown hair slicked back, and green eyes. He looks about my age, maybe a bit older.

I sit down, then change my mind and remove my coat.

"Can I get you anything?" He hands me the menu.

My stomach is coiled up in knots. There's no way I can eat. "I'll just have an espresso for now, please."

He orders coffees for both of us and pays for them.

"Thank you for coming all this way, Richard. I really appreciate it."

"It's no problem at all. When I heard you'd called my mother…" He shakes his head. "Would you mind if I showed you a photo of Alison?"

"Please. I'd like to see her."

He pulls out a slim wallet from his back pocket and opens the flap. Under a clear plastic window is a photograph of him and, I assume, Alison. They're in a bar, he has his arm around her shoulders and his chin resting in the palm of his other hand. She has light brown hair, tied up in a ponytail. She's holding a champagne flute and toasting to the camera. They have the same green eyes. They're both smiling. Other than both being female and around the same age, there are no similarities between us.

"That was her last birthday," he says wistfully.

"She's beautiful."

He stares at it for a little longer, then closes the wallet and puts it back in his pocket.

"She was beautiful. Inside and out."

Richard can't stop talking about her. I learn that she was two years older than he, and that she loved being a big sister. That they got along really well, better than most siblings, according to him.

"I really hope you can help me out, Katherine. I really want to understand what happened to Alison. It's been haunting me for two years."

"Richard, I'll do whatever I can. I promise you that."

"Thank you. It means a lot."

"Why don't you start at the beginning."

The waiter arrives with our coffees. We pull apart and fall silent. When the waiter retreats, we both take up our respective positions, elbows on table, leaning close to each other.

"They met in a restaurant back in Manhattan. Alison was having lunch and when it came time to pay, she realized she had lost her wallet. She told me a nice woman at the next table overheard and offered to pay. They exchanged phone numbers so Alison could pay her back later. That's how she met Eve. It went from there."

I nod. Interesting. Already, I'm picking a similar M.O. Seems like Eve has a knack for being in the right place at the right time. Just when we need her.

"My sister and I saw each other occasionally, mostly at family gatherings. We did talk on the phone regularly. In these conversations, she would mention Eve, in passing. I got the sense they'd become really good friends. They did a lot of things together."

"Did you ever meet her?"

"Twice. The first time when I dropped by her place to borrow a vacuum cleaner. Eve was there, I said hello, didn't really pay attention. I was only there a few minutes."

"You didn't find her attractive?" I ask, then I regret it immediately. Why did I say that? I know why. Mark fell for her, so why wouldn't Richard? Up until then, he had been looking down, stirring a spoon slowly in his coffee cup. Now he looks up at me, slightly puzzled.

"Sorry. Ignore me. What about the second time?"

"It was much later. I hadn't seen Alison for a while, until my mother's birthday. Alison looked awful. She wouldn't talk about it. Afterwards I called her, suggested we meet up, she didn't want to. She kept making excuses. I'm too tired, I'm not very well, I just want to rest…"

I get goosebumps hearing this. It's all so very familiar.

"I should have tried harder. It just wasn't like her."

"You really can't blame yourself, Richard. You have no idea how good Eve is at controlling others."

He runs a hand over his face. "I asked questions, of course. Are you okay? Is it work? She'd just been through a pretty grueling court case. Did it have to do with that? I'd ask. I couldn't get it out of her. She would just assure me she was fine, just tired. She did the same to our mother. My mother told me that Eve was the one answering the phone. She told my mother Alison didn't want to speak to her. You can imagine how devastated my mother was. After a few weeks of this, her avoiding us, I went to her apartment without calling first. Eve was there. Turned out she had moved in, in the spare bedroom. It was strange. I didn't know Eve had needed a place to stay, or why Alison would invite her in like that."

I nod, but I don't interrupt, even though I have so many questions that are tripping over each other in my brain.

"I did see Alison that day. She was in bed. She looked awful. Tired, hollow. I remember the dark rings under her eyes. Like she wasn't sleeping at all. She was so thin."

He flicks a glance at me and shakes his head, then squeezes his eyes shut and runs his thumb and forefinger over them.

I want to put my hand on his arm, but I don't.

Richard continues. "I wanted to take her to a doctor, but she wouldn't budge. 'At least come and stay with me,' I told her. 'You shouldn't be here by yourself.' And something really creepy happened then. Eve came in. She stood in the doorway, and she said, 'She's not by herself, she's got me.' I realized then she'd been listening to us the whole time. She walked in and sat next to Alison. And I swear,

Katherine, I saw Alison recoil when Eve did that. I swear to God, Alison was frightened of her."

"How long after they met did this happen?" I ask.

"About three months."

I shudder. I wonder now if the worst is yet to come, with Eve. It occurs to me she is insatiable. She enjoys it so much, this slow torture. If I manage to find the money she wants, would she really stop? Set me free? Or is that part of the fun, this giving, and then dashing, of hope?

She won't stop. I know that already.

I should ask Adley about that. Adley the Wi-Fi genius. Did she really leave you alone after you gave her money? Because I have no doubt there's been an exchange of cash there. All her victims had recently come into money, so at some point, she makes her move. That's how she makes a living. A million dollars for your freedom. Or whatever you can spare.

Richard has fallen silent. "What happened then?" I ask softly.

He hasn't touched his coffee yet, but he keeps stirring. The spoon clinks against the porcelain. "She called me one night, crying. She said she'd done something terrible. And that she couldn't live with it anymore. 'What did you do? Whatever it is, sis, we can sort it out,' I told her. She whispered into the phone, she said Eve knew what had happened. I asked her, 'What does Eve know? What has she done to you?' I could tell that whatever was going on with Alison, whatever was making her ill like this, Eve had something to do with it. That's the last time we spoke. Two days later, she was dead. An overdose."

"Oh, God! Richard, how awful! This is ... I don't know what to say."

He wipes his eyes with the palm of his hands.

"Can I ask you something?"

"Sure," he says, shaking himself out of it. I look behind my shoulder, to make sure the young couple at the table behind us isn't listening.

"Are you sure your sister killed herself?" I whisper.

He nods. "There was a suicide note."

"Oh. I see." There goes my theory. I'm disappointed. I was sure he was going to accuse Eve of murder. We could have investigated the case, together. We could have cracked it, proved that Eve was responsible. She would have gone to jail. I would have been free.

"She mailed it to me."

"I'm sorry?"

"The suicide note."

"Mailed it?" I'm astonished. Suicide notes are usually left at the scene, right? They don't usually get mailed. One would think that by the time you've reached the post office, bought the stamp—because who keeps stamps handy these days—and stuck the letter in the box, you've had time to change your mind. If you're determined to die at your own hand, do you really want to risk it? But then, even before he says it, I figure it out.

"She didn't want Eve to find it."

The letter, Richard explains, was really a confession. There had been a party, upstate. They went together, Eve and Alison. It got late, Alison drove them home, even though she'd drunk too much. There was an accident. She hit someone. A man. She killed him. That's what she said, in the letter. *I killed a man.*

Chapter Thirty-Five

Something is wrong with me. It's as if the world around me is shifting. Everything is wavy and strangely distant, like I'm looking through thick glass. Even the sounds are coming from far away, distorted. There are black dots dancing in front of my eyes and I grip the edge of the table.

Richard has a hand on my shoulder. "You're okay?"

"Sorry. Some water would be good," I manage to say.

I can barely breathe. I don't understand what's happening. I don't understand how it's even possible that Alison Walters' story is the same as mine. What are the odds that Eve was involved in the exact same scenario twice? They're so slim they're fucking microscopic, that's what they are. Eve is either one very unlucky woman, or she—I can't even bear to formulate the thought. She... engineered these accidents?

"Here." Richard has returned with a glass of water that he almost shoves against my lips.

"Thank you," I say, wiping my mouth with the back of

my hand. I take a moment while he stares at me with concern. "Keep going, I'm all right now." I say.

His eyes search my face for reassurance.

"Go on," I say again.

"Alison had been through that court case I mentioned before. If it came out she'd been involved in a fatal hit-and-run, while drunk, it would have been all over the papers. She freaked out. She wrote in the note that she drove off and left the man to die. You don't know my sister, but she was the sweetest, kindest girl you could ever meet. You might think I'm biased, but it's the truth. I can't believe that she would leave this man to die by the side of the road. But in the end, it crushed her. She fell into a deep depression. I would say that it killed her, except it's more complicated than that. You see, Eve had been in the car with her. She was the only person who knew what had happened. In her letter, Alison said that Eve had been able to keep the case from being investigated. But she'd also wanted a lot for that. After we buried her, I found out that most of Alison's money, the big payout from the court case, had already been spent. I don't have evidence for it, but I believe she gave that money to Eve. I believe that Eve was blackmailing my sister. She left town, too, you know? Eve. My sister was supposed to be her great friend, and she didn't even turn up to her funeral. She was already gone. Just as well. I think I would have killed her myself."

I've taken hold of a paper napkin and I'm rolling it and unrolling it on my lap, tearing off bits of it in the process. Anything to hide my shaking hands. Someone drops a plate behind us. It breaks on the tiled floor and makes me jump.

Richard leans forward. His tone urgent.

"But I checked everywhere. I went to the police station.

I searched online, I poured over the news archives…" He takes a sharp breath. "There was no hit-and-run on that road, Katherine. Fatal or otherwise. Not that week, not that month. It just. Didn't. Happen."

"What?"

"Never happened."

It's me now, who leans in, the corners of my mouth drooping.

"But I saw it," I hiss into his ear. He recoils.

"What are you saying? You weren't there!"

"No, no, no," I assure him. "You don't understand." My eyes dart around the café to make sure no one's listening in. I'm still whispering.

"Someone did die. I'm sure of it. You may not have found evidence of it, but Alison would have known. She would have felt the impact. She would have seen the man lie dead beneath the wheels of her car. She would have seen the blood oozing from his head. I know I did." He doesn't look convinced. In fact, he looks like he wants to leave. Fast. I grab his wrist. "The same thing happened to me," I hiss.

I never speak of him, the man I killed that night. I never search for him online or ask Eve if she has any more facts about who he was.

The truth is, I don't want to think about him, and if I do, I quickly banish him from my thoughts with a virtual finger-flick. Because I'm afraid. I'm afraid that I might have seen him that night, standing on the edge of the road, and in my crazy state maybe I pressed down on the accelerator instead of the brake. I'm afraid that maybe I'm the one who's evil. Maybe I deserve everything that's happened to me.

One person in a hundred is a psychopath, give or take,

which is a hell of a lot when you think about it. I know Eve is one, but I once thought that I too might be one. It's not something I think about, ever, the truth is, the accident wasn't the first time I killed someone.

But I don't tell Richard this of course. We've only just met.

Chapter Thirty-Six

I do tell Richard about what happened to me, that night with Eve. What choice do I have but to trust him? We're in the same boat here, more or less, both of us broken by a psycho. Still. It's not easy admitting to anyone, let alone a virtual stranger, that you've let some poor soul die alone in the woods, and it was all your fault.

I tell him about the dinner, about going to the club and how I suspect she spiked my drink. I skip the part about smoking a joint. He gets the picture. I shouldn't have been driving. I said that to Eve, I tell him, but she made me feel like I was being overly cautious, like I wasn't living up to her opinion of me. "You have to understand Richard. She seemed so ... extraordinary. Beautiful of course, but that confidence and that self-assurance she has, you just want her to like you..."

Stupid much?

Anyway, I'm not proud of it, I say. I have a daughter. If she ever got behind the wheel after a night like I'd had? She'd be grounded for life.

"I hit something, Richard. I know I did. I hit it hard

and when I came out of the car, he was there."

We sit huddled together, our heads almost touching, going over the facts as we know them. We agree about what is possible, and what is not. We agree that the odds of these experiences being so similar, Alison's and mine, and also being real, are pretty much non-existent. He says "unlikely," but I don't like that word. I never have. Too unresolved.

"I'm calling it," I tell him, slapping my hand on the Formica tabletop. "The odds are nil."

I am comfortable in this conversation. After all, probabilities are my favorite topic. It's only when he says, "Are you sure it wasn't a dummy?" by which he means the victim, that I get a prickle of alert—it's the word: *dummy*—to the fact that I should be at work. I straighten up quickly and dive in my bag for my cell. It's after two pm and I have missed four calls, all from Eve. She's sent one text: *Where the fuck are you.*

But the strangest thing happens. My heart doesn't race like crazy, I don't begin to sweat, I don't rush to stand up and run out of the cafe, leaving Richard to pick up the tab. Instead, I find that … I don't care. Well I do, a bit, but nothing like I would have, say, last week. It's really very relaxing, this feeling. I send off a reply. *Atwood House. Emergency. C u tomorrow.*

"Did your car need any repairs?" Richard asks.

"It has a dent. But I haven't had it looked at. I haven't even driven it since, except to put it in the garage."

"Come on, let's go." He stands up and retrieves his jacket from the back of his chair. "I'll get this," he says, pulling out his wallet from an inside pocket.

"Where are we going?"

"We're going to take a look at your car. I never thought to check Alison's, and then my mother sold it. She didn't know anything of course, about the accident. She just had no use for it. Only sad memories."

"So, hum… Do you know much about cars?" I ask. We're standing in front of it now. The garage door is wide open, which means we're in full view of the neighbors, which makes me feel a bit nervous, but the light is better that way.

"I've tinkered with a few in my time."

"That's funny. I wouldn't have picked you for the type."

"No? Why not?"

I shrug. "I don't know." I was going to say he seemed too bookish for that. But I wasn't sure if he'd think that was a good thing or not.

He walks around it. "Nice color," he says. It's white. I almost tell him, technically, white is not a color, and even if it were, it's not particularly nice. It's not like yellow, for example. Or green. Now those are nice colors. But I keep my mouth shut. Instead I watch him crouch at the front and examine it closely, running his hand over the depression.

"Come and have a look at this."

I bend down, peering at the spot he's pointing to.

"Was that there before the accident?" he asks.

"That's where I hit—that's the point of impact. I'm sure of it."

"I'm no expert," he says. "But that looks real low to me. Did you see the guy? When you hit him?"

I try to think back. "When I hit him? No."

"But he—or whatever it might be—would have been

right in front of you, you said so yourself." He points again at the dent.

I shudder. "I know it sounds weird, Richard, but I didn't see him. That's the truth."

I scratch my head with both hands. "It's just confusing, the memory of that night is so... foggy. I remember being lost, the GPS, and the radio, it was really loud. That's right. I couldn't hear what she was saying, and I went to turn it down. That's when I got distracted. I wasn't looking at the road when I hit him."

He thinks about this for a moment. "Don't you think it's strange? That you were distracted at just the right moment?"

I nod. Because it comes back to me then. After the accident, after she drove us home, she said something like I'd hit the guy. Like it was my fault, and I got angry because I did think she was giving herself a pass, and she had a lot to do with what happened. Including putting the volume up so loud. I did blame her that night, for pushing me, for distracting me. But I didn't think she had done it on purpose."

"What did Eve do then? After the impact?"

I take a moment to think about it. "Oh, my God." My hand flies to my mouth.

"What?"

"She was hurt. Or I thought she was. She was bent over as low as she could. Her head was on the dash. She was moaning, in pain. I remember panicking, thinking that she was really hurt. For a couple of minutes there, I wasn't looking at the road. I was looking at her. Trying to help her. She made sure of that."

"Let me ask you again, do you think it was real? The guy you hit? Could it have been a mannequin?"

"I doubt it. I couldn't see him very well, and I didn't touch him, but he sure seemed real. And he was bleeding. Definitely bleeding."

"Okay. Maybe she had an accomplice. While you're busy making sure she's okay, the accomplice slips in position. He would have been waiting in the shadows." Then seeing my face, he says, "Did I say something funny?"

"It's just that we sound like a couple of TV detectives. You especially. Sorry. Ignore me. As you were, Sherlock."

"Hey, don't knock it, we're really getting somewhere here."

I touch him on the shoulder. "I know. You're doing great."

We're both silent for a minute, each of us entangled in our own thoughts. "But what about the impact? I did hit something..."

"I know. I'm thinking about that, too." He bends down to check the bumper again.

"Wait a second." I rush out of the garage and over to the side of the house. Richard follows me. I run my hands over the branches of the short cypress near the fence, pushing them apart.

"If you tell me what you're looking for, maybe I can help?"

"Just wait. Shit. Where is it?"

Then I find it. Caught in the lower branches of the side hedge. It's soggy and darkened from weather damage, but here it is. The strip of cloth I had pulled off the day after the accident. I brandish it proudly. "What do you think this is? It was caught on the license plate."

He takes it from me, lifts it up. "I'm not sure. Did it come from his clothes?"

"I don't think so. He was wearing a soft black hooded

jacket. And jeans. Dark jeans. I don't remember seeing this on him."

"It's like... Burlap?"

I reach to touch the fabric and our hands brush briefly.

"Let's go and have a look," he says. "Maybe that'll give us a clue."

"Look where?"

"Where you had the accident."

"What, now?"

"Yes."

I don't like the sound of that much, but then I think about it some more, and I still can't see why it's a good idea.

"There might be something there, something they left behind," Richard says. "Maybe even something that will explain this." He waves the piece of fabric in the air.

"Fine." I pull at one glove using my teeth, one finger at a time, and get my phone from my pocket with the other.

"Come on, let's go."

"Give me a minute. I'm calling for a ride."

He points back at my Honda. "What's wrong with your car?"

"Nothing! I just haven't... I don't..."

He waits for me to finish, his head tilted to the side.

"I told you already. I haven't driven the car since that night."

"But why?"

"I'm just not comfortable, that's all."

"Okay." He nods, takes a moment, then he says, "But it didn't really happen. We know that now."

I bite the inside of my mouth. "I wish you'd driven from New York." I say.

"Yeah, well, I flew. Can we go now?"

Chapter Thirty-Seven

"Normally, if you hit someone at a certain speed, they'll flip onto the hood. That's basic physics. What you've described, the guy ending up right in front of the wheels like that, it just doesn't make sense."

"Well he didn't flip onto the hood. Even in my inebriated state I think I'd have noticed that."

This feels good. We're doing things, we're taking charge. We are investigating the case. We are taking destiny into our own hands and I like it. When I turn into Hammond Pond Parkway I find I'm okay. It's broad daylight, there's plenty of traffic, and it's not raining. All of that helps.

We park the car on the embankment, as close to the location of the accident as I can remember.

"Well, here we are. What are we looking for again?"

"Anything that doesn't belong here."

We walk up and down a hundred feet or so, scanning the area, our eyes trained onto the ground. I prod a discarded Coke bottle with my toe.

"It's been weeks, Richard. What could possibly be here after all this time?"

"Something like this," he says, bending down. In two strides I am by his side. We both crouch and check the edge of the road.

"What is it?"

He picks up what looks like dirt to me, drops it in the palm of his hand, but something about the color feels wrong, like it doesn't belong here. We look around, looking for more, but it looks like it's just there, in that spot, over the edge and onto the grass on the embankment.

"It's sand," he says.

"Sand?"

We stare at each other, then we blurt it out at the same time. "Sand bags."

"Oh, my God, that's the bit of fabric!"

"Burlap," he says. "It must be from the bag, it caught on your license plate."

I clutch both hands to my head. I'm hyperventilating. I think I'm in shock. "I drove into a sand bag?"

"Looks like it."

"But why?"

Except I know why. There's only one explanation. It's the only one that makes sense.

"All of it," I make an expansive but irrelevant gesture around me, "was staged?" And then I burst into tears. Happy tears? Sure, of course, hey I didn't kill anybody lately. That's always good news in my book. But why me? I've let her ruin my relationship, ruin my job, any prospects of buying into the company. I've lost so much because of her.

At least I found out before I gave her the money she

wants. Because let's face it, I would have found a way to get that money.

In the car on the way back, I keep asking the same question over and over. "It wasn't real?" I've asked fifty times since we came to the conclusion about the sandbag.

"She's been working on this scam for years, we know that now. You never stood a chance, Katherine."

"The heartless, fucking bitch."

"Yep, you can say that again."

"She picks people—women, they're all women, did you know that? Women who have come into money! But also are isolated."

"Alison had recently broken up with her partner. She also just went through a grueling court case."

"If Eve thinks the target is easily manipulated…"

"Then she blackmails them."

I shake my head. "But in my case, she misjudged it. She thought I had inherited a lot more than I did. My mother came from money, but it's long gone. The house in Kirkland Place, it's not worth as much as she thought."

He gives me a surprised look.

"It's a prestigious address," I say, "but it's a small house, nothing like its neighbors. And I've put it up as collateral for my mother's care. I couldn't sell it if I wanted to. So yes, she miscalculated this time."

"I bet she was disappointed."

"She's still after me for a million bucks. But it's not just about money for her. She's a psycho. She wants complete control over her target. She wants to break them. Emotionally, financially, physically… It's all a game to her. A sick game." Then I see his face.

"Sorry. You know all this already."

"That's okay." We're both silent for a moment, then he says, "There has to be an accomplice. That's the guy who is dead, except he isn't. Just a bit of makeup for the blood. They pick a quiet part of town…"

"Must be the guy I saw."

His head turns sharply. "What guy?"

I told Richard already about being in the condo, about how I found his sister's details. But I'd skipped the bit about being almost caught, until now.

"Jesus, Katherine." He runs a hand over his face. "These people are dangerous."

"I don't think he saw me."

Then I bang my hand on the steering wheel. "I can't believe I fell for this shit." I mentally retrace my steps. From the moment Fiona called me to say something had happened to my mother, right until now. I see myself offering Eve a job. Letting her stay in Kirkland Place. Giving her money. Losing my mind.

I think about Uncle Bill who is so connected and powerful he can stop the investigation in its tracks. Although that part is probably not as farfetched as you might think. You don't have to be especially cynical to know that it happens all the time. There's a lot of corruption in the world.

I tell Richard about Uncle Bill. "*My uncle the cop*, Eve calls him." I explain how she wheels him out, metaphorically speaking, whenever I looked like I might not give in to her.

"Alison wrote that Eve had been able to keep the accident out of the news, thanks to her police contacts."

"I guess she's got a big family."

"Helpful, too."

"Always handy to have a few uncles in the police, I find."

He laughs. I do, too. By the time we get back to my house, we're hysterical.

Chapter Thirty-Eight

I reach for the pad next to the door, ready to turn off the alarm, but it's already off.

"Abi?" I call out. I look up the stairs waiting for her. "I thought we agreed, alarm on, in or out!" There's no reply. I walk through to the kitchen and find the note on the table.

At Paige's. Back for dinner.

"Okay," I say, taking off my coat and sliding it on the back of the chair. "Let's make those calls."

We sit together on the couch. I'm the one who suggested he comes back with me. I want to keep knocking off those dominoes, keep finding things she lied about. I want Richard with me, so it's us against the psychopath.

He leans forward, his forearms on his thighs. He looks comfortable in my space, which is nice. Our thighs touch, barely.

I call the Brookline police station and ask about the hit-and-run. We know it's not real, but we agree it's good to confirm. At some point, we're going to confront Eve about all this (oh, the bliss) and the more facts we have, the better.

I tell the person at the other end that I'm doing research on fatal car accidents in the city, particularly the hit-and-run variety. "We're looking at occurrences of such accidents in the Boston area over the last six months." Richard nods at me, approvingly. Someone puts me through to someone else, and I repeat my story a number of times until someone says that I'll have to come in and fill out the paperwork.

I make a joke about paperwork ruling our lives. Officer Joyce, my interlocuter, commiserates. We joke about KPIs and how bureaucracies killed everything that was ever good about anything. We flirt. I used to be okay at flirting, back in the day, when I wasn't a sad shadow of myself. I guess it's like riding a bicycle though, it comes back pretty quickly.

"That accident in Hammond Pond Parkway back in late January," I say now. "January 24th to be exact. I haven't been able to find a reference to it, can you look it up for me?"

"Hammond Pond? Mmm. Rings a bell," he says. My head turns sharply and Richard clocks the look on my face. His mouth opens. My heart sinks. Did we really have it all wrong?

"No, wait," Joyce says. "I'm looking at it now. The evening of January 24th you said?"

"That's right."

"Nah. That was different. I can't find an accident for that day, for that location. Which means there wasn't one."

I raise a hand toward Richard and I sit up, very still. Like a dog that's picked up a scent.

"What did you mean, what was different?" Richard stares at me with a question in his raised eyebrows.

"There was a call in that night. We think it must have been a prank. Looks like there were roadworks barriers erected on Hammond Pond Parkway, north of Route 9. All lanes. Someone called it in because they couldn't get their car out."

"I don't understand, why would they call you?"

"There was no roadwork. They wanted us to come and do something about the barriers. It was almost one in the morning when we got the call. There was no record of *any* roadwork carried out that night. We sent a car, just in case. The officer reported that all barriers were gone by the time they got there."

"So it wasn't true?"

"No, it was true, CCTV confirmed it. Someone drove up in a van, blocked the road, came back forty-five minutes later and removed them. Same on the northern side, too, near Beacon Street, also for forty-five minutes. License plate illegible. We think maybe they were selling drugs down there. Didn't want the patrol to disturb them."

"Seems a bit radical, no?"

He laughs. "Yeah, I'd say. Amazing what people come up with. But no harm done in the end, none that we found, anyway, so it was either a prank, or a well-organized, late-night drug-fest."

I remember how quiet it was. The eerie feeling of being the only car on that road. I don't have anything else to learn about this. I make vague promises to come in and fill out the paperwork. "I look forward to meeting you," he says. Before I hang up, I ask if there's an officer by the name of Bill Howinski at that same station.

"Howinski? Never heard of him."

When I tell Richard about the barriers, he is speechless. Then he shakes his head and chuckles.

"What's so funny?" I ask.

"Are you kidding? This scam gets better and better! They sure went to great lengths to make sure there would be no other cars, no one around to help you."

"Exactly. I don't see why it's funny."

He shakes his head. "Sorry. You're right." He runs his hand over his sleeked dark hair. I wonder if he uses some kind of product to make it stay like that.

I give him a small smile and pat him on the shoulder. "It's okay. I'm being a bit oversensitive. This is a lot to take in."

Next: the Boston Herald. I tell Richard that Eve showed me two articles.

I open their website and type 'hit and run, Hammond Pond Parkway' into the search bar. I honestly think I would die if a million recent articles came back and it turned out that the sand was irrelevant and that yes, Eve was unlucky enough to be involved in a hit-and-run, not once but twice, and Officer Joyce does not know how to search a database.

But other than an ad at the top (*Call us now to avoid a hit and run charge!*) which almost makes my heart stop, there's nothing relevant. We try a number of variations on that search for good measure, but nothing relates to a hit-and-run in the area around that time.

"It's not there," I say, stating the obvious.

"There were no articles about Alison, either," Richard says. He clicks on the contact link. "You want to call?" he asks. "Or shall I?"

"I'll do it," I reply, and call the City Desk.

"Dawn Blake," the voice says, brisk and professional.

I tell the same story I told Officer Joyce. About doing

research on fatal car accidents in the city, particularly the hit-and-run variety. Dawn Blake isn't very interested in helping me out. She directs me to the website, the archives, the search bar.

"I was wondering if every hit-and-run would be reported in the Herald," I ask. "Fatal ones, I mean."

"Yes," she says. "We don't have so many of them that they don't get reported. If somebody dies, of course we report it. Do you know anything about a hit-and-run?"

"Do you ever take the article down, after reporting it?" I ask, ignoring her question.

"Ms…"

"Frost," I reply. My alter ego. "Kara Frost."

"Ms. Frost, the only reason we would take an article down would be if it was inaccurate or if legal told us to. And even then, it's more likely that we would keep the article up but post a correction. Are you referring to anything in particular?"

"I was under the impression there had been an accident, that involved a death, in Hammond Pond Parkway, late last month. I can't find a mention in your paper."

I sure hope I won't regret this. If something comes up about it in the future, she's bound to remember. *Oh yeah, that woman who called, Kara Frost was it? Very strange. She knew about it even though we didn't. Kept asking if we'd taken the post down.*

"Hold on. Let me take a look," she says. I've piqued her interest. She's gone for a short while, leaves me to pass the time with one of Vivaldi's Four Seasons, I don't know which, and when she comes back, she says, "There's definitely no report of a hit-and-run or a homicide of any kind around that time in that area. Where did you say you were calling from again?"

"Okay, thanks." And I hang up.

So it was all a mirage. Except I did see those articles, and I keep saying that to Richard but he's as stumped as I am. "I wonder if Eve did the same with Alison, showed her some fake online report to terrorize her into submission."

"I'd say that's highly likely."

"Where did you say Eve showed you the articles?"

"At the office, on her computer, why?"

"When are you back at work?"

"Tomorrow." I can't wait. "I wonder if she'll bring up Uncle Bill," I say, and we both crack up.

"We need to check it, her computer."

"We do, do we?" I reply, smiling. Although at this point, do I care anymore? Maybe she showed me a doctored photo. It doesn't matter. It's not real. Everything else is just details.

"When do we confront her?" I ask.

"I have an idea, about those articles, how she did it. Let's see if I'm right first. Don't say anything to her yet. Let's catch up again tomorrow and come up with a plan." Then he says, "I didn't bring my laptop with me, do you mind if I search some more?"

"Help yourself. I need a shower. Take your time."

I go upstairs and within minutes, I'm standing under the hot spray of water. I let it get as hot as I can until it burns my skin. I wash my hair. I massage through a conditioning treatment. I even shave my legs while I wait for the treatment to work its much-needed magic.

Because Eve was right about one thing, I did let myself go.

I select a light beige cashmere turtleneck sweater and a pair of black skinny jeans with a double zip on the waist. I really like these jeans, but I only wore them once or twice because they were too tight. Now they fit perfectly. So there you go. Every nightmare has a silver lining, after all.

"Any luck?"

Richard shakes his head and closes the laptop.

"Nothing. I went through Wayback machine—" he sees the puzzled look on my face— "it's the internet archive. It stores versions of web pages across time. I thought maybe Eve had a way of posting an article just for a day, without anyone knowing, just long enough to trick you, or Alison. But there was nothing." He picks up his jacket.

"Do you want to stay for dinner?" I ask. I study the contents of the fridge. Mustards in various flavors, pickles, grilled peppers, horseradish. No real food.

"No thanks, I'll go back to the hotel."

"I don't blame you," I say, thinking that there's no way I could rustle up a meal from what's in front of me.

That's when Abi walks in. She unzips her coat. The snowflakes that have been sprinkled over its edges float to the floor.

"Hi, sweetheart. Hey, how would you feel about pizza for dinner? I am absolutely grocery shopping tomorrow, I promise—"

She pulls her hood back. "Mom?"

I smile at her. "Yes, baby."

She stares at me. "You look different." It's not a question. She doesn't go straight to her room, the way she usually does. Instead she walks right into the kitchen and throws her arms around me. My daughter has not hugged me like that in ages. It's wonderful. I hug her back.

"Mom?"

"Yes, baby."

"I can't breathe."

I laugh and release her.

"You're back," she says, frowning.

"Yes, baby, I am." I pull her to me and kiss the top of her head. My beautiful girl. She smells of pine. She pulls away and stares at Richard, who is looking at his feet, his hands in his pockets.

"Who's this?"

"This is a friend of mine. Richard, this is my daughter, Abigail. You're sure you won't stay for dinner? It'll be take-out."

He smiles, and nods.

"Okay, thanks. That'll be nice."

Chapter Thirty-Nine

I wake up refreshed, no dreams, no sleep interrupted by night terrors, just one long, restful slumber. I forgot how good it felt, to sleep. Then, even better, I actually *forget* for a moment that my psychopath is nothing more than a cheap charlatan, a peddler of mirrors and lies, an ordinary, run-of-the-mill con artist, and as I fully emerge into consciousness it all comes back to me. It's like being ten years old and remembering it's Christmas morning. I am so excited to be alive, I throw the blankets off and spring out of bed. No more dragging myself through the fog of life bullshit.

I've done nothing wrong.

I take my time, because why not, and cook Abi some breakfast. Abi is delighted to see me up so early. It's all over her face, even before she wraps me a warm hug, an Abi hug.

"I love you so much, Mom."

"I love you, too, baby." I should say that I'm sorry for putting her through so much grief, but there will be plenty of time for that. We are not out of the woods yet.

I make her an omelet—that's another thing she loves.

233

Just plain omelets. And some toast. She chatters about last night's rehearsal (awesome) and the day ahead (geography, not awesome), while I mentally prepare for my next call.

"Are you rehearsing with Paige again after school?"

"I don't think so," she says. "I'd rather be home with you."

After Abi leaves, I pick up my cell and call Adley. Wi-Fi Adley. When she picks up the phone I blurt, "Don't hang up. It's Katherine. You want to hear this, I promise."

Then I tell her about Alison, and by extension, Richard. "There's a lot of us, all sharing the same night-mare: the utterly convincing lie that we have accidentally killed someone, and then left them to die by the side of the road. I only have four names, plus me, but there's bound to be more."

I ask her, is that what happened to you? Did you think you ran over someone one night, on a dark, isolated stretch of the road? When you shouldn't have been driving?

She lets out a sob. She doesn't answer. I understand. She doesn't know who I am. I could be an associate of Eve, for all she knows.

I tell her about bags of sand, and that the supposed dead person is just an accomplice with a bit of cheap makeup. But we both know the power Eve can yield. It's the inexorable path to insanity that gets you in the end. You give her what she wants because you want it to end. By then the accident doesn't even seem real anymore.

"You haven't done anything wrong. You never did."

"I think I always knew, deep down, that something wasn't right," she says in a low voice. "But I didn't trust my own instincts."

"I know."

"What are you going to do?" she asks.

That's a very good question.

Richard insists we need to expose her. That's one option, I agree. A good one, and let's call it Option A. Between Adley, Richard and me, surely we can make the case, bring her to justice for all to see (especially Mark). Let's put her in the public square and give her a good flogging. Send her to jail, see if she can hustle anyone in there.

Then there's option B. I haven't told Richard about option B, whereby I tell Eve what I know, and then we swap roles: I become the blackmailer, and she gives me lots of money every month to keep my mouth shut. I like this one, too. A lot. Even if it's just for a little while, just to see the look on her stupid face.

I get to work, late, and all eyes are on me when I cross the floor to my office. Maybe everyone thought I'd gone for good, never to return. My phone pings, with a text. I almost stop in my tracks reading it. It's from a contact at the FDA. It's unexpected, and very interesting, and I immediately decide not to share it with anyone.

Eve greets me halfway with a loud, "Hi, Kat! Did you have a nice day yesterday?" Meaning she's forgotten why I wasn't at work. I quickly slip my phone into my bag as she takes my elbow, leading me into our office. She closes the door and hisses in my ear, "Do you have my money?"

"What? No! I told you already. I don't have that kind of money, Eve, I just don't."

"Well you better do something about that, Katherine Nichols, because we have a problem."

"Really?"

She crosses her arms over her chest. "Mark wants to let you go." She searches my face for a reaction. My first thought is, *Option B then*, and then for good measure, I clap my mouth with one hand. "Let me go?"

"I know," she says. "It's bad. With the fees for your mother's nuthouse and all that, and your kid, fuck, I don't know how you'll cope. Although you realize I don't give a shit about all that. Your problem, not mine. But it does put us in an awkward position because heck, I'm stuck here." She looks around to make the point. "Not ideal. You need to sell your folks' house to give me my money since as you point out, there's no other way. If you don't have a job, I can see how you'll try to delay everything. Play the victim card, you know? Poor little Katherine, broke, unemployed, loser. Not good. For me, that is."

She pulls her chair closer to me. "I told Mark, Mark babe, too harsh, I said. Especially in her state and all, but he said there comes a time in every company where you have to realize that some people are not a good fit. His words not mine."

She gives me a sorry smile, waits for me to say something.

"Oh, no," I say.

She raises a hand, palm facing me. "I have a solution." She taps the side of her head with one finger. "You'll find I'm smarter than you thought, Kat. Checkbook balancing notwithstanding."

"Oh, good."

"I will soon be taking over your position. It's all been arranged. I will be director of the New Business section. Isn't that cool? To be honest, and this stays between you, me, and the goldfish bowl, I have no idea what I'm doing. I don't need to, since I have you. But it's going to look odd if Mark lets you go and I leave at the same time. So, Kat, I had to argue your case, and to keep you on in a way that works for everybody, I suggested you work for me!" She claps her hands. "What do you think?"

Before I have time to respond, she says, "Drop in pay. Big drop in pay. Had to happen because I get a big salary increase, see? Of course, you do. You can add *and* subtract."

She's interrupted by Caroline who pops her head round the door.

"Hi, you two," she chirps. "Katherine, you look better," she adds, almost disappointed. "Wow, Eve, nice dress! Where'd you get that?"

"Thanks Caro! I got it last weekend." She stands and does a little twirl on the spot, letting the dress fan out. "From Serenella."

Caroline goes up to her, eyes on the dress, and fingers the fabric.

"Wow. Very nice. Expensive?"

Eve does a show of rolling her eyes. "Don't even ask. Impulse buy, too. Cleaned out my savings account!" she laughs.

"Well, good for you!" Caroline gushes. "You have to treat yourself sometimes. Because if you don't, who will? That's what my mother used to say."

They both chuckle away, and frankly, Option B, where I get to blackmail the blackmailer, is looking better and better by the minute.

"You're ready for the new business meeting?" Caroline says.

"New business meeting?" I repeat. New business meetings take place on Mondays, and I wasn't here on Monday.

Caroline shakes her head. "Eve will bring you up to speed."

"That's exactly right. Give us a minute, will you, Caro? We'll be right there."

"You bet, doll," Caroline says, retreating.

Once she's out of earshot, Eve says, "You weren't here on Monday. What the fuck was I supposed to do? I had to come up with an excuse and move the meeting."

"Oh, right, makes sense."

She stands up now, extends a hand. "What have you got?" she asks. "Hit me with it. What sparkling new start-up do you have up your sleeve? Come, give it up."

"I don't have anything."

She puts her hand on her hip. "You must have something, I'm the new business director. I can't go into that meeting with no new business to suggest!"

I shrug and open the door. "You're coming?" I say. She's standing there gaping. But they're all at the conference table now, watching us and ready to go. There's nothing Eve can say or do.

"Okay! Thank you for joining us," Mark says. He smiles at Eve and frowns at me. "Okay, everyone, first I want to congratulate Eve on her promotion. Eve is now director of new business. Thrilled to have you, Eve! Congratulations from all of us. I know you'll bring much success to our little firm." He lays it on a little thick I think, but everyone claps, myself included.

She raises both hands. "Please, it's nothing. Don't, really." She blushes prettily and smiles lovingly at Mark. It's unbearable.

Then we get down to it, and of course, after that charming introduction, what else can Mark do but turn to

Eve and say, "Please, director of new business, what have you got for us today?"

It's hilarious. He stretches one arm over the seat behind him and pushes back against the table so his chair balances on its two back legs. He's beaming. He's so happy, so proud of his little protegee, he just can't wait to hear what she has to say, and neither can I.

Eve turns to me, she's smiling, but her lips are thin and pale. I raise my eyebrows. She turns away.

"Katherine has been working on something for me," she says. "Katherine? Care to share? Where is that at?"

I make a show of how confused I am. "Mmm..." I lay one finger on my lips, crease my forehead, and finally I say, "I have no idea what you're talking about."

She makes a short, frustrated click of the tongue. "Of course. You haven't been around much." She sighs. "That's too bad."

"What was it?" Mark asks, glowering at me.

"Search me," I say.

She clears her throat. "Excuse me," she says, reaching for the water jug. Mark is already on his feet, pouring a glass for her.

"Thank you, Mark. Okay. So this is...okay. It's different, but as director of new business, I think we should branch out." Mark nods, his face a picture of happy anticipation.

"So. There's a new shoe designer that's been on the news lately because her husband was arrested for exposing himself in a park somewhere. Did you see that? Gross, right? If you haven't, check it out. Grab a tabloid, she's all over it. She's got a Japanese name. Anyway, she's in the news a lot, mostly because of that, and her shoes are awesome so why don't we invest in that? Japanese designers are big. It's bound to pay off with all the publicity her husband has generated for her. Like, our work is done here, right?"

Complete, total, silence. I turn to Mark. He's smiling, in that one-sided curl up way he does when he waits for the punchline. There's no punchline. Then it dawns on him that she's not kidding, and I want to laugh so bad I have to cough to hide it. I note that no one hands me a glass of water.

"And still looking at PellisTech. You remember, the very exciting prospect I identified recently," Eve says now.

I'm thinking, recently not, that was weeks ago, but never mind. Mark nods thoughtfully, but I can tell he's waiting for, well, new business. Not new business from three meetings ago.

Mark nods as if he's processing all that, as if any of that was in fact new business.

"Anyone else?" he says. "Okay, then I guess we're done here!"

Chapter Forty

"You two-faced little bitch. You just did that to embarrass me," Eve snarls. It goes without saying we're now back in the privacy of our office.

"In what way?"

"You know very well in what way. You were supposed to have compiled a list of prospects, Katherine. Or haven't you heard? You work for me. You've been demoted. In fact, I think you should call me Boss from now on. Oh, I know." She waves her finger at me. "You're trying to weasel your way back in. You want Mark back. You want to show off how smart you are, how nothing can happen without you. You think I don't know what you're up to?" The waving finger is now poking at the air very close to my face until she remembers that we're in full view of the others and she wipes something from my cheek. "There. Better," she says sweetly. Then between gritted teeth, like a ventriloquist, she says, "You just want to make me look bad. I'm onto you, Katherine."

"I'm really not—" but Caroline taps on the glass and mouths *coffee?* to Eve.

241

"Coming!" she chimes gaily. She grabs her coat, and on the way out she stops and looks me up and down. "You are looking better."

"Thank you."

I take my seat at my desk and finger the various Post-it Notes spread around my desk. She leans behind me and whispers, "Don't make me call Uncle Bill."

After she's gone, I call Richard.

"She's driving me crazy. There's no way I can pretend to be scared of her now, she'll figure out I know something."

"Hang in there, Kat." It's the first time he's called me Kat. "Can you check her computer? I have an idea about how she tricked you with those articles."

"Okay, what's the plan?"

"We know the article doesn't exist, but you've seen it. I'm wondering if she, or someone she knows, could have created a dummy website, a holding page, and made it look like the real thing. We're looking for a domain name that *sounds* like the Boston Herald. Can you open her browser?"

I go to her computer, enter the password, which I'm pleased to see she has not changed.

"Looking good. She hasn't cleared the cache, by the looks of it she never has."

"Okay, that's excellent."

I tell Richard I'm putting the phone down, and I scroll through the browser history until I reach the dates.

It jumps out at me. I pick up the phone again. "You're a genius."

"Am I?" I can hear the smile in his voice. "What's the link?"

"Bostonheraldtoday dot com."

He whistles. I click on the link, and my breath catches. It's the same article. The page has the exact same layout as the online Boston Herald, complete with ads and banners, footer menu links, logos, everything. But when I click on any link, anywhere on the page, I get nowhere. Just the same page reloading.

"Amazing. Like I said, you're a genius."

"Thank you, I'd like to agree with you, but I build websites for a living, so it was pretty obvious."

I hear a noise, I realize it's Mark. "Fuck!" he yells out, hitting the top of his desk with his fist. Then he turns to me. "Katherine! Get the fuck in here!" he bellows.

"I have to go," I tell Richard and hang up.

Everyone has looked up, their eyes following me as I cross the floor to Mark's office. I close the door behind me.

"What is it?"

"What the fuck is wrong with you?" He swivels his monitor so it faces me. It's a video. It takes up the whole screen.

It's me.

"Oh, my god!"

It's me, dancing at the club. It's the video Eve took on her phone that night.

"Where did you get that?" But then I recognize the site. It's on fucking YouTube.

"Max forwarded it to me."

"Max?"

"Our client, Max."

"Oh, that Max. Wow, how did he know about it?"

Mark points to the video title: *Katherine Nichols, Rue Capital's Secret Weapon*

I can't believe she did that. Actually, correction. I can

believe it. I wonder when she put it up? Must be ages ago, before she realized she needed me here.

"What's wrong with you?" Mark says. "Do you know how this makes us look? Why would you put something like that up?"

I reach for the keyboard and press the spacebar. The video freezes right at the point where I put the tip of my finger into my mouth.

"Oh, fuck! This is bad! Are you out of your mind? And why would you mention Rue Capital?"

My heart sinks. "I didn't put this up. And if anyone should be embarrassed, it's me, so I don't know why you're so upset about it." I take another look at the still image. I am dying inside. I groan.

"You think this is funny?"

"No!"

"Okay. We're done. You're fired, Katherine. Get the fuck out of here."

"You're firing me? You can't fire me, Mark."

"Can't I? Seriously? I should have fired you a long time ago. Your work is shit, Katherine! There. I've said it. For weeks now, you contribute nothing, your reports are sloppy, nonsensical even. You take time off without the courtesy of—"

I raise my hand. "Fine. I get it."

"And now, this? I wanted to let you go, Katherine. I should have done it then. But Eve insisted. You can thank her for that. She's the only reason you still have a job."

"Right," I snort. "She's an idiot. You know that, right? She understands nothing about our business. Surely you've figured that out by now, after the Japanese shoe designer exhibitionist husband..." I make circles with my index finger near my temple. The classic sign for crazy.

244

"Don't do that," he says.

"Do what?"

He shakes his head. "Never mind."

I rest my hands on this desk. "I built this company, Mark. Rue Capital was just a shitty little firm that never picked a profitable startup until I showed up. You shouldn't fire me, you should give me a bonus. You should beg me to stay. Give me a raise. And make it big, because Rue Capital is nothing without me."

Possibly, I went too far. Mark really believes that he is responsible for the company's success, and that I just helped along the way. I just told him he's irrelevant.

He stares at me, mouth open. There's a single black curl on his forehead, like an insolent strand that doesn't know its place. He blows it out of the way with a puff of air and a forward chin. And before I can stop myself, I sit down, reach across and take his hand in mine.

"Mark, I beg you," I plead. "I love you, and you love me, Mark, I know you do."

He recoils, horrified. "What the fuck? Are you completely out of your mind?" His eyes dart everywhere, except on me.

"I know things haven't been perfect between us," I continue. "We all have good days and bad days and it's true, I've possibly had a few bad days. But there are reasons for that which you can't possibly understand. We love each other, you and me. Remember how we love each other? It's not too late. I love you, Mark. I'd do anything for you."

"You're crazy, you know that?" he says, his lips dripping with contempt.

"No, I'm not, but *she* is. She's evil, Mark. I swear to

you. She's the devil. You need to get away from her because otherwise, it's going to end in tears. Trust me."

He stands up now. "Are you threatening me?"

"Threatening you? I'm trying to help you!"

"Okay, that's enough. Pack your things and get out. And don't come back! You hear me? You're fired, Katherine Nichols!"

"But I…"

In the end he threatened to call the cops on me, his face almost purple with fury. People were staring on the other side of the glass and when I came out it felt like the walk of shame, all the way back to my office.

I put my coat on, slip my bag over my shoulder, and pick up the photo of Abigail and me from my desk. It was taken when she was five years old and sits in a brushed wooden frame with a small blue starfish at the top. Abi made it at preschool for Mother's Day. I slip it into my bag and as soon as I'm out in the street, I call Richard.

"I just got fired," I wail.

"Then I'm going to go find a nice bar and buy you a glass of French champagne to celebrate your dismissal. I'll text you when I find one."

"Okay. And the first bar you see will do. Doesn't need to be nice."

Chapter Forty-One

"I was like, fire me already! What do I have to do!" I laugh. It's good to laugh at Mark, even if the story I just told has nothing to do with what actually happened. Anyway, laughing is better than crying, which is what I was doing when I first walked in.

"What a jerk," Richard says now that we've finally calmed down.

"God. Tell me about it."

"Christ, what an asshole. What did you ever see in him?"

I smile at him. He's laying it on a bit thick, but I suspect he's trying to make me feel better. I suppose all this must remind him of Alison. He must have been a very protective brother, and those urges to defend and protect are transferred onto me. It's not unpleasant. It occurs to me I've never had that, someone standing by me, angry on my behalf. Wanting to protect me.

No. It's nice, it's flattering, but it's too early. I twist the stem of my glass between my fingers. "To be fair, when

Eve decides to use her charms, there's not a lot anyone can do."

"Bullshit!" he scoffs. "Don't defend him, Kat."

"I'm not—"

"He's a piece of shit."

He drains the last of his glass, turns the empty bottle upside down in the bucket and signals the barman for another. But the barman is joking around with two young women who were playing pool earlier and are now seated at the other end of the bar.

"Sorry," he says. "I'm angry, about everything. I shouldn't take it out on you, or him."

"You can take it out on him all you like. Doesn't bother me."

He smiles and we look at each other for a while. I feel the blush burn in my cheeks, a window of possibilities opening. He leans in until his lips touch mine, and I decide it's not too early, after all. It's nice. I lose myself into the kiss, until we part, minutes later.

"This is a fine establishment," I say, wanting to diffuse the awkwardness of the moment. The bar is called The Dive, and it fits. It's like stepping back in time. The seventies, most likely. Above the pool table in the corner are faded posters of rock stars. It's actually not that bad, although the carpet could do with a wash.

"You did say pick the first one I came across," he says, and I laugh.

"Sorry, I shouldn't have done that, the kiss…" He reddens. "You're vulnerable. That was wrong."

"Don't apologize too much!"

He smiles. "You're going to be okay?"

I shrug. "I'll get another job."

The barman finally notices us and returns with another bottle of sparkling.

"So that's it," Richard says, raising his glass. "It's over. Cheers to that. It's time to expose her, Katherine. There's no point in waiting."

I nod, tracing the path of the bubbles on the side of my glass.

"Best thing is to go to the police. The sooner the better. Tell them everything."

"You're coming with me, right?"

He nods but he looks away. "I need to speak to my mother first."

"Can't you do that now? Call her this afternoon."

"I'm really sorry, Kat." He takes a breath.

I blink, confused.

"The truth is," he says, "I don't think I can put my mother through all that. Alison was the apple of my mother's eye. She will never recover from her death. But I can't be dragging Alison's name through the mud like this. It'll kill my mother."

My eyes widen. "Through the mud?"

"You know what I mean. There'll be a court case. Everyone will know Alison... what she did."

"Left someone to die," I say.

He nods.

"But it wasn't true!"

"Alison didn't know that. That's what people will remember about my sister. I have to think of my mother. You understand that, don't you?"

"Oh, my God! What about me? What about my name being dragged through the mud?"

He reaches to touch my cheek again, but I brush his

hand away. "You can defend yourself, Kat. You're not dead."

"I don't believe this." I slide off the barstool and snatch my jacket.

"Don't go, Katherine. Come on."

"Richard. Thank you for helping me, I don't know that I would have figured it out without you. But you bailing out now? When we're almost at the finish line? You're a coward."

"Don't say that."

"You said so yourself, it's the right thing to do, to stop her. But you want me to do it alone."

"There's going to be a court case—"

"Exactly. And you *should* be a part of it, for Alison's sake. Instead you're leaving me to face it alone. What will everybody say about me, when they find out I thought I'd hurt someone and did nothing? What about my reputation being dragged through the mud?" I put my hand on his chest. "It's going to be my word against hers, and that's not enough. The case can only be made if we all speak up."

"I can't."

I'm outside now, Richard has followed me.

"Kat! Please!"

"Everything okay, Katherine?"

It's Amy. Amy from work. She's standing right in front of me, frowning at Richard. He gives me a pleading look.

"What do you care?" I snap at her and walk away.

I sit at the closest bus stop and pull up my phone to call Adley. There are dozens of texts and messages from Eve, of course. *I just heard. I'll sort it out. You should have waited for me.* Then later, *Call me immediately. Get the fuck back here, Kat! What's gotten into you?*

I wipe them all, even the ones I haven't read yet.

I tell Adley about the latest developments and the fake news website. "We have to go to the police, tell them about the scam."

"What's the charge for something like that, do you know?"

"Good question," I say. "I don't know but I can find out." I pause. "It means you'll have to come here, so we can go to the cops together."

She doesn't speak. "Or I could come to you," I say. "We could begin the process over there."

"I don't think so, Katherine. I'm sorry."

My heart sinks. I press the heel of my hand between my eyes. "If it's just me, it won't work. I have no proof."

A bus arrives. Half a dozen passengers step out. The driver looks at me. I shake my head and the door closes.

I explain to her about Mark. About how Eve turned her charms on him just to spite me. About me getting fired. "I'll be dismissed as a jealous, disgruntled ex-employee slash ex-lover. If it's my word only, it'll never hold."

"What about Richard?" she asks.

"Richard won't do it, either. He doesn't want to put his mother through the shame of it all." I snort audibly at that.

We're both silent for a few moments. I wait for her, with my eyes screwed shut in earnest prayer. *Say yes, say you'll come, say you'll do this with me please, I don't want to do this alone. I don't want to be alone.*

"I want to talk to the others," she says. "If I can get at least one more to agree, I'll consider it."

Okay, it's not what I hoped for, but it's not bad. I

ponder the suggestion for a moment, and come to the conclusion that in fact, maybe it's better.

"I've only got another two, apart from you, me and Alison Walters, but I couldn't locate them. One woman who'd just gotten divorced, and another whose parents died in a car crash. Although I haven't tried very hard, yet."

"Can you give me the details? And I'll have a go?"

"Okay, but for the time being let's keep it between us, the victims."

"Inside the victims' circle," she says.

"Yes. And I'll send you the pictures I took from her files. That's everything I have. I'll do it right now."

After we hang up, I scroll through the images on my phone, going back in time, searching for the snaps through the camera photos, and when a large man comes and sits down next to me, and he says, "Do you mind?" I slide farther down the bench without looking up, because my heart is in my throat and I swipe again, faster this time, through albums and timelines and back again, and I open different apps because now I'm confused about where I stored them, and another bus comes and I'm vaguely aware of people getting off and on and I'm still sitting there with my fingers now frantically moving on the screen but I know by now that they're not there. The photos I took at Eve's condo, the photos of her files, they're gone. Someone wiped them.

And that can mean only one thing.

She knows.

Chapter Forty-Two

I'm home, breathless, my heart pounding, and I check my laptop immediately. I am relieved to see the four images are still here, on my computer. I immediately email them to Adley.

Then my doorbell rings.

"Where the fuck have you been? Why aren't you taking my calls?" My psychopath is standing at my door, one hand on her hip. She pushes past me and walks right in, unties the belt of her coat.

"I got fired, haven't you heard?"

"You should have waited for me. I could have fixed it." She drops her coat on the couch.

I laugh. "Fixed it? You're the one who put it up on YouTube!"

"It was just a joke. I didn't expect Mark to see it. I didn't expect his client to send him the link. People are so uptight! Anyway, I removed it." She brandishes her phone and shows it to me. 'Video unavailable' it says.

"So you can come back to work. Your online reputation is restored."

"I'm not going back to work."

She sighs. "Aren't you going to offer me anything? A glass of wine, maybe? Or have you had enough for today?"

"What do you want, Eve?"

"I want my money."

"I don't have time for this. You need to leave." I grab her coat and throw it at her.

She folds her coat and lays it on the couch, drops herself next to it. "It's because of Mark, isn't it? I pushed you too hard. You're weaker than I thought, Katherine Nichols. I do love him, you know. And he loves me. I admit that at first, I just wanted to teach you a lesson. You think you're so much better than me, I couldn't resist. He was surprisingly easy to seduce, too. Odd, don't you think? Considering the two of you were … you know, in love? Or maybe it wasn't the two of you. Maybe it was just you. Maybe you're not so smart after all."

She puts her hands on either side of her face. "Oh, can't you count, Eve? Me, I have a master's in mathematics! And I sure know how to pick winners! I am so good at everything! But you, Eve! Imagine not being able to balance a checkbook! Can you type?" She narrowed her eyes at me. "Yeah, I can type. Turns out I can add, too. All the way to one million bucks. So where's my money, Einstein?"

"I'm not giving you any money. Even if I wanted to, I don't have it."

"You'll figure something out. After all, there is so much more I can do to you. I barely got started."

She picks at imaginary lint on her skirt, and without looking at me she says. "How's your new boyfriend, by the way?"

"My new boyfriend?"

"Rumor has it you're already at the lovers' tiff stage. Didn't take you long to get over Mark after all."

Amy. She saw me, us, outside the bar, just a little while ago. Went straight back to the office and told Eve. What the fuck is it with everybody?

I check my watch. "I don't have a new boyfriend. Shouldn't you be at work?"

She shrugs. "Must just be a rumor then. Have I told you about my uncle Bill?" She smiles sweetly.

I smile back, mirroring her. "Have I ever told you about my uncle Trevor?"

She rolls her eyes. "Sure you have. He took you in, poor little stray puppy that you were, and your baby. And now he's dead. Boohoo."

"He used to come into my room and rape me." She rolls her eyes again, but I raise a hand. "Really, you want to hear this, I promise." I sit down opposite her. "I was a slut, he said, and everybody knew it, by which he meant, Abi. Exhibit A, over in the crib. So, on those nights he came to teach me a lesson. That's what he said. I told my aunt Maud and she said I was lying, and if I kept that up I'd be sent off to a foster home where no one would be so nice to me, and they'd take Abi away because clearly, I was unfit to raise her. And also, I could kiss my education goodbye.

"The first time my mother came to visit I begged her to take me away. I'll be good, I said, I promise. I'll never cause any trouble again and I'll do anything, just let me come home."

"'I'm working on it,' my mother said. 'Your father is still very angry though, so it may take a little while. But I'm trying.'

"When I told her about Uncle Trevor, her eyes filled with sadness, and pity, and after an eternity she said, 'It's best if you don't lie anymore, honey.' Turned out Aunt Maud had already warned her about my outrageous 'fantasies' as she called them. So yeah, in the end, I gave up. My dad never forgave me, and I never went home.

"I heard them argue once, Aunt Maud and Uncle Trevor. She told him to stop doing it because if I ever got pregnant, I'd tell my parents it was him and what if they did a paternity test? Then they'd lose all that money. You see, Aunt Maud knew all along it was true, but she was more worried about losing the money my father was paying her every month to look after me.

"So I went to the doctor and said I had insomnia, I was desperate for something. He prescribed me some sleeping tablets."

Eve is crossing her legs, smoothing the creases in her dress. She's pretending to be bored but I know she's listening.

"That night," I resume, "I may have mixed those pills into their drinks. I may have waited until they fell asleep and I may have gone into their room and lit one of Uncle Trevor's cigarettes, which I may have left burning on his pillow. Maybe it took more than one cigarette, but eventually, and this part is not in dispute, they both burned to death. My only regret is that they were asleep. The firemen said it was so fast, Abi and I were lucky to get out of there alive."

Her mouth twitches, and she rubs the back of her neck.

"That's what being pushed too hard looks like, Eve, so I don't know, but you might want to rein it in. And I'll tell you one more thing. I don't think you're in love with Mark, because I don't think you're capable of it. You just wanted to get at me because that's what you do. You like to hurt people. Just like Uncle Trevor. Tell me Eve, will you still love Mark when he's broke? Because you might be impressed by the shiny cars, the prestigious address and the expensive stationery, but one thing you might not know, is that Rue Capital, it's all paid for by Sonya's money, not Mark's. I wonder if she'll keep financing it when she finds out about you. Someone will have to, because with me gone, that place won't turn a profit anymore. I thought I'd mention it, seeing you like money so much. Now get the fuck out of my house."

Chapter Forty-Three

One day, two days, three days... I wait, I don't even know what for. At least Abi is keeping herself busy. She's either at school or with Paige or hanging out with her friends. I have to remind myself she's sixteen now, and she's growing up. She had dinner at Clover's last night with her friends, or so she says but I found an earring in the laundry basket the other day, a small gold butterfly with two green stones in the center of each wing. It had caught on a thread of her blue top. I left it on the kitchen table and the next morning it was gone. When I commented on it that evening, she blushed. "Is it new?" I asked. "It's pretty."

She mumbled something in reply like 'sort of' and changed the subject. *My little girl has a crush on a boy.* Should I be worried? Of course not. I just need to get this business with Eve sorted out, then I'll have all the headspace in the world for my girl.

But I've heard nothing from my psychopath since I threw her out the other day. No calls, no visits, no emails. No Uncle Bill threats. Now I wish with all my heart I hadn't told her off like that. Eve knows. She went through my phone, checking up on me. She found the photos and deleted them. She knows I'm not scared of her anymore.

I should have kept up the pretense because I don't know what she's going to do now, and that part is driving me crazy. I'm on high alert all the time, listening closely for strange noises in the house, looking out for her wherever I go, jumping whenever the phone rings. I am literally hoping to hear from her. How fucked up is that?

It's Sunday. I need to talk to Mark. Away from the office and away from Eve. I bet he hasn't told Sonya yet so I go to his house where again I am greeted by Man in Grey Suit. He doesn't remember me from the other day. To be fair, I've washed my hair since then. I've cleaned up. I look human.

He tells me that Mr. Rue is not at home, but Sonya must have overheard because she comes into the hallway. "It's all right, Alex. I'll see Ms. Nichols."

I'm taken aback by her words and it puts me off balance. Unsettled. She gives me a small smile. "Come with me," she says.

I follow her into the living room, a lovely, elegant room with lots of light and fresh flowers in tall vases. It's all very nice. Very warm and very expensive.

"Can I get you something? A glass of water, maybe?" she asks.

"No, thank you." It dawns on me that she doesn't look too good after all. She's not in her perky yoga outfit of course, she's wearing black slacks and a green turtleneck, a pair of earrings almost matching the color, emeralds probably. Her blond hair tucked behind her ears. It's her face though, that's giving it away. The purple half-moons under her eyes.

I pause, searching for words. "Sonya, you know who I am, right?"

"Of course. Mark has told me a lot about your work for us. It's nice to finally put a face to the name. And to be able to thank you in person."

"Thank me? For what?"

"For being such a great asset to us. I understand you've managed to grow our little company considerably. We've doubled in size and tripled in profit since you joined us. I'm sorry you left, for what it's worth."

I nod my thanks. "Can I ask you a question?"

"You can try, if I can answer it, I will."

"Are you ill?"

She recoils, her shock evident in her frown and the slight flush that's appeared on her neck. I don't know why I asked. I knew the answer to that question the moment I saw her.

"It's just that Mark told me you've been battling with a … condition. For some time. Years, in fact."

She looks at me, tilts her head slightly. "Why are you really here, Katherine?"

I remember the last time I came to see her. I was determined to find out if Mark had been lying to me about the state of their marriage. I don't even care anymore. I don't need to ask her, I know he's been lying to me. The whole time.

"I didn't leave exactly. I got fired," I say now, for no particular reason.

"I heard. Is that why you're here? You want me to talk to Mark?"

I shake my head. "No. There's no need. I'll find something else."

"Good," she says. "Because Mark doesn't live here anymore. The only conversations we're going to have are going to be through our divorce lawyers." She tilts her head and adds, "You didn't know? About him and Eve?"

"I knew. I didn't know he was living with her. I didn't think you knew, either."

"He's not living with her. He's at the Plaza. Or that's where he went when I found out and I threw him out."

I let out a low whistle. "Can I ask how you found out?"

"Eve called me."

My jaw drops. The shock must be evident on my face and she asks if I'm all right.

"She called you? When?"

"Last Thursday afternoon. Mark left that night."

"Jesus."

"You still haven't told me why you're here looking for Mark."

I ignore the question. "What did Eve want?"

"I'm not sure that's any of your business."

I search her face for a clue, but she just looks sad.

"Sonya, I need to tell you something." I tell her about Mark and me because I have to. It's part of this story. I'm embarrassed and ashamed, I tell her. I thought you two had split up, I really did. I'm so very sorry, I say, over and over again, even though it's not my fault, is it? I'm only guilty of being gullible. Did gullibility kill the Kat? I've slept with her husband and now I can't remember why I ever thought it was going to be okay.

"It's been going on for months. He said he was waiting for you to get better before moving out. But he said you'd already split up."

She looks out the window, lost in her thoughts. "I knew," she says.

"You did?"

"I didn't know it was you. But I knew there was someone. The telltale signs, you know. The phone calls he'd disappear to take, the last-minute change of plans where he would come home and go out again, pretend it was something at work. He used to say he was going to the gym on Sunday afternoons, over on Charles Street. I walked past that gym once, when he was supposed to be there. They were closed for renovations. When he came home, he did what he always does after a workout, he went to have a shower. I asked him where he'd been. He maintained the lie. He even commented on how busy they were. So yes. I knew."

"And you never confronted him?"

"No."

"Why the hell not?"

"Does it matter now?" she asks.

"No."

"Because if you must know, I thought he would tire of it, you, whoever it was."

Her words hurt, but they don't shock me. I probably would have thought the same.

"Mark and I were going to buy you out of the business, as soon as the SunCell round was completed. Did you know that?"

She laughs. "Buy me out? Now that the company is finally making money? You must be joking. Or very rich. I poured millions into Rue Capital. It's only been making a profit for the last two years. Thanks to you, I might add. Mark never managed to do what you did."

"He said he owned half of Rue Capital."

"Then he lied to you. Mark couldn't possibly own half of Rue Capital. Mark has no money of his own. I pay him to manage the firm. He is my employee. It's true that Rue Capital was his idea, and that I have no interest in it, beyond being its only backer. He thought he could make a success of it. He didn't. Until you came along. When it looked like you might be leaving us at the beginning of last summer, he was very concerned. Not overtly, but enough for me to notice."

"Leaving you?"

"An offer had been made, hadn't it? DMC? That was the rumor. Mark said he'd take care of it so you wouldn't leave. He'd find a way."

I look away. That offer was supposed to be confidential. I was all set to take it until… Denver.

Fucking Denver. The conference. The first time Mark and I slept together. The lie about Sonya and their impending separation.

Everything had been a lie. He never intended to leave her for me. The fucker was just stringing me along so I wouldn't quit.

"You're sure I can't get you anything? A glass of water?"

I look up at her and for a second I don't remember where I am, or why I'm here. Then it comes back to me.

"When Eve called you, what was she like? Was she friendly? Or did she want to gloat about Mark?" I ask.

She blinks. "She was surprisingly friendly," she says finally. "She was also very … remorseful. It seems that Mark has lied to her, too. She didn't know Mark was still married. I don't think Eve and Mark have a future. Put it that way."

I can feel my pulse thumping in my throat.

"She knew he was married. Trust me. She's lying to you. There is something very calculating about Eve. She's a very dangerous woman, and I suspect she's coming after you."

She recoils. "After me? What on earth does that mean?"

I consider telling her everything, about the accident, how Eve came after me, but I stop myself.

"Eve runs some kind of scam. She goes after wealthy single women, befriends them, then finds a way to blackmail them."

"You're joking."

"No. She came to see me last Wednesday," I say. "The day I got fired. In my rant I told her that Mark was broke, and the money flowing around him and Rue Capital was yours. At the time I didn't think it was completely true. I thought he had brought something in. I was just being spiteful."

She raises one eyebrow.

"The thing is, I think she believed me. I don't think she gives a shit about Mark. She's called you to tell you about their affair, why would she do that? She could have just broken it off with him, you would have been none the wiser. No. She wants you alone, without him. She wants you vulnerable. You're next in her sights, Sonya. She's going to run the scam on you."

Chapter Forty-Four

Sonya doesn't reply. I can see she's trying to process everything I've said.

"If she calls and asks you out, for dinner, to a party, anything in the evening that involves alcohol, will you call me right away? I know it sounds crazy, but maybe together we could find a way to entrap her. I could give you a small camera, we could hide it in the car. Then no matter what happened that night, we'd have it on tape."

She actually laughs. "Why would I do that, Katherine? You're not making any sense. And if what you say is true—and it's a big if—and Eve is coming after me as you say, why on earth should I put myself through that? Why wouldn't I just say no to her offers of friendship?" She tilts her head at me and smiles.

"Because we have to stop her, that's why. Everyone is scared. But she's coming after you now, I can feel it. She'll call you, she'll charm you. But it won't be long before she pounces. She really is evil, Sonya. You have to help me stop her. We have to put her in jail."

I take my things and stand. She walks me to the door.

265

She has one hand on the doorknob and the other extended to shake mine.

"One last thing," I say. "SunCell. Sorry, but it's a dud. You need to get out."

She recoils at my words. "But I thought—"

I fish around my bag for my cell. I really need to get another bag. One with pockets. "Here," I say, brandishing it. I show her the text I received last week, the day I got fired.

I never told Mark this, but I happen to have an inside man at the Patent & Trademark Office. It's a guy I went to college with. I came across his name on some paperwork—Jason Federer—and I got in touch. Jason and I now have an arrangement whereby whenever we consider whether to invest in a company, if their technology is patent dependent, he'll pass on information to me before it becomes public. In return I make sure he gets a piece of the pie. Mark thinks I get it right one hundred percent of the time because I'm *crazy* smart.

I show Sonya Jason's text. *Will be rejected due to lack of detail and inaccurate descriptions.*

That showcase by Eve? Unhooking the cell and shutting down the building? That was a bit of theater. We tried to make it work with the real thing, back when I was going to present, but we couldn't store enough power for long enough to make it work. The company said they'd accidentally given us a faulty battery. Same with the next one. I should have realized then, but frankly I was so focused on getting the round completed and buying Sonya out, I believed what I wanted to believe.

"I don't think it works yet. They're probably on the right track, but they're exaggerating their claims and it's not a good sign. The backers will have to wait a long time to get their money back, if at all. You do what you want Sonya, but Vlad has committed a lot of money, and I don't think you want to mess with Vlad. Or his money."

"Have you told Mark all this?" she asks, not unreasonably.

"No."

I can't wait to call Adley. I want to tell her about Sonya, and that maybe we can convince her to help us. We'll have to tell her more, but it's worth it if we can catch Eve in the act. I think Sonya will help, if we explain. I can feel it.

I'm almost at my house when I hear him. "Katherine!" I turn, and it's Richard. He's smiling, his hands deep in his pockets. His hair is not as sleeked back as last time, some of it has come down over his forehead. I like it better that way. He pushes it out of the way. It's the wind. He pulls out his earbuds and for a second a waft of loud beats floats out to me.

I point to the earbuds. "These things will make you deaf, don't you know?"

He shrugs, smiles, and shoves them in his pocket.

"You're still here?" I ask.

I was mad at you, I want to say, real mad. But I don't because that's left me. It feels so long ago, even though we're only talking days.

"I thought you'd be gone back to New York by now."

"I should be, my boss isn't happy with me. But I keep delaying."

"Why?"

"I've been thinking about you. And about what I said. About leaving you to face it all on your own. You're right Kat, that was wrong of me."

"Okay…"

"I should go to the cops with you. Tell them everything I know. I've decided, Katherine. I'm not going to let you down."

I can feel the grin spread over my face. I put my arms around his neck. "Thank you. It means so much, Richard, you have no idea."

He laughs and I release him. I put the key in the lock and open the door. "There's been some new developments."

He raises an eyebrow. "Oh?"

"Yep. Come inside. I'll tell you all about it."

I'm bursting to tell him about Sonya, and how maybe, just maybe, with her help, we can build a very strong case against Eve. I'm pleased to see Abi has armed the alarm this time. She's not home which is good because there is so much I need to discuss with Richard.

We throw our coats over the back of the armchair and I'm about to tell him when my phone rings.

"Just a second. It's Adley. Hi, Adley! I have some news."

"Me, too," she says.

"Oh, my God, you've managed to track down the others." Richard is sitting next to me now and I squeeze his knee in excitement.

"Not yet, but I did speak to Mrs. Walters, Alison's mother."

"Really?" I say this slowly, drawn out, *rreeaalllyy?* because I'm surprised she even got this far. "And?"

"She said I was crazy."

I'm disappointed, but then I tell myself we never thought Mrs. Walters would listen. Maybe we'll have to leave Alison out of the case, after all. "She didn't want to listen to me either, if that's any consolation," I say. "I only made headway because Richard got in touch."

"And I told her that. But that's the thing…" she hesitates.

"What?"

"She said Alison doesn't have a brother."

Chapter Forty-Five

Richard is turned toward me, his eyebrows raised, a questioning smile on his lips.

What did she say? he mouths.

I'm still holding the phone, looking right into his eyes, willing myself to stay calm, but it's no use and the panic rises in my throat and makes my eyes swim. My lips begin to tremble. I'm vaguely aware of Adley's voice, *you're still there?* and it's as if a shadow passes over his face. I watch his features rearrange themselves from innocent anticipation into cold fury.

I didn't hear the front door. It's only when Abi sings out "Hi, Mom," that I realize she's home now. Hearing her voice breaks the spell. I quickly tell Adley that I'll call her back and plaster a smile on my face as I rise to greet Abi.

"Hi, baby!"

She stops. "What's wrong?"

"Nothing's wrong, why?"

"You know that saying? You look like you've seen a ghost? Well that's you. Right now."

I laugh. She's undoing the buttons on her coat and I

put a hand on her chest. "Don't. You'll just have to do them up again. Paige is waiting for you at her place."

"What?" She pulls her phone out from her pocket. I'm about to tell her I'll drive her there, but Richard's hand is on my shoulder, his fingers digging into the flesh below my collarbone. He squeezes so hard I have to hold my breath.

"Hi, Abigail," Richard says.

"Hello," she replies, cautiously.

I grab her gently by the shoulders and turn her around. I want to whisper into her ear. *Go, and call the police right away. Tell them to come here. You go to Paige's,* but he's too close to me. I can't risk it. Not with Abi right here.

"Get on the bus. Just go, Abi, okay?"

She shrugs me off. She's annoyed now, she thinks I don't want her here, and she's right. She thinks I am pushing her away because I want to be alone with Richard.

She leaves without a word. I wait until she's closed the door after her and I kick back with the heel of my boot, hitting him in the shin. He lets go of my shoulder with a cry of pain and I leap forward, my arm outstretched toward the front door but he's on me in seconds, he grabs my hair and pulls hard, knocking me to the floor. The side of my face hits the console table and the pain explodes in my temple. For a moment I think I'm going to pass out.

"Get up," he says. He's standing in front of the door, barring my way.

I put my hand on the side of my face, and with the other push myself onto my knees.

"You're the motorcycle guy." My voice is shaking.

He puts one hand under my arm and pulls me up. "You got me."

I wobble back to the living room with Richard propping me up. I'm too shaken to get away from him. I sit on the couch, my hand still against my cheekbone.

"I really didn't want this to happen," he says.

"How did you find me?"

"I followed you."

"When?"

He laughs softly. "The day you went to Eve's condo. You were hiding in the closet. I saw the broken china on the floor. Then I heard you. Frankly, Kat, you were hard to miss. You were pretty noisy. I waited for you downstairs and I followed you back here."

I remember that day. The creepy feeling that I wasn't alone.

"I was crouching under that window, right there." He points to the window behind me. "Listening to you make those calls."

"Is your name really Richard?"

"Yes."

He begins to pace the room. "This isn't good, Katherine. You were not supposed to find out about me."

"Why did you tell me how she did it? You gave the whole game away, why?"

"Haven't you figured that out yet?"

I shake my head.

"I wanted her to get caught. I wanted her to suffer, the way she made me suffer."

"How—"

"Four years, we've been together, her and I. And I never did anything but love her. I was at her beck and call. I'd do anything for her. I *did* anything for her. We've been running this scheme for most of it. We've made a hell of a lot of money from it." He pokes at his own chest with an angry finger. "And I did all the work. I find

272

the location. I get the sand bags. I put barriers up if I have to keep other cars out of our way. I'm the dead guy. I clean up afterwards. And after all that, she fucking dumps me?"

"Oh, God."

"Four years, Katherine! Then one day, just like that, she tells me it's over. We're over. The scam's over. Princess Eve wants to settle down. She wants to have kids! Fuck! But not with me! Can you believe that? She's met someone new, she says. That asshole, Mark fucking Rue! And what am I supposed to do? Get on my bike and ride into the sunset by myself? After everything we've gone through together? After everything I did for her?"

"I think she's going to break it off, with Mark. She found out he doesn't have any money."

"I know," he replies.

"You do? How?"

"She wants me back."

"Really? So that's good, right?"

"Yes, it's good. It changes everything. Except now there's you, Katherine Nichols."

Oh, God. I press the heel of my hand in the space between my eyes. "Abi's going to come back. I don't want her—"

"And I don't want to either, Kat, but maybe you should have thought of that before."

I'm at a loss why any of this is my fault. "I haven't told anyone, about the scam," I say. He shakes his head at me. "You've told everyone, Kat. Don't lie to me. You told your little friend Adley…"

"Does Eve know? That you—"

"Told you everything? No. That would defeat the purpose, wouldn't you say?"

"But if I'd gone to the police, wouldn't you get caught, too?"

"I wasn't going to stick around, Katherine. We still have a lot of money. Plenty for me to start again somewhere else. I'd have been long gone by the time she gave them my name."

We're quiet for a moment, he's still walking, thinking. So am I.

"She knows, she found the photos I took of her files, on my phone. She deleted them."

"That was me," he says.

"You?"

He nods. "Jane White. Divorcee. She knows me. And my name. We did a variation of the scam for her benefit. We swapped roles, Eve and me. If you'd managed to track her down, you might have found out about me." He grits his teeth and wags his finger in my direction.

"But you got your little friend to fucking call Alison's mother. Now you know about me! You have ruined everything!"

I've begun to cry. "I'm sorry," I whisper. "Tell me how to fix it. I'll call Adley and tell her something, that I had it wrong—"

"Don't be fucking stupid."

He paces some more, up and down and back again.

"Where's Eve now?" I ask.

"She's waiting for me." He flicks his wrist, checks his watch.

"Maybe you could go away, like you said, together. Start a life somewhere else. Get new identities." I wipe my tears with one hand. "You could leave now, couldn't you?"

He shakes his head. "We're doing one last job. Later today." He taps on his watch. "We'll leave after that."

I'm about to blurt it out. *What? Sonya? But...*

But Sonya lied to me, that's what. I guess she didn't believe me after all. I sigh. What did I think? I'm up against Eve. Everybody always believes Eve over me. They've probably had dinner already, Sonya and Eve, at that *nice little Italian restaurant around the corner.* She seduced her already. I was too late.

At least I warned her. She'll see it coming, hopefully.

My head is still throbbing. There's a bump the size of a small egg next to my right eyebrow. "I need some ice." I point toward the kitchen with my chin. "Can I?"

He takes a look at the side of my face, frowning.

"Okay. Go and get it," he says. I walk unsteadily into the kitchen. He's right behind me. He leans against the wall as I get some ice from the freezer and drop the cubes into a kitchen towel.

We return to the living room, with Richard leading the way. There's a desk lamp on the table behind the door. One of those brass ones with a green glass shade. I reach low as I walk past and pull the lamp cord from the socket and it comes quickly. He turns around and I lift the lamp and bring it down on his head but I'm scared to hit too hard and the first blow doesn't land. It just makes him gasp. I do it again, harder this time. It's horrible. By the third time he has fallen to the floor and I drop the lamp.

He's moaning, writhing on the floor. I step over him and run out the door. At the last minute I turn around and glance down the length of the hallway. Richard is still lying where he fell, moaning, his head in his hands. I slam the door shut and run.

Chapter Forty-Six

I don't have my phone, I don't have any money, I don't have my jacket and I don't have my keys.

I'm running to Hilary's house. I'm running to Abi. Everything is a blur and I almost collide into the man with the dark overcoat who stopped abruptly outside the news-stand. I don't wait for the lights to change, and I only just avoid the blue sedan, slap one hand on the hood to propel myself as the car honks, but I'm running. A woman walks out of Tatte Cafe and I knock her Styrofoam cup out of her hand and she shouts, "Hey!" but I'm running. I turn the corner and slip on the icy metal grate. I get up instantly, ignoring the pain that shoots up my hip and I keep running.

By the time I get to Hilary's house my breath is hot and hurts my lungs and I have a stitch in my left side. I bang on the door. I'm shouting, hitting it with both hands and when Hilary opens, wide-eyed and teary, I almost fall inside. I put my hands on my knees and catch my breath.

"What on earth happened?"

I press my hand against my ribs on one side. "Is Abi here?"

"No, should she be?"

"Where is she?"

Hilary puts her arm around my shoulders. "What's wrong? Come and sit down."

"I told her to come here. Is Paige home?"

"Not yet. She'll be home soon. What's happened?"

I need to calm? down. They're obviously together. There's no need to panic. "Can I borrow your phone?"

"Of course, do you want some water? Come and sit down." I say yes to water and sit down on the dark velvet couch.

My whole body is shaking. I'm still finding it hard to catch my breath. Hilary arrives with her phone and the glass of water. I gulp it greedily with one hand and press in Abi's number with the other. It goes straight to voicemail. "Hey, sweetie, it's Mom, I don't have my phone, I'm with Hil. Can you call Hilary please? As soon as you can, okay? Or come here. Even better. I need to know where you are, okay?"

Hilary brushes her fingertips against the side of my face. "Jesus! What happened to you? Did someone do this to you?"

"Oh Hil…" I drop my head in my hands.

"Tell me what's happened?"

"There was this guy at my house—"

"At your house?!"

"I had to run away!" I wail.

"Did you call the police?"

I shake my head. "There's no point. He'll be gone by now."

"Who was he? Do you know?"

I nod. Through my sobs I manage to tell my story. I tell her about Eve, about the accident, about the blackmail.

"But it wasn't real, you see? It's this scam she runs on people, people like me. She thought I had money because of my mother's family. She set me up. And I'm so stupid I believed it! All of it!"

"Oh Kat, this is just awful! You should have told me!"

I scoff. "Told you what?" I wipe the snot off my nose with my sleeve. "That I hit someone with my car? That I drove away and then he died? That I was drunk?"

"I would have helped you," she says. And I believe her now. She would have. Hilary is a much kinder soul than she had me believe. I reach for a Kleenex from the box on the side table and blow my nose.

"Then this guy, he tracked me down. He told me some bullshit story about being the brother of one of Eve's victims. He told me how she did it."

"Is that the guy? What's his name? Richard? Your new boyfriend? Did he do this?" She turns my face so she can see the side. I touch the bump gingerly. "He's not my boyfriend for fuck's sake."

"I'll get you an ice pack." She stands up. "We need to call the police."

I grab hold of her wrist. She winces. I let go. "How do you know about Richard?"

She blinks. "Abi told Paige. She said you have a new boyfriend called Richard. I don't think she was very impressed, according to Paige, anyway."

I look away. "That's right, Abi met him, the same day I did. He was there when she came home." Hilary rubs her wrist where I held it just now. "Sorry," I say, then I notice properly her drawn face, her red rimmed eyes. "Are you okay?" I ask.

278

She does a quick flick of the head. "It's not you, it's—"

"Why would Abi think he was my boyfriend?" I narrow my eyes at her.

She thinks about it for a moment. "She said you looked happy. Happier than you had been in ages."

"Oh, God." I groan. "He's not my boyfriend. He's Eve's accomplice. He tricked me. He came to my house..."

"Does he know you're here?"

"No! He has no idea. He doesn't know anything about you. He's never met Paige—Oh, Christ! How stupid of me! Can you call Paige? Now? See if Abi is with her?"

"Of course." But then the door opens, and Paige appears. I stand up immediately and look behind her.

"Is Abi with you?" My tone is too harsh and Paige blinks at my words.

"No."

"Where is she?" I've grabbed her by the arms and Hilary gently pulls me away.

"Paige, honey, when's the last time you saw Abigail?"

She shrugs. "I don't know. At school, on Friday I guess."

"But you rehearsed together yesterday!" I say.

Paige frowns at me. "Rehearsed?"

"Yes! Your play, you two rehearse all the time, here!"

"We only rehearsed here once, for fun, ages ago," Paige says, just as Hilary adds, "Abi hasn't been here in weeks. Not since we went to the movies, that's at least two, maybe three weeks." She turns to Paige as if seeking validation, but Paige just looks confused. She pulls at a strand of her hair.

"Dinner! The two of you had dinner with your friends, at Clover's, last night."

Paige shakes her head and Hilary says, "Paige was here last night."

"So where is she?" I'm still holding Hilary's phone and I dial Abi again. Hilary is asking Paige where Abi might be. As I leave another message on Abi's voicemail I overhear Paige say something about 'her friend'.

"Of course! She's got a boyfriend!" I grab hold of Paige's hand. "That's it, isn't it? She's with her boyfriend. What's his name? He's from school, isn't he? What's his name Paige!?"

"Abi doesn't have a boyfriend, Mrs. Nichols—"

"She does!" I'm squeezing her hand and she winces. It's all I can do not to shake her. "You just said—her friend —who is it, Paige? Tell me!"

Her bottom lip wobbles. Hilary lays one hand on my arm. "Kat…"

"It's your friend," Paige says. "She hangs out with her all the time now. She said not to tell anyone!"

I release her, put a hand on my chest. "*My* friend?"

"That woman at your house, the night we had pizza, the one who had the video!"

Chapter Forty-Seven

It's Eve, she's with Eve. They do stuff together ... takes her shopping ... buys her things ...

I close my eyes, press my fingers against my temples.

Been going on for ages ... she's teaching her to drive...

I snap my head up. "What did you just say?"

"They hang out—"

"No. Something about driving."

"She's been teaching Abi to drive. It's only been a few days."

Paige has begun to cry softly. Hilary comforts her with soft words. "It's okay, honey."

"What's going on, Mom?" Paige asks.

"But... Eve doesn't have a car?" I direct this at Paige.

"That's what Abi said."

My thoughts are jumbled up, falling over each other.

"How did it start, do you know?"

"We bumped into her, one time, at Porter Square. She was super friendly, she said to Abi that she was worried about you."

Bumped into her. Right. As if Eve hadn't planned

all this.

"She took us to get some waffles. That's how it started. After that Abi would go and hang out with her."

"But where?" I ask.

"I don't know, shopping and stuff."

"This is crazy. Why would Abi not tell me about this?"

"Because Eve said she was helping you, and it was better if they talked without you knowing. That's what Abi said later. Eve told her you were suicidal, but you were on heavy medications. It was important to leave you alone and not make you stressed."

"Oh my God!" This is all my fault. I take Hilary's phone from her again but I can't remember Eve's number. I try Abi but no reply.

"Where the fuck is she?" I mumble. "Why isn't she picking up?"

Fragments of sentences collide my head. *Rumor has it you have a new boyfriend… Abi said you looked happy. Happier than you had been in ages… She's teaching Abi to drive… Eve is waiting for me… She wants me back… We're doing one last job. Tonight. We'll leave after that…*

And that's when I know. It comes to me, fully formed and terrifying. I know what Eve is going to do, and it's so evil, that it makes the room tilt.

"Paige, thank you for telling me all this," I say. "Now I need to talk to your mom, do you mind leaving us, please?"

Paige turns to Hillary. "Go on, honey. Go to your room. We won't be long."

"Okay if I call Abi?" she asks.

"Yes!" I reply. "Call Abi, text her, message her, anything to try to get in touch with her. But don't say anything about Eve, please. Just tell her to come here right away."

I wait until she's safely out of earshot.

"Eve knows about me and Richard. I'm sure of it. Amy, the receptionist at work. She saw us and told Eve. I didn't worry about it then, because I thought Eve and Richard had only met once or twice, years ago. Even if Amy had described him, it wouldn't have meant anything to Eve. That's what I assumed." My tone becomes more urgent. "But you heard Paige just now. Abi's been talking to Eve. You yourself knew about Richard, Paige told you, because Abigail told her." I can barely breathe when I say it. "Eve knows that Richard—her accomplice—and I have been seeing each other. She must know he's blown the whole con wide open. Now Richard believes that Eve has changed her mind and wants him back. Really? Even now she's found out he betrayed her?"

"She's got an agenda."

"That's right. And Richard still thinks she's in the dark, about him talking to me. But he said they're doing one more job. Why would she do that? I know it's a scam, she knows that. Surely it's not worth the risk, running it again here? So soon? She must assume I'm talking to the cops, or I'm about to."

"What do you think she's up to?"

"That's the problem, I don't know. But I thought she was reeling Sonya in. Now I think she's going to involve Abi somehow." My voice cracks. Hilary's hand clasps her mouth.

"Are you sure?"

"Almost."

Hilary looks away, a single frown line between her eyes. "But you said this whole scam was about blackmail. Why would they want to blackmail Abigail? Abigail doesn't have this kind of money? They must know that?"

"I don't know, but I think she's about to do something terrible, some kind of ultimate act of revenge. Oh God." I bite my knuckle. Hard. It's like a release. I pull it out and check. You can clearly see the marks my teeth left.

We call Paige back out of her room. "Where do they go, to teach Abi to drive?"

"I don't know, I'm sorry!"

"Did she reply to you? Anything?"

She shakes her head. "But I know where she is."

"What?"

Paige offers her phone up for us to see. The screen shows a map, with a bunch of names below.

"What is this?"

"Find my Friends. It's an app."

I snatch it out of her hand. There's a photo of Abi in a circle, hovering over the map. I tap it and it zooms in.

"This is where she is?" The three of us are bent over the screen.

"Yes," Paige says. "She's not taking calls but her phone's on."

"The cemetery!" Hilary and I say in unison.

"Why didn't you say that before?" I snap.

Her face, that was so filled with pride just now, crumbles.

"I didn't think…"

I reach out to her, kiss her on the forehead. "I'm sorry. Sorry, Paige. This is great. It's better than great, it's wonderful. Thank you."

The cemetery.

"Can I take your car?" I blurt out to Hilary.

"I'll come with you. We're taking your phone Paige, all right? We'll bring it back."

Chapter Forty-Eight

"I thought the cemetery would be closed by now," Hilary says.

"It's Sunday, maybe they stay open later. Can you please hurry?"

I've said that a hundred times already and it's only been five minutes. My eyes are trained on the screen. I watch Abi going around the avenues and back again.

"Can you believe it? Teaching Abi to drive?"

"Well technically, she's old enough to drive," Hilary says. "But she should have asked your permission. Definitely."

"You don't get it. It's not about that, is it? It's an excuse to get Abi in the car. If anything happens to her, I swear…"

We're at the gate, and Hilary was right, they're closed. Not what I expected. Hilary parks the car, and we get out to look around.

"What do we do now?" I wail. I try Abi again. No reply. "I don't understand. She's definitely in there. Look!" I angle the phone so Hilary can see. We stare at Abi's photo moving up and down and around, inside the cemetery.

"Let's try this way," Hilary says. We walk briskly along the perimeter of the wall. My eyes are glued to the screen until Hilary grabs me by the shoulder. "Here!"

I look up, she's right. The wall has ended and been replaced by an iron fence and one of the spikes is missing. It's narrow, but we can just squeeze through. Just.

"I think she's this way," I say.

Hilary is peering over my shoulder. "I think she's over there," she points in a different direction and now I'm not sure.

"Look, Crystal Avenue." I point at the sign. We start to run, then take a wrong turn, backtrack, and five minutes later, we're here. We're standing in the middle of one of the avenues, right where Abigail should be.

"Where is she?" I check the phone screen again and it looks like we are in the right place, but there's no Abigail and no car. And then I see him, through the dark, naked trees and about a hundred feet ahead, on the other side of a landscaped section.

Richard.

He hasn't seen me. He's concentrating on his task, his head down, a dark hoodie over his head, but I know it's him.

I turn to Hilary. "Stay here," I whisper, and bring a finger to my lips. Then I crouch and scurry through the shrubbery, getting as close as I can without alerting him to my presence. He's panting, dragging a bag of sand into the road. I get a bit closer. He's moving in a certain way, then I get it. He's got his earbuds in.

I return to where Hilary is waiting, hiding behind a tree.

"We're not too late. Thank God."

She closes her eyes briefly, lets out a breath of relief. "What do we do now?"

"Call the police. Just get them here. Tell them there's been an accident, and the cemetery gates are locked. I'll—"

But then I hear it, and it's like an electric current running up my spine. I sprint back through the shrubbery. Richard is still up there, but the road curves at this point so he's partially hidden by trees and the edge of a large headstone. And then the car comes into view. A small black car I've never seen before.

They're going too fast. Even from this distance I can see it's Abi behind the wheel. I run toward them, waving my arms and screaming. "Stop the car! Stop the car, Abi!" But they're going so fast and I can see her face is distorted, she's crying, I see that now, she's screaming. *Mommy!!!!*

But she's not going to stop and something is very wrong and Eve is leaning against Abi but Abi is shouting something and I'm still screaming "GET OUT OF THE CAR!" and I stand with my hands on my head and I turn and Richard seems so far away barely visible around the bend with his back to us and I scream his name but he doesn't hear me and I shout again "GET OUT OF THE CAR!" and I want to step in front of it and stop it with my bare hands and my baby is shrieking and I shout again with all the air in the world… *GET OUT OF THE CAR!*

She flies at me, my baby. I have my arms out and she lands on top of me. She's jumped out of the car. We're on the ground, my shoulder wedged hard on the curb. Everybody is screaming, and there's a terrible, terrible noise after that, and I don't want to look.

Chapter Forty-Nine

She killed him. That was her one last job. Her last Hoorah! To kill Richard, the treacherous accomplice. He thought it was a real job, of course, and that he still had at least fifteen minutes before they showed up. But she tricked him. She timed it so he'd be taken by surprise.

In the end, he was the mark.

It was clever, to use Abi. Would I speak out after that? If Abi had been behind the wheel? Unlicensed, speeding, and guilty of killing—and this time, I really mean killing—someone? Eve thought she could swing it so Abi really believed it was an accident and that she was at fault. But when I showed up, Abi tried to stop the car, but Eve wouldn't let her. She took hold of the steering wheel and pressed her foot on the accelerator. Abi tried to fight her off and Eve went crazy. She was almost on top of her, she just wouldn't let go but Abi managed to get out anyway. I thank the universe every day for that.

All that came out at the trial. Eve was found guilty of first degree murder and she's in jail now. For life. I heard she was appealing but I'm not worried. I can't imagine the odds are in her favor.

One good thing, if you could call it that, was that no one brought up the scam she was running. Certainly not Eve herself, and when you think about it, why would she? Extortion is a felony in this state. It wouldn't have done her any favors. So the police, the prosecution, they all thought Eve had killed Richard out of jealousy, that we were bound up into a sordid tale of lovers and betrayals. Me and Mark, Eve and Mark, Richard and me. Which meant Adley and I didn't have to testify. None of us victims did.

But Adley and I, we tracked them down in the end, the victims, the ones we knew about. And we found three more, three other women. Maybe there were others, we don't know. But the ones we reached out to, we told them the truth.

It never happened.

It didn't give back what they lost, but it enabled them to move forward.

Chapter Fifty

There's a new sign in the lobby today. I stand below it, with a grin on my face. *Rue & Nichols*, it says, in great big letters. I like it a lot, although I was hoping for *Nichols & Rue* but I got overruled. Sonya said she's paid enough to have her name upfront. They're not together anymore but she's kept the name. It's a brand, she said. That's all.

We're in a different building, too, thank God. None of those heavy steel beams and oversized clocks. Our office is warm, pretty. We have drapes, too, which Vlad really likes.

Things got a bit messy when Sonya kicked Mark out of the business. She didn't even have to pay him a cent, which means he's even more broke than ever, but that's beside the point. She asked that he immediately stop the SunCell funding round and pay back the investors, but he refused. Even faced with the prospect of the patent application being rejected, and the value of the product being, well, nil, essentially, he wouldn't budge. He said SunCell will get it right eventually, and the next patent was bound to be successful. Bound to, he said. As if he'd know. And anyway, it wasn't against the law to get it wrong, he said. He's right, technically, but everyone would lose their money. I would have loved to see Mark explain to Vlad why his ten million dollars disappeared into thin air.

I wasn't there when Sonya fired Mark, and she said he was 'beyond shocked'. But what could he do? For all his bluster and his fast cars and ostentatious writing implements, he was still an idiot. No, that's not what I was going to say. I was going to say, he was still an employee. And Sonya was perfectly entitled to fire him. And Vlad got his money back, with a personal card from Sonya, explaining the situation, and that from now on, she and I were taking over. He came in and thanked us personally. "It's not every day in my business you meet people with principles," he said. "That takes guts." He's still our best client.

Of the original team, we only kept Liam (Head of IT) and Aaron the legal guy (Head of Legal). That's it. Plenty of jobs out there for the rest of them, and I don't miss them.

Wi-Fi Adley is now Head of Innovation. I headhunted her and she moved from New York. She's awesome. But we knew that already.

Hilary runs our public relations department. My dear friend Hilary. Hilary and Henry are no longer together. It turns out that he was a rather controlling prick. Maybe even violent, but she won't discuss that. She wanted to work, would have loved to work, and he forbade her. Twenty-first century Henry forbade his wife to work. So, there you go, when people make snide comments at you, criticize your choices, are always quick to judge, maybe it's not you they resent, maybe they're just scared.

I'm talking about me, by the way, not Hilary.

Hilary had her own shortcomings, but she turned out to be a wonderful friend, the best I could possibly hope for and more than I deserved. And if I can help her in any way? Try and stop me.

My mother died, peacefully, two months ago. It was a relief in so many ways. I kept the Kirkland Place house in the end, and Abi and I live there now. Sasha came over from LA, and with Hilary, they helped me catalogue and auction the contents of the house. As it happened, there were a lot of valuable items. Works of art, beautiful pieces of furniture, books, including a very expensive, very rare first edition of one of the founding works of the theory of probability.

I couldn't help but think of Eve after I auctioned the lot. Just that book came to over thirty thousand dollars, so yes, I made a lot of money from that auction. Where would she be now, if I'd paid her out? Not in Framingham correctional institution, that's for sure.

I couldn't resist. I sent her a postcard. Not anonymous exactly, but you certainly wouldn't make out my name from the scribbled signature. But she'll know.

Hey, Eve, guess how much I got for the contents of my house? Just a hair over a million dollars! Can you believe it? One million dollars! What are the odds?

Acknowledgments

I am very fortunate to have some wonderful people in my corner. They help me produce a better book and I am very grateful to all of them.

A heartfelt thank you to my fabulous editor Traci Finlay, especially for her brilliant suggestions and her wonderful enthusiasm!

An equally heartfelt thank you to Mark Freyberg, for again generously taking the time to answer my questions on all things legal.

Thank you to my family, my lovely friends who cheer me on above and beyond, and especially to my husband who is there for me in too many ways to list here.

And to you, dear reader, thank you for reading this book. It means the world, always.